The Chancellor's Foot

A Novel

Ron Atkey

Little, Brown and Company (Canada) Limited
Boston • Toronto • London

Canadian Cataloguing in Publication Data

Atkey, Ron
    The chancellor's foot

ISBN 0-316-05627-8

I. Title.

PS8551.T54C5 1995   C95-931686-8
PR9199.3.A75C5 1995

Cover design: Tania Craan
Front jacket photos: Masterfile (Parliament Buildings) Barrett &
                MacKay; (Money) Mark Tomalt
Author photo: Morris J. Fish
Interior design and electronic assembly: Pixel Graphics Inc.
Printed and bound in Canada by Best Book Manufacturers Inc.

Little, Brown and Company (Canada) Limited
148 Yorkville Avenue, Toronto, Ontario, Canada

For Marie

This novel is set in 1984–85 primarily in Montreal and Ottawa, two culturally and politically interesting cities, albeit in different ways. All the characters exist only in the author's imagination and bear no relation to people in real life.

Prologue

"Equity is a roguish thing. For Law we have a measure, know what to trust to; Equity is according to the conscience of him that is Chancellor, and as that is larger or narrower, so is Equity. 'Tis all one as if they should make the standard for the measure we call a "foot" a Chancellor's foot; what an uncertain measure would this be! One Chancellor has a long foot, another a short foot, a third an indifferent foot 'Tis the same thing in the Chancellor's conscience."

John Selden
1584—1654

(reprinted from *Table-Talk: Being the Discourses of John Selden Esq.*, E. Smith, London, 1689)

Chapter One

As the Air Canada flight glided westward along the southern rim of the Laurentians on its way to Mirabel Airport, Antoinette Belair turned away from her companion Marcel Gagnon and cast her eyes over the snow-covered hills to the north. The vague outlines of carefully carved ski runs dotting the distant horizon came into view. She knew that, not far beyond, the pristine slopes of Mont-Tremblant arose majestically from the floor of the tree-covered valley and still frozen tiny lakes. For her, this brought back memories of fast skiing, exciting parties and great sex.

It was less than two months since she had laid cautious plans to protect the bundle of American cash delivered to her in the lobby of Le Quatre Saisons Hotel in downtown Montreal by Gus Bertolini's courier, up from New York that cold day in February 1984. The two million dollars delivered had been all in thousand-dollar bills. She had sewn five hundred of these into the lining of her over-sized black leather bomber jacket, according to firm instructions from Marcel, her aging European lover and procurer of the valuable "China white" heroin from Burma via Marseilles. She had worn this jacket when she met him in England.

"Hello, I'm Alan Chant. Who're you?" the tall, angular skier ambled towards her late one Saturday afternoon in the Bistro Bar at Tremblant Inn. He had thick, tousled brown hair and wore a fashionable Descente one-piecer. With her flashing dark eyes, long auburn hair, shocking-pink ski wear and well-proportioned body, Antoinette found it easy to attract the good-looking ones. This was her usual Saturday après-ski activity, and on this particular February day, Alan Chant was her target.

"I'm Antoinette."

He looked at her quizzically. "Antoinette—?"

"Just Antoinette." She smiled flirtatiously. "That'll do for now."

He grinned. "I see. A mystery woman. Any point asking what you do?"

"I ski and have fun, work when I have to. What do you do?" She flashed him her "genuinely interested" look, already having suspected that he might be a stockbroker or a lawyer.

Alan took the bait, offering first to light her cigarette. "Well, I have a small law office in Old Montreal. I try to help out thieves, prostitutes, criminals and the occasional nice person who has an unfortunate run-in with the law." Alan smiled, trying not to sound patronizing.

She studied his boyishly attractive face. She saw confidence, warmth and just enough earnestness to suggest reliability. This one clearly had promise, she thought to herself.

She'd been mystified, then terrified, when, two weeks earlier, Marcel's New York contact had warned her at Le Quatre Saisons: "Take twenty-five percent for your supplier and deposit the rest with someone you can trust who we can contact here in Montreal, just in case, God forbid, you and Marcel don't come through."

She'd fretted over this "deposit" requirement and wondered what suitable unsuspecting person she might recruit. In the meantime, she'd purchased a small, brown, leather attaché case with a lock and a hand strap. It barely held all the money, but fit neatly into her suitcase and went with her everywhere.

"Any plans for dinner?" Alan whispered in Antoinette's ear after several drinks.

"None that would interest you, big guy." Her smiling gaze continued to penetrate his casual veneer, and she squeezed his hand ever so gently. "But I could shake loose about nine if you happen to come by Express Disco downstairs at the Inn here. Where're you staying anyway?"

"Just happen to be booked into a room here. But if I show up at nine with my dancing shoes and you're not there, I'll come looking for you. I can be very aggressive."

"Should I be frightened? Or maybe just excited? Aggressive men are my specialty." Antoinette took a drag on her cigarette and exhaled languorously.

"Don't force me to go all the way around the lake to Cuttles to embarrass you in front of your friends. Be here at the disco at nine. I'll be plenty aggressive, don't you worry."

Antoinette was impressed. Alan had figured out that she was staying with a group of friends in a condo at Cuttles Inn across the lake. She'd rejoin them for their usual Saturday supper at the local pizzeria in the village. Then she'd beg off to return to get ready to go dancing with her new-found prize.

Alan's training as a criminal lawyer had served him well. When she was in the washroom, he'd spied beside her cigarettes a book of matches bearing the distinctive "Cuttles" logo. He'd seen "units twenty-two and twenty-three" scribbled on the cover. He'd made the calculated guess that she was staying there and he'd carefully watched her face when he first mentioned the name of the well-known winter weekend haunt of the Montreal glitterati. No further confirmation was needed.

Antoinette arrived at Tremblant Inn at ten past nine. Inspired by Rod Stewart, Madonna, Whitney Houston and Phil Collins, she and Alan kicked up a storm on the dance floor, every part of their bodies moving with reckless energy. Their frenzied movements continued on a more intimate basis back in his room, with Antoinette's gyrating hips, muscular legs and hardened nipples challenging Alan to his physical limits on at least three occasions before daybreak. She knew in the back of her mind that this one-night stand would serve her mission well.

By the time the invitation came to ride back with him to Montreal Sunday afternoon, she was satisfied that he was indeed a lawyer and could be trusted.

"The snow was fabulous this morning, wasn't it?" Revving the black BMW up to 140 kilometers per hour as he headed south on Route 117, Alan decided to take the high road as a conversational opener.

"It would have been even better if we'd hit the slopes before eleven," she teased. "But you insisted on ordering us that big breakfast. Guess you thought we'd have to replenish all that energy — you were great last night. Do you give those kind of performances on a regular basis?"

"Only twice a week, but during ski season even less," grinned Alan, "because I really like to be the first to tear down those freshly groomed hills, and that means early to bed the night before. Anyway," he added, "you were pretty imaginative yourself. Not bad on the slopes, either. Frankly, I was surprised that you kept up with me!"

"When it comes to cutting an edge, I'm second to none," she boasted, knowing full well that he'd been truly impressed with her prowess. She'd insisted that he ski with her that day.

As a teenager, Alan had competitively raced the gates every winter weekend in the Eastern Townships. At one point, he'd even dreamed of trying for a spot on the national ski team, which would have entailed quitting school during the winter months. His father Sam had vetoed that idea — no child of his was going to drop out of university. Now, at age twenty-six, Alan was finally ready to admit that Sam had been right.

As the car approached the turn-off to the Autoroute des Laurentides, Alan sensed a mood change in his attractive young passenger. The carefree and cheeky *bon vivant* had become serious and vulnerable. Alan tried to deflect whatever might be coming. He aired his usual gripes about the BMW, complaining about always having to take his prized possession for repairs during the cold weather. There was no way he was going to be sucked into anything serious with this young woman. He was already feeling guilty about the previous night. Sexual escapades were not his regular weekend bill of fare.

"I need your help, Alan. It's not just any lawyer I need but someone I can trust to look after something important. And not to talk about it." Antoinette's cocky smile had vanished, replaced by a look of fear and foreboding.

Alan sensed a trap. "Sure, you can trust me. But are we talking about something personal or legal?" He ran a hand nervously through his hair.

"Well it's both — I don't think you can separate it that way." She hesitated. "My father died last month. He left me some confidential papers that he wanted me to keep under lock and key until the first anniversary of his death. He passed away on January 10th and I've had a lot of difficulty handling it for the past month. Believe it or not, this is the first weekend I've been out since."

"Quite a coming out for you, Antoinette." Alan couldn't resist. She didn't smile. "I'm sorry," he said softly, kicking himself for being flip.

"You've got to understand. I made a promise to him on his deathbed. It's not a large package. It all fits into a small attaché case. It was important to him that nothing happen to it for one year. I don't want to let him down."

There were tears in her eyes. Alan instinctively patted her knee. "Don't worry. I'll do whatever I can to help."

"Alan, I've got the case with me. It's with my gear in the trunk of your car. Can you keep it at your office? It'll only be for a year, then I'll pick it up. By that time, papa's affairs can be wound up."

Alan couldn't help but notice the strange and somewhat erratic tone she used in speaking of her father, a tone that fluctuated frenetically between reverence and revulsion. He hesitated. He decided not to ask just what the package contained, for fear of being professionally implicated in something he didn't want to be a part of. "I don't do successions work in my practice. But I know two or three notaries competent in this field who could help you out."

"Alan, that's very helpful, but I'd really rather you stay on top of the situation yourself," she pleaded.

Alan didn't need any further explanation. But she rambled on. "I'm feeling so alone. I need a little time to get my act together. Please, take the attaché case and keep it — my father insisted that his papers be properly protected. You can call me with the names and numbers of those notaries. I'll get back to you, and you can send the case to whoever I choose." She paused. "But it may be a while, I need a little time." Her eyes were imploring, almost fearful in a way he had not seen the previous evening.

Alan was reluctant to get involved, but with Antoinette's sexual delights still fresh in his mind, he felt perhaps he owed her something. He would call her the following day with the names of the notaries, and then wait for her to get back with delivery instructions. Meanwhile, the small attaché case could be locked up in one of the filing cabinets at his office.

When they stopped for gas at St-Sauveur, Antoinette had

him open the trunk of the BMW and she rummaged through her suitcase. The locked attaché case had been tucked away under her clothing. Alan took it from her. He placed it in his large lawyer's briefcase lying on the back seat of the car, and twirled the combination dial to ensure that it was locked. This was not the first time that Alan's trusty old briefcase had been used for important papers in transit.

The plane touched down on the mottled black tarmac with a thud, the wing flaps went up and the reverse jet propulsion went into action to slow the heavy Boeing 747 to a stop on the icy runway. Marcel was surprised that it still seemed to be winter in Canada, even though it was April. Having seen the daffodils and tulips on the drive to Heathrow, and with memories of sunny Marseilles, Nice and the Mediterranean still fresh in his mind, the cold, gray arrival at Mirabel was a sobering experience.

An elevated bus carried Antoinette, Marcel and the other passengers from the tarmac directly to the fluorescent-lit terminal, disgorging them in front of the smiling, freshly scrubbed customs officers lined up in a row ready to process their papers.

As he took his bearings, Marcel could not help notice the large, cavernous nature of this terminal, obviously planned by a benevolent government that had anticipated far more air passenger traffic than had actually materialized. He quickly concluded that, compared to the bustling Nice International or the busy Terminal Three at Heathrow, this airport was having trouble justifying its existence.

"So this is the gateway to North America and my new life," he whispered to Antoinette. Nonetheless, he was amazed at the friendliness of the commissionaire who went out of his way to help guide them into line.

"Passport, sir. You two traveling together?" the customs officer asked with a French accent quite unlike any Marcel had heard for a long time.

"Yes, this is my daughter, Antoinette. We've been over for a brief vacation in London," explained Marcel carefully, in French. He put on his best Parisian accent, which he had scrupulously practiced to camouflage his Marseilles roots. Before leaving France, he had made other preparations. Antoinette had suggested a plan for getting Marcel into Canada illegally, based on the fact that she had possession of the passport belonging to her late father — and Marcel's old war comrade — Roger Belair.

Roger Belair had been born, as stated in the passport, in Pont l'Évéque, a small village in Normandy. When he was twelve, his father, a fitfully employed laborer, decided to move his family to Montreal and try his luck in the New World. With Roger's passport in hand, Marcel's very un-Québécois accent made perfect sense. Now he only had his appearance to worry about.

Marcel was a few years younger than Roger, but not enough, he hoped, to arouse suspicion. They both had brown eyes and gray hair, and Marcel had grown a thick beard like Roger's to hide the difference in the shape of their mouths. In London, he had a barber cut and style his hair like Roger's. With any luck, he would pass.

The middle-aged customs officer, trying unsuccessfully to adopt a classic French look with his droopy mustache and nonchalant demeanor, squinted intently at the passport photos of Roger and Antoinette Belair. He was taken aback by the contrast between the two pictures: the beautiful and sultry daughter and the worn-out and world-weary father. Looking up at Marcel, he was relieved to discover that the father was actually better looking and less tired than in his photo — probably the invigorating influence of his vivacious young daughter, he thought to himself.

"Did you buy anything when you were in England?"

"Nothing other than some very expensive meals, marvelous plays and a very expensive hotel suite," Marcel responded with a smile, having anticipated this question. Looking the customs officer squarely in the eye, Marcel appeared to challenge him to probe deeper — a calculated gamble that the best defense was a good offense.

"Well, looks like you enjoyed yourself. Can't charge you duty on those items. Go ahead." The officer had tacitly conceded victory. He handed them customs clearance forms, signaling them to proceed to the baggage arrivals area. His scribbled inscription permitted Marcel and Antoinette to whisk right by the brown-uniformed immigration official standing in wait for travelers identified by customs for interrogation. The pair picked up their luggage at the baggage carousel and marched out into the Quebec cold as ordinary residents of Canada returning from a family vacation.

As he jumped into the Mirabel taxi behind Antoinette for the ride south to Montreal, Marcel Gagnon permitted himself a tiny smile of self-satisfaction as he clutched his overstuffed valise. Ownership of four kilos of pure China white while poised on the doorstep of America, just 600 kilometers from a reliable New York buyer who'd already laid down a sizable deposit, wasn't a bad way to get started in the New World.

Antoinette had other thoughts, some of them troubling. She'd call Alan Chant in the morning.

Chapter Two

Disdainful but curious, Alan Chant adjusted his red and blue striped suspenders, straightened his Hermès tie and strode quickly into the Grand Salon at the Queen Elizabeth Hotel that April evening in 1984. Since the ski season had ended, he'd found himself taking on more legal work than he could handle. Though he'd promised his father he'd go to a political dinner that night, he was running late. "Christ, the old man says Savard's gonna be the next prime minister. Only three years out of law school, and I'm hobnobbing with the top guy," Alan had explained to his partner Guy Doucet as he rushed to leave the office. Guy would be there for another two hours.

"Alan, you'd better move it. You're never on time! You know how Sam hates that."

"What's a car dealer know about being a lawyer, Guy? Does he have the faintest idea what we do in this office? Probably thinks I'm a dilettante who spends most of my time at the ski slopes chasing women."

Earlier, Alan had tried to be charitable. "Dad's worked hard — he's never had much in the way of outside interests," he'd explained to Guy. "Politics are something new and exciting for him."

That morning, Alan had been doing a legal aid stint on

the third floor of the Palais de Justice, representing people in trouble with the police who couldn't afford a lawyer. There'd been four adjournments, five remands, three bail applications and two sentencings. Only one guy had gone to jail, a doper, a creep.

Alan did this duty work because he believed in helping the underdog — the disadvantaged and destitute everyone else rejected. McGill University Legal Aid had taught him that. The pay was lousy, sixty-five dollars an hour, very low for a partner at the up-and-coming law firm of Chant & Doucet. Though they were only a two-man shop, word had it they were destined for great things.

For Alan, though, legal aid work was like visiting your mom on Mother's Day — she likes it and you feel good. Besides, Montreal courts really worked a double standard if you let them get away with it. The poor got screwed unless someone forcefully intervened and reminded the judges of their duty to be fair. It was the sort of challenge that Alan thrived on, maybe even the reason he was attracted to law. But it could be discouraging, demeaning and occasionally dangerous.

At his fashionable pine-filled walk-up offices at 127 Rue St-Pierre, just south of Place d'Youville in Old Montreal, the afternoon had brought bigger challenges: a lucrative divorce case (with his good looks, he seemed to attract beautiful wives deserted by wealthy husbands), and a small investment dealer charged with fraud by the Quebec Securities Commission. "Think of it," Alan told Guy, "each case brought in retainers of ten thousand dollars just to get started. Not bad for an afternoon's work."

Alan's partner was pleased. Guy had run unsuccessfully in the 1976 Quebec election as a Péquiste, as members of the separatist Parti Québécois were known, six years before Alan had joined him in the practice fresh from law school and his call to the bar. Obviously Doucet's earlier political candidacy had paid off. He had been named special prosecutor by the Parti Québécois attorney-general of Quebec in over thirty criminal trials in Montreal. This work had become the firm's bread and butter.

Guy was a practical-minded lawyer known for his ability to cover all the bases so he had urged Alan to get involved in politics with another party, perhaps at the federal level. Instinctively, Alan had resisted — at least for the moment.

The stench. Puke, urine, shit, smelly armpits, all rolled into one. That's what Alan remembered the most from the first day he entered Courtroom 17 as legal aid duty counsel. At first he thought the odor came from the filthy holding cells in the basement where all the street hookers, transvestites, winos and petty thieves had been herded over the previous twelve hours.

Then he realized it wasn't just the result of sloppy maintenance by underpaid city staff. This horrible smell came off the bodies of these wretches — a sickly mixture of sweat, sour milk, rancid butter and stale tobacco that labeled these poor souls as hopeless rejects and inferior beings deserving little compassion and respect.

Alan managed to fight off feelings of nausea, revulsion and condescension that day. Whether it was his mother Laura's example in her quiet support of the Salvation Army and its charges in Pointe-Claire over many years, or the gentle but effective prodding of his McGill "Ethics and the Law" professor who preached "justice for all" at every opportunity, Alan soon came to recognize his special calling. For the next little while, the lower criminal courts in Montreal would be his arena in which to serve mankind through the pursuit of equal justice. Once the goal was in sight, dealing with the ugly smells, the indignities, the creeps and the assholes was easy.

The elder Chant was indeed annoyed, but quietly. "Seems like Alan got hung up at the office," he whispered to Jean-Marc Labelle, who ran the biggest car rental agency in downtown Montreal and was Sam's best customer. Beads of sweat ran down Sam's back, but were hidden by his expensive Hugo Boss suit. Savard and his entourage would soon make their entrance. Sam desperately wanted Alan at his side when the bigwigs approached him. Deep down, he felt that running the largest Chev Olds dealership in Montreal wasn't enough. Having a son who was a partner at a law firm and a star graduate from McGill Law School improved his image.

"Hi, Dad, Mr. Labelle. Sorry I'm late. A major case came in at the last moment — had to take instructions." Without intending it, Alan was beginning to sound like an English barrister at Lincoln's Inn.

"Take instructions? For Christ's sake," Sam muttered beneath his breath. Outwardly, he beamed.

Introductions to the "beautiful people" at Sam's table followed: Ned McRae, the tall, gangling, forever smiling senior partner at Rayment Leclair, Sam's auditors, and a political sycophant responsible for retaining his firm's fair share of federal Crown agency audit clients; Serge Gendron, a dapper advertising executive with an Armani suit and perfect teeth, one of Savard's key bag men; Gilles Lavoie, the earnest but ineffectual member of Parliament for Ste-Foy in suburban Quebec City whose most memorable attribute was his curly hair; Bertrand Grandmaison, a high-powered, handsome Outremont businessman with a long-time history of loyal party support; and Felicia

Fortin, a striking middle-aged tax lawyer with noble Italian and French ancestry, a partner in a large downtown firm that counted Sam as a key client.

In his rougher moments, Sam described Felicia as "the beautiful broad who helps me screw the government."

Not a bad assemblage at five hundred dollars a pop. Where else could Sam, for a tax-deductible four grand, get so much influence, glamour and a chance to be seen as one of Savard's insiders? The opportunity to show off his talented son to the prospective prime minister and his cronies was a bonus.

The room smelled delicious and masculine, an intriguing combination of high quality roast beef, aromatic eau de toilette for men and the occasional Cuban cigar. The television lights were focused on the entrance nearest the head table and giant screens carefully placed in each corner were showing a continuous montage of beautiful Canadian scenery.

Suddenly, the raspy voice of Bruce Springsteen singing "Born to Run" crackled over the loudspeaker. The suits and their ladies marched slowly towards the head table. Like trained seals, the crowd stood up immediately and clapped politely. They were awe-struck by this grand entrance of their hero with the broad smile and flashing eyes, the object of their largesse and their expected vehicle for achieving power in Ottawa.

"Pretentious bastard — using an American pop singer for his entrance," Alan brooded. "Is he bringing a presidential podium too?" If it had been him, he'd have used something by a Canadian, say Burton Cummings and "I've Got My Own Way To Rock." Yet, without really knowing why, he was clapping along with the rest.

The saying of the grace, the introductions and Savard's

speech were all standard political stuff. "Why have him speak first, before we eat?" Alan asked his father, his handsome high forehead furrowing for the first time. "I missed lunch today since Court went late — Christ, I'm famished."

"Try to understand, Alan. Savard and his people are pros — they want to hit the evening TV news with this speech. That means into the can and down to the studio before eight-thirty. We want a shot at 'The National.' The convention is in less than two months and this is the best way to reach delegates across the country." Sam was already sounding like an insider.

Alan shrugged and hungrily munched on another roll as Savard wound up his pitch for economic renewal, Canadian unity and better relations with Canada's American neighbors. "I need your help to make Canada strong!" he intoned, with unctuous sincerity.

"Let's get out of here," snarled the cameraman behind Alan's table. Coming before the closing of Savard's speech, this interruption at first struck Alan as rude and insensitive. It reminded him, though, that just by being in this hall, he had the jump on all those unsuspecting Canadians who did not yet fully appreciate that Savard was headed for the top. He watched the videotape being slapped into its case by the television crew and hustled out to a waiting car, its images to be transmitted within the hour to more than three million homes.

After soup, Chateaubriand, poire Belle-Hélène and cognac, the band started playing. "God, they've flown in Hagood Hardy from Toronto. Would you believe it?" Alan winced. "That geriatric music from 'The Homecoming' — here in Montreal! Oscar Peterson would have been better."

A burly advance man whispered to Sam, "Jacques's making the rounds. Your table's next."

Selwyn House, on Côte St-Antoine, was unlike any other private school in Montreal. Its prefect system was designed along English lines to teach young gentlemen aged fourteen to sixteen how to handle authority over other young gentlemen just slightly their junior. A wide array of disciplinary measures was available — detentions, quarter laps on the track, messenger service, even caning by the headmaster in serious cases.

For five years, Alan dreamed of being a prefect. He remembered vividly the date and place when he was called out of his grade eleven class to the headmaster's office to get the word. Access to power was like an aphrodisiac to him even then, though the responsibilities that went with it eventually prevailed. Alan actually felt humble and vowed never to abuse power like so many around him already had. It was almost three months before he handed out his first detention.

Sam proudly announced to his assembled table, so all could hear, "We're about to be visited by the next prime minister of Canada."

Alan spied Savard, bathed in TV lights, striding towards their table. He was smaller than he looked on television. But there was no mistaking that silver-gray hair, those perfect teeth, the flashing eyes, the joie de vivre, the ooze of confidence and power. Savard seized Sam's hand, letting him decide the order of introduction. He'd known Sam for just five years, and only in passing, but he greeted him now like a lifelong friend because he needed his support, along with that of all the others, in the upcoming campaign.

There was a blur of charming remarks, followed by

fawning responses from everyone in Sam's lair. Savard's eyes fixed on Alan. He mouthed the words, "Who do we have here?"

Savard knew very well that Alan, an only child, was the apple of Sam's eye. Alan smiled, confident that he could handle being singled out for special attention.

"Pleased to meet you, Mr. Savard — enjoyed your speech," Alan lied. But now he was hooked. It would only be a matter of weeks before the call came. His partner Guy would be very happy.

Chapter Three

"Susan Belair, is it really you?" Alan called after the attractive woman running towards the large glass doors that formed the entrance to the Palais de Justice at the corner of Notre-Dame and St-Laurent in Old Montreal. As her feet beat out staccato steps on the stone stairs, Alan noticed the shapely, muscular legs beneath the skirt of her stylish black suit. Her blond ponytail and red hair ribbon bobbed up and down in unison and a well-worn briefcase dangled loosely from her left hand as she firmly clutched the day's file in her right.

Susan was tempted to ignore the greeting. She was in a hurry. It was ten minutes past nine and court started at nine-thirty sharp. Her client, a young Haitian woman charged with shoplifting who would be deported if she were convicted, had already been waiting for almost three quarters of an hour, and Susan had yet to meet her. But the voice calling after her had a strong ring of familiarity. It had been too firm, too insistent and too "Anglo" to be just another client waiting to chat or complain.

"It *is* you. Haven't seen you since third year at McGill," he said as he caught up to her. Alan had been at least ten feet behind. Thrusting his large frame forward two steps at a time, he was slightly ahead of her in their mutual quest to open the two sets of heavy doors. "What are you doing here in uniform? Thought you were going into immigration work with the blue jean and denim shirt crowd."

Susan looked slightly irritated. "This *is* immigration work, Alan Chant. My client is alleged to have stolen two hundred dollars' worth of children's clothing. If I don't get her off today, she'll be shipped back to Haiti before you can blink." Then she allowed herself a smile, as though finally taking in Alan's attractive looks. "It's really great to see you — heard you joined Guy Doucet in a new partnership in Old Montreal and are already the lawyer of choice for Montreal's white collar criminals." Alan smiled wryly. She had managed to both flatter and insult.

"Listen, I'm in a real time bind, Alan — haven't even met my client yet and she's number five on the list. I'll have to catch up with you later. Could we do lunch sometime?"

"How about today, say at Les Filles du Roi at one o'clock? My morning's ending reasonably early — entering a "not guilty" plea on a trafficking charge — making an election and setting a date for one of the Conditti brothers." Alan spoke rapidly, trying quite unsuccessfully not to sound like a name dropper.

"Sure, as long as my client's case is disposed of by lunch time. Give me your card, and I'll call your office to confirm. But if you don't hear from me by twelve-thirty, assume that I can't make it. Now buzz off, big shot, I've got work to do that involves *real* justice."

She gave him a warm smile and a friendly wink. "Hope to see you later."

For Alan, the wink brought back memories of Susan, the spunky French-Canadian law student, always a bit impertinent in class but pulling it off with a combination of brains, charm and sex appeal.

Alan had never asked Susan out at McGill because he was heavily involved at the time with another student (Gail Leahy, he remembered unpleasantly). But he had fantasized more than once about a relationship with Susan, given her magnetism and the allure of her sensual beauty, intellectual inquisitiveness and apparent commitment to fighting injustice. She had a certain mysteriousness and flair, which he figured derived from her Québécois roots.

Sam had always warned his son about being seduced by the many French beauties who populated social and professional circles in Montreal. But somehow Susan was different. Word had it at McGill that her real name was Suzanne. Apparently she had changed it just before entering McGill Law School to please her father, who wanted her to become proficient in the English language and mannerisms.

Alan finished his assignment that morning for Tony Conditti by ten-thirty, having agreed to a date for trial in September. It was only a seven-minute walk back to his office, where a mound of files awaited his attention.

"Alan, phone call for you," said Hélène Lambert at twenty-five past twelve. Hélène was Alan's secretary who also served as switchboard operator, scheduler and research assistant at Chant & Doucet. "It's Susan Belair from the Palais de Justice."

Alan had begun to despair and was relieved to hear from her. "Just finished two minutes ago, Alan. Got an acquittal out of old Thibodeau, would you believe it? Is lunch still on at Les Filles du Roi?"

Alan tried to be nonchalant yet enthusiastic. "Yeah, I

think so. I'll have Hélène confirm the reservation. Hold on for just a minute." He put Susan on hold for two minutes, knowing full well that the reservation was secure, and carefully consulted his pocket diary. He got back on the line. "Yeah, sure, it's a go. I'll see you there at one. It's table number four, the one at the rear. I'll bet you have a happy client. Congratulations!"

Alan hung up the phone as Hélène entered his inner office, which occupied a small but charming corner of an old Montreal building. The office featured exposed brick, rough-hewn timbers, wooden plank floors studded with large wooden nails, a large pine desk with an antique phone, an old dry sink serving as a credenza and a leather couch covered with a richly textured afghan knit by a gifted Quebec artisan from the Gaspé. Guy's office was a larger version of Alan's, although he had begun to sully the old Quebec image by introducing a few modern furniture pieces of glass and steel.

"Why did you keep her on hold for two minutes?" Hélène asked innocently.

"Had to check my schedule to see whether I could manage a full two-hour lunch at Filles du Roi. This is not going to be a grab-and-run situation. Could you reschedule my three o'clock appointment with Frank Russo to four?" Alan responded, trying to sound casual about putting personal interests ahead of business.

Russo was a high-profile commodities broker who had been charged under the Quebec Securities Act. Alan had to tell him later that he would have to arrange alternate counsel, since at the end of the month he was taking a leave of absence from the firm for a couple of years to go to Ottawa. There he would be working for Jacques Savard, the new leader of the Opposition. Russo would be disappointed but at the same time impressed that Alan was attaching himself to the person likely to be the next prime minister of Canada. He would feel that the counsel Alan chose for him, likely his senior partner Guy Doucet, would be able to protect his interests, aided and abetted by his important new political connection in the capital.

Les Filles du Roi had been a culinary institution in Old Montreal for many years. From the street, its dark stone exterior was inconspicuous except for the two impressive brass coach lamps mounted on either side of the under-stated entrance. Inside, the rich, dark pine furniture was gently accented by antique lighting fixtures and magnificent handmade quilts adorning the red brick walls.

To complete the seventeenth-century mood, the staff were dressed in early Québécois *paysan* costumes — the men as farmhands in their Norman-inspired coveralls, red neckerchiefs and floppy berets, the women as farmhouse girls with colorful long skirts, white lace hats and blouses, and lots of cleavage. "Les filles du roi" were originally single young women dispatched by the French kings to the colony of Quebec to keep the working men company so they wouldn't leave Quebec, and to start a home-grown rather than an imported population. They were immediately prolific.

Susan arrived first and was greeted warmly and respectfully in English as "Mr. Chant's good friend" by Michel, the fastidious maître d' who had been there for more than twenty years. She was immediately shown to table number four. Michel offered to safeguard her briefcase in the manager's office and, without being asked, brought her an ice-cold bottle of Perrier complete with wineglass and a twist of lemon. "Nice touch. Guess he knows what the Anglos and their friends want at lunch — a cool drink and a clear head," she thought to herself, cynically. Still, although Susan was no Quebec nationalist, she wasn't sure whether she should resent the fact that Michel seemed to have assumed she was English.

It struck her that, while Perrier was nice for quenching thirst, she really preferred a glass of good red wine. Her case that morning had been a tough one and she was tempted to order a glass before Alan arrived. But that might have been a little forward since she hadn't seen him for three years. She remembered that he seemed somewhat straight-laced at McGill, appearing more interested in getting good marks and going home early for a good night's sleep than joining the beer and pizza crowd at Amelio's when the library closed at eleven o'clock.

"Hi, Susan, sorry I'm late. Recovered yet from your ordeal this morning?" Alan broke into her thoughts, politely kissing her on both cheeks before sitting down. "My God, has Michel brought you nothing more than a Perrier? Let's get you some wine — *qu'est-ce que c'est que tu préfères — du rouge ou du blanc?*"

"Red," she responded with a smile. "Your accent needs a little work." Susan knew that Alan would be working as much in French as in English, given his case load in the Montreal criminal courts. She also remembered his moot court presentation in second year at McGill, entirely in French. She had thought at the time that it was not at all bad for an Anglo.

Her most vivid memory, however, was his performance on a panel at a law school conference on protecting native rights in the James Bay area in the face of a massive hydroelectric development by Hydro-Québec. She had admired his incisive mind and social sensitivity as he urged a reasonable balance between economic development and protection of an important minority within

Quebec. Alan's closing remarks remained fresh in her mind: "Above all, Quebec must be fair to all its inhabitants as we march forward into the twenty-first century."

This had not been popular with the *nationalistes* in the student body who had been critical of native obstruction of Quebec economic independence. But it had struck a positive chord with her.

Although the bottle of Moulin à Vent was more than half gone, the waiter had wisely been reluctant to interrupt their animated and what appeared to be highly personal conversation. At last he came to their table.

"Pour madame, la brandade de morue aux raves, avec une salade verte," Alan said, after scanning the menu. *"Et pour moi, le lapin au poivre, avec une salad verte."*

Susan had asked Alan to order for her. "You probably come here more often than I do," she teased. "Immigration law doesn't buy a lot of fancy lunches." Alan had responded immediately, going to the "specialités de la maison" section of the menu. He'd ignored price and chosen the most exotic items.

"Do you like fish?"

"Yes, love it — as long as it's fresh and from Canadian waters," she'd answered.

So he had decided on the cod, no doubt caught from the Grand Banks off Newfoundland. For himself, the rabbit seemed appropriate — tasty but not too heavy, since he still had work to do that afternoon.

"Any symbolism there, Alan?" Susan had asked mischievously. "Rabbit for you, fish for me?"

Alan had paused a moment, then gave it his best shot. "You swim fast, I run fast. Either way, we get where we want in a hurry," he'd said, lamely.

"You could have ordered turtle soup for me — I noticed

it on the menu. Then we could have assumed the roles of tortoise and hare. That might have proved a better fit," she'd laughed triumphantly.

"Well, Susan, I'll be honest. I thought about that briefly. But there are two problems with that fable. First, I don't see us in competition with each other. In fact, there may be a lot of things we can do together. Second, I don't like being the hare, because I'm not going to lose whatever race we get into. I'm only interested in a win-win situation for both of us. Now, let me tell you about my new job in Ottawa. Starts next month."

Alan and Susan covered a lot of ground over the next two hours. They dissected their professors at McGill (some had inspired, others had disappointed or angered, and one had been fired from the university). They compared summer jobs (Alan had planted trees in northern Ontario, Susan had worked as a waitress in Pointe-au-Pic). They described their first job as lawyers (before joining Guy Doucet, Alan had done his *stage*, or articling, at Richard et Langelier, a well-known Montreal criminal law firm whose senior partner had been *bâtonnier*, or head, of the Montreal bar; Susan had been unsuccessful in lining up a job for her *stage* with a large firm in Montreal and ended up working for the Immigrant Aid Society of Greater Montreal, which had eventually led to her own immigration practice at the corner of Park and Milton).

As the discussion turned to personal matters, they shared their family problems. Alan complained mildly about his materialistic father who seemed concerned most about driving the most expensive and flashiest car he could lay his hands on, as long as it came from General Motors. Susan was still distraught over the death of her father five months previously, particularly since they'd had a falling out just before his death. She also had concerns about her younger sister, Antoinette, who had abandoned her education far too early and was getting caught up in the Montreal film crowd for all the wrong reasons.

Suddenly, Alan made the connection between his February escapade at Mont-Tremblant, with its reminder sitting in his filing cabinet back at the office, and the attractive woman across the table from him. He looked suitably sympathetic and then set about subtly changing the subject. He hoped Susan didn't notice.

Eventually they turned to their own personal lives, at least those parts they cared to talk about. Alan had played the field since law school. After breaking off with the detested Gail Leahy he'd had no time to develop any serious relationship with one exception — Jane Buckingham, an aspiring Junior Leaguer from Westmount who had ultimately proved to be too socially aggressive for Alan.

Susan had had two serious relationships, one with an older stockbroker fresh out of his first marriage and more impressed with his own huge ego and sizable bank account than with Susan, and the other with the assistant conductor of the Montreal Symphony Orchestra. He had rekindled Susan's interests in the arts but had been unable to accept Susan's intense desire to make her own mark in a profession that he neither appreciated nor understood.

Finally, they got into the professional intricacies of their recent cases, with Alan letting Susan go first. She explained how she had convinced Judge Thibodeau that her Haitian client did not really have criminal intent the day that she took the clothing from the children's department at the Bay. Alan talked about Chant & Doucet's first case under the Quebec Securities Act, representing Frank Russo, which, if successful, would likely lead to further lucrative assignments for the firm.

Susan and Alan ended their long lunch at twenty past three, finishing with soufflé au chocolat and cappuccino. With difficulty they tried to re-focus their minds and bodies on the remainder of the business day that awaited them. Alan had his rendez-vous with the obnoxious Russo at four. Susan was scheduled to see a Cuban refugee who was coming back for a second meeting with supposedly firmer evidence to buttress his already shaky story.

"Susan, can we do this again soon? I haven't enjoyed a lunch so much in a long time," he said as he kissed her not on the cheek but squarely on the mouth. Her lips were warm.

"Lunches like this are generally very difficult for me," Susan said to a temporarily disappointed Alan. "But I've been known to accept dinner invitations, particularly on the weekend." She surprised even herself by her forward response.

Alan hardly missed a beat. "This Saturday night, dinner at Les Halles. And no appointments afterwards, please," he said with only a hint of questioning in his voice.

"Shall I meet you at the restaurant, and at what time?" she asked, tacitly acknowledging her acceptance.

"I'll pick you up at 4854 Côte-des-Neiges at the corner of Queen Mary, apartment 304, telephone 932-4174." He grinned. "That's why I was a bit late for lunch — you weren't listed in the phone directory so I had to go to other sources. How about seven-thirty?"

"Sure, Saturday night is fine, but make it eight-thirty. I'm playing tennis until seven at the Mount Royal, and need time to get home and change."

Alan was impressed. Here was someone as active as he was, with an interesting career as a lawyer and apparently part of the social set from the Mount Royal Tennis Club. Located on Gray Avenue in Westmount just below Sherbrooke, it had twelve courts, a respectable but not spectacular clubhouse, an outdoor swimming pool and a comfortable balcony — truly an ideal place for the upwardly mobile.

"You're on. No problem." He gave her one last peck on the cheek and hurried away, trying to shove the anticipated dinner date out of his mind so that he could deal head on with Russo.

On the following Sunday, a few minutes past noon, Alan finally left 4854 Côte-des-Neiges in his black BMW after a wonderful dinner at Les Halles, a long rapturous night and a leisurely breakfast of fresh orange juice, eggs benedict, croissants, black coffee and *The New York Sunday Times*. Susan had another tennis game at the Mount Royal at one-thirty and kicked him out to get ready.

Chapter Four

"**L**adies and gentlemen, we have the results of the fourth and final ballot," intoned the chair of the leadership convention, his warm, crooked smile a contrast to the electric tension that pervaded the arena.

"In alphabetical order: Joan Forrester — 1,418." He spoke slowly and deliberately. The crowd noise began to swell in the left center of the stands and a noticeable collective groan could be heard at the far right end.

"Jacques Savard — 1,569." He had barely finished before the Savard supporters erupted in a deliriously jubilant frenzy, assured now that their hard-fought battle to achieve party leadership for their hero was finally over.

It was a warm September afternoon, the Thursday before Labor Day. So much had happened in the intervening three months that the convention now seemed like the distant past, thought Dr. Tom Baldwin. Thanks to the early resignation of an elderly member of Parliament from Montreal and the cooperation of the prime minister, a by-election had been called in late July and Jacques Savard had won handily. Now Tom stood in front of the Parliament buildings in Ottawa, about to visit the office of the leader of the official Opposition. He was a man of medium height and solid build, with warm, hazel eyes, a clean-cut jaw and a pleasant, open face. Although prematurely gray, he appeared youthful and energetic, partly because he kept himself in superb physical shape.

When he'd got out of the taxi at the west door of the Centre Block, Tom found himself almost involuntarily looking up at the Peace Tower. Silhouetted against a cloudless sky, it struck him as a comforting, familiar symbol of orderly government and Canadian-style democracy.

On arriving in the foyer of the ground floor, he presented his credentials to the commissionaire, who looked up at him with friendly curiosity. With most members of Parliament back in their ridings preparing for the upcoming election, people around the Hill tended to be tourists or House of Commons staff. Visitors like Tom, a stranger important enough to have an appointment with Savard, were apparently a rarity.

"Yes sir, I 'ave your name 'ere on my list." The commissionaire had a strong French Canadian accent, which reminded Tom, a westerner, that Quebec was just across the river. "Monsieur Savard is expecting you at three in room 409 S. You can take the elevator or the central staircase. If you take the stairs you will pass the House of Commons on the second floor and the prime minister's office on the third. Monsieur Savard's office is on the fourth."

Baldwin chose the stairs. The last time he'd seen the Parliament buildings he'd been a teenager on a high school trip and he hadn't paid much attention. He slowed as he passed the outer doors of the House of Commons, shut down and silent for the summer. The bright afternoon sun filtered through the stained glass windows lining the upper level of the chamber, and he was impressed by the rich green and gold light that lingered there.

Reaching the fourth floor, he was still uncomfortable with the thought that the occupant of this ornate historical office on the south side, which had housed Canadian prime ministers and opposition leaders since the turn of the century, had been his mortal enemy only a few months ago. And now he was about to meet him to discuss prospects for a new job after the impending election.

As he approached the reception desk, he was met by Jacques Savard's personal secretary, a charming, well-dressed francophone woman in her late forties who clearly presided as the gatekeeper for the office. On their short walk to Savard's suite, she pointed out the small, functional office of the newly appointed executive assistant. Tom spied a tall, tousled-haired young man wearing fashionable navy blue and red suspenders. He was leaning back in his executive leather chair with his feet — shod in glossy black loafers — on the desk. He was totally absorbed in what appeared to be an intense telephone conversation. The secretary explained that he was a civil rights lawyer by the name of Alan Chant, just up from Montreal. Recently hired by Monsieur Savard as a senior staffer, he was an example of the sort of new talent the leader had been able to attract to work for him in Ottawa.

The walls of Savard's office looked bare, probably because his retired predecessor, who had moved out only in July, had removed all his personal memorabilia — family portraits, political photos, gifts from visiting dignitaries. But the carved wooden desk was a masterpiece. The mahogany wainscoting and the rich-looking bookshelves laden with parliamentary tomes lent a certain weighty aura to this special workplace of such famous Canadians as Diefenbaker, Pearson, St. Laurent and King.

The leather furniture had that old English club look, eminently suitable for those who had seen or done it all. As he awaited Savard's entrance, Tom wondered how many important people had sat in those impressive chairs over the years, how many potent political plans had been hatched within these four walls, and what great influence events within this august room must have had on Canadians over the years.

Savard's entrance was almost anticlimactic. He was much smaller than he had appeared at the leadership convention and more personable. "I need talented people like you in my government, Dr. Baldwin. That's why I'm glad you've decided to take the plunge in Regina East."

"Pleased to help out, sir. Don't have much experience in organized politics but I'll do what I can out in Saskatchewan. Hope my medical background might come in handy once we're over the election." Savard smiled politely but said nothing. He knew Baldwin would be angling for the health and welfare portfolio after the election — the medical doctors coming into the House for the first time were all the same. He was relieved that Baldwin had the good sense not to ask outright.

"Very impressive office you have here, Mr. Leader. I'm honored that you suggested I visit here today," Tom said, trying to break the uneasy silence following his last remark. "And congratulations on your by-election victory, sir."

"Thanks. I don't plan to be in this office too long, Dr. Baldwin. We're all gunning for the bigger offices downstairs and the prime minister's suite in the Langevin Block across the street. Haven't even unpacked any of my personal stuff yet."

That explained the bare walls, thought Tom. If nothing else, the man was confident.

"Once the election's called," Savard went on, "I expect to be out of here onto the hustings for the duration. Don't want you or any of the other star candidates to even dream of coming to Ottawa until you're officially declared the winner on election night." Savard paused and held out his hand. "Now, if you need any information or organizational help, call my people at party headquarters. If there's some emergency requiring my personal attention, call my assistant Alan Chant just down the hall. Good luck!"

◆ ▼

Baldwin had reason to marvel at the fast pace of events. It was less than six months since he'd been approached as a non-political but prominent young Regina physician, to come out and meet Joan Forrester, an aspiring candidate for the leadership of the opposition party in Ottawa. She was a middle-aged Toronto lawyer, a courtroom veteran. Though never elected to political office, she promised vision, good judgment and intelligence.

That cold March night at the "Meet the Candidate" reception at the Ramada Inn in downtown Regina, Baldwin had been impressed not so much by her rhetoric as by her body language, her demeanor. ("All politicians sound the same," he observed to his wife Carolyn on the drive home.)

By the way Forrester walked, smiled, frowned, listened, laughed and even flirted, she projected a basic honesty and integrity that was all too rare among elected people. As a professional, Baldwin could see why Forrester had been successful in the courtroom — she could establish a presence, a rapport with the judges before whom she appeared. The thought struck him that she might achieve the same success with the voters, long grown weary of self-centered, arrogant politicians who didn't listen or try to understand.

For Tom, Joan Forrester had something extra despite her mature years. "God, she's impressive," he thought to himself as he watched her confidently work the room. He noted her warm smile, her firm bosom, broad shoulders and dark hair swept up in a chignon. Her fashionable knit suit, in a rich teal blue, accentuated her slender legs. He wondered if she had a man in her life.

The questions served up to Forrester that night at the Ramada Inn had been easy enough. What's the number one issue facing the nation? ("People have lost faith in their elected representatives.") Can you speak French well enough to be party leader? ("*Assez bien. Je consacre une heure par jour à mes études.*") What's your prescription for pulling Canada out of the economic recession? ("Reduce the deficit and find ways for the private sector to create more jobs.")

But it was a lengthy answer towards the end of the question period, which had followed the traditional open bar, coffee, tea and stale sandwiches, that impressed Baldwin the most. Questions had been fired staccato-style from the audience, all of whom had been standing with drinks or coffee cups carefully balanced.

From the corner of her eye, Forrester had noticed a diminutive, bespectacled Chinese male trying valiantly to get in a question. Because of his weak voice and his small stature, he was having no luck. Baldwin recognized him as Dr. Stephen Wong, head of anesthesia at the Regina General Hospital. "Look, Carolyn, it's Stephen. I bet we're the only two doctors here," he whispered to his wife.

"Excuse me, ladies and gentlemen," Forrester interrupted politely, "there's a gentleman in about the third row who's been trying for some time to get in a question. I'd like to hear him. We've got to give everyone here a chance."

"Miss Forrester, what is your position on Canada's

immigration policy?" the doctor asked.

That was a loaded question, here in a hotel room in downtown Regina. Forrester knew that more than half the people in the room would want a more restrictive immigration policy. But the questioner — his accent from his native Hong Kong barely suppressed — would probably favor a more open one.

"That's a good question, Dr. Wong." Astutely, Forrester had managed to make out the name tag proudly mounted on his left lapel. "All of you know that this country was built on immigration — for example, we had large and significant movements of people from the Ukraine and Poland at the turn of the century." It was smart politics, thought Tom, to start with these groups since many Ukrainians and Poles had settled the prairie provinces, including Saskatchewan.

Forrester went on to detail various waves of immigrants and refugees that had swept Canada since the mid-1800s, careful to include the Chinese. Although this was basic high school history for most people in the room, the crowd seemed rapt. Then she paused, ever so slightly shifting gears.

"However, there is one thing that I would try to do differently, that is, to make the immigration admission process fairer — to establish a clear set of rules under which people can come to Canada based on individual merit or close family ties. This would involve the elimination of queue-jumping and illegal immigration that the present government has permitted for too long."

Forrester appeared almost judicial as she looked people directly in the eye. She finished with a warm smile aimed at a pleased and comforted Dr. Wong, who envisaged easy entry for many of his medical school classmates stuck in mid-career in the Royal Hong Kong Hospital. Others in the room interpreted Forrester's answer as signaling a tightening up of immigration, and they too were pleased.

Trust and confidence permeated the room. Everyone seemed to feel, Baldwin observed, that whatever their individual views they could count on Forrester to be just and impartial if she became party leader and prime minister.

Carolyn jokingly chided Tom on the way home. "I'm surprised you were taken in by that smooth woman and all her 'vision, judgment and intelligence' stuff. She's in good shape, though, for someone who must be close to fifty — I bet she's had lots of younger lovers your age. Maybe I should be worried."

"She's forty-seven." Shooting back a wry look, Tom knew that Carolyn could read him like a book. He was indeed taken in — but not for the reasons she suggested. Carolyn, always loyal, was too attractive, intelligent and self-confident in her own right for Tom to even dream about infidelity.

But he did feel that evening a rekindling of his latent interest in politics, suppressed since his undergraduate days at the University of Saskatchewan at Saskatoon. He had been president of the student council when he decided that he wanted to go to medical school at the University of Toronto and would need to commit all his time and energy to first getting in and then getting through the course.

"Maybe I'll get involved in her leadership campaign, Carolyn. They want me to run at the delegation selection meeting for our constituency next month. There'll be six chosen from Regina East and the convention's scheduled for the second weekend in June. It won't take that much time. Damn it, the clowns who are running the government now have got to go, and I think she'd make an attractive alternative."

Carolyn chuckled mischievously. "Is it the 'alternative' part that really interests you, or is it the 'attractive' part?"

Tom hardly heard her. There was more on his mind than getting elected as a delegate in April and spending a long, hot June weekend waving placards in a crowded, smelly arena in Ottawa. He had become aware that there was no serious candidate to challenge the government incumbent in Regina East, a milquetoast character who had distinguished himself through invisibility both in the nation's capital and in his own riding.

At age thirty-eight, Tom was a surgeon with a specialty in obstetrics. He had become chief of the medical staff at the Regina General Hospital, the city's largest — an unprecedented achievement brought about by hard work, professional competence, smart politics and good luck. His two main contenders for the post had effectively canceled each other out. Dr. Theodore Luns, respected by other doctors, was too disdainful of the General's board of directors, believing that no one without medical training had any right to make decisions about the hospital. Dr. Bertha French, while highly regarded by the board, was universally disliked by her professional peers because of her huge ego, inability to be a team player and her autocratic style.

Tom, with no perceived enemies, had run up the middle as the compromise candidate.

Having reached his professional goal at such a young age, Tom had wondered what challenges would come next. He could not imagine remaining chief of the medical staff for the rest of his working life.

"Come on, Tom, it's Saturday night and the party starts at

nine. You'll never get a girl sitting on your butt working out biochemistry formulas."

The University of Saskatchewan in 1971 was a good party school, in spite of, or perhaps because of, its relative obscurity and the long prairie winters. Even though they'd broken up, the Beatles were still popular, Simon & Garfunkel appealed to the dreamy set, and bellbottoms and long hair were the rage.

"Nope, gonna finish this assignment tonight 'cause tomorrow's committed," Tom confessed to his roommate in the student residence. "I'm chairing a Student Christian Movement conference all afternoon and evening tomorrow, and I'm going to church in the morning."

"You're getting religious on us, Tom. Loosen up for Christ's sake and get into the mainstream."

"The mainstream?" Tom snapped. "I know where that is and I'm in the middle of it. Do you know how many SCM members there are at the university? And they're all going to vote on election day."

Friday was voting day at the university. There was a huge storm and many students had partied late the night before, so voter turn-out was only twenty-three percent. Tom won the presidency of the student council with fifty-four percent of the vote.

When the result was announced, Tom felt tears welling up. Impulsively he put his arms around Forrester. She was too polished to let this syrupy young Regina doctor, her Saskatchewan organizer, distract from the dignity of the moment of her expected loss to Savard. Gently, she moved him aside with a kiss on the cheek and whispered "Thanks." Maintaining her composure and warm smile for the benefit of the four million TV viewers, she moved majestically out of her VIP box towards center stage.

Everyone watching knew what had just occurred. The forces of organization, money, pragmatism and sycophancy had prevailed over the powers of principle, integrity, imagination and feminism. The leadership campaign had been hard fought, but the clever and handsome Savard, using all his glib charm and not inconsiderable energy, had outgunned Forrester on three fronts: he had raised far more money, he had obtained early and binding commitments from key Quebec organizers, and he had projected a more "stable" image — in other words, delegates were just not ready to accept a woman as leader.

Forrester was gracious in defeat. She kissed Savard on both cheeks, held up his arm in a symbolic gesture and asked that the result be made unanimous.

Tom was devastated. Everything had revolved around Forrester — his decision to become a delegate and to be away from the hospital and Carolyn for all of convention week, the call from Forrester asking him to be Saskatchewan organizer and finally the approach from the Regina East riding president asking him to seek the nomination for the general election expected in the fall. Now, all this effort seemed wasted.

Tom had made the mistake of believing that his own organizational success in the nine Saskatchewan constituencies was being repeated across Canada. Through Tom's efforts, twenty-eight Saskatchewan delegates had been committed to Forrester, with only eleven for Savard and fifteen undecided. But Forrester had not done as well in other parts of the country. In Quebec the francophone Savard was more appealing, and in rural and suburban Ontario, with their large numbers of delegates, Forrester was viewed as left of center.

From the nearly deserted VIP box, which twenty minutes earlier had been a hive of frenzied activity befitting a prospective prime minister, Baldwin watched glumly as Savard strode to the podium to give his acceptance speech.

"Does this guy stand for anything?" he thought, forcing himself to listen. Something inside Baldwin told him to give Savard a fair hearing, no matter how loathsome he seemed.

By then most of the seats around him in the arena had been vacated. Tom couldn't bring himself to attend Forrester's wake back at the Chateau Laurier Hotel. He sure as hell wasn't going to intrude on the victory party of all those smarmy Savard supporters either. Feeling empty, he caught the last flight out of Ottawa that night and reached Regina via Toronto mid–morning.

Chapter Five

After the leadership convention, the nation had responded favorably to Savard's call for party unity, national reconciliation and economic renewal. But there had been much grumbling, fomented by media opinion, that the party had squandered the opportunity to select its first woman leader, however inexperienced.

Serenely, Forrester had remained above the fray, enjoying the wave of public sympathy but politely and properly asserting her unequivocal support for Savard in the battle to defeat the government in the next general election.

During the summer run up to the election, Savard had taken two significant steps to help heal the rift arising from the leadership campaign. The first was to name Forrester deputy party leader. The other was to personally telephone all Forrester organizers who had not publicly criticized him and who were perceived to have a future in the party as candidates or organizers.

A startled Baldwin had received one of these calls. Moreover, Savard knew from his thorough staff that Tom had been considering the nomination in Regina East. He encouraged him to run, with the guarded suggestion of even better things to come if he won and the party formed the government. He had even suggested a meeting with him in Ottawa. Flattered but confused, Tom had called Forrester in late August.

"Don't be silly, Tom. In politics, loyalty can be transferred. Run for Savard in Regina East, I'm going to run in Toronto St. Paul's." Baldwin was flabbergasted. He had fully expected Forrester to return to her law firm now that the brass ring was no longer there for her.

That Savard would win the October 28 election was a foregone conclusion by voting day, given the erosion in public support for the government party and voter demand for change. Savard had also surrounded himself with an effective team of attractive new candidates and hand-picked professional staff, some of whom had little experience in organized politics but who brought a new idealism and commitment to the public good, all with favorable results in the press and the polls.

The fact that Savard did not make Forrester deputy prime minister following her decisive election victory in the Toronto riding of St. Paul's was a bit of a shock. It suggested that he was either disappointed in or intimidated by her during the few months that they had worked together. Her consolation prize was the justice portfolio.

That Savard would call Baldwin and ask him to be minister of immigration was also a surprise. Nothing in his training or political background had prepared him for this onerous and controversial portfolio. What did he know about the intricate rules of immigration or the huge immigration bureaucracy in Ottawa-Hull, across the country and in foreign posts? And what did he know of the sharp-tongued immigration lawyers in Toronto, Montreal and Vancouver who were always attacking the minister or taking him to court?

The first congratulatory call he had received, just minutes before the swearing-in on November 12th, had come from Forrester. "Well, Dr. Baldwin, we're in it together now. You and I, we're very different people — different background, different age, different region, different gender. But maybe we share some of the same values. Remember, no matter what the pressure, the screaming, the complaining, the whining — above all, try to be fair."

Tom had thanked her politely and put down the phone. He stared out at the Peace Tower, clearly visible from his window at the Chateau Laurier, for a long, introspective five minutes, not quite sure of what lay ahead. Thinking back to the day he had become president of the university's student council in Saskatoon, he remembered all those enthusiastic SCM members who had braved the weather to vote him in and the high expectations they, like the voters of Regina East, had had for him.

Resolutely, he had straightened his bow tie — now a trademark for this political physician from Regina — collected Carolyn, who had been waiting patiently, and had taken the elevator down to his limousine and departmental driver, Denis Forget, for the brief journey to the swearing-in at Rideau Hall. Regina General Hospital seemed a long way away.

"Minister, we received a call from the Prime Minister's Office a few minutes ago. They want you to see the candidate they've chosen to be your executive assistant," said Martha Kulyk, the imperious secretary, interrupting Tom's reminiscence of those recent pivotal events. Tom was organizing his desk in the immigration department's offices at Place du Portage Phase IV in Hull.

"Well, sure — what time?"

"He'll be here at four o'clock this afternoon — name is Alan Chant, a young lawyer from Montreal. He's been working in Savard's office since the summer. This could be beneficial to us, but we don't know too much about his background. Hope he's a good one." She turned to leave, then added, apparently insensitive to the fact the government had changed, "The last one nearly sank us when he became power drunk."

Tom wondered whether he had made the right decision in keeping Martha on when he became minister. But he had opted for her experience and had tended to dismiss any suggestion that she might not be totally loyal to him, even though she had been secretary to the minister of immigration in the previous government.

What was particularly galling to Tom, however, was the prospect of having someone in higher authority actually select his executive assistant, the person with whom he would spend most of his waking hours as minister. This person, his alter ego who could make important decisions in his name, also determined whom he should or should not see and was responsible for running his office and hiring his political staff. The only redeeming feature was that this man seemed close to Savard, which might come in handy if there was a dispute with another minister. Tom regretted not having introduced himself to Chant when he first visited Savard in Ottawa in early September.

Savard had wanted it that way for all of his ministers — far better to secure some direction and control from the center as well as to establish regional and cultural balance in each minister's office. What better way to protect a naive, unilingual, newly elected Regina doctor in the immigration portfolio than to assign him a savvy bilingual EA who had worked the criminal courts in Montreal, had been part of the Savard election machine and purported to understand ethnic Canada?

Baldwin's haughty secretary opened the door to his office. "Dr. Baldwin, Alan Chant here to see you." She spoke just loud enough to tell both Tom and Alan that, while the government might have changed, she was still in charge of this office.

"Please bring him in, but first make sure you offer him a coffee, soft drink or whatever he wants," responded Tom, desperately trying to make a point in this petty little battle for office supremacy. Thirty seconds later, Martha Kulyk returned with Alan Chant in tow.

Tom had already made up his mind. He was going to get along and not buck the system. Savard had already shown that he picked the brightest and the best. He'd just have to trust him.

Alan let Baldwin speak first. He'd learned at Selwyn House that this was a mark of politeness to a superior on first meeting. "Welcome to the immigration hotbed, Mr. Chant. I'm glad to have some capable company."

"It's good to be here, Dr. Baldwin. I'm honored to have the opportunity of working with you. The prime minister said you were the brightest new guy with the toughest job in town," Alan responded, trying hard to make it sound like the supreme compliment but also letting Baldwin know at the outset who had really hired his executive assistant.

Baldwin tried to break the ice. "Let's cut the formalities and the bullshit. When we're alone, first names only — I'm Tom and you're Alan, okay? You know and I know why and how you're here, and I accept that. We both have the same boss and if either of us screws up, we're both toast."

Alan smiled and gave a slight nod. Encouraged, Tom plunged on.

"I've looked over your CV and I like what I see. It seems you didn't come to Ottawa because you needed the work. You had a good law practice at Chant & Doucet but the system sought you out because you had something to offer. Same with me. Chief of the medical staff at a major hospital in western Canada was pretty secure, but the chance to contribute in the larger sense was too good to pass up. We're partners in this job, Alan," Tom confided, with a warm, knowing look that only a physician can muster when sharing serious truths.

Alan could sense that the bond of mutual respect was already established, with friendship not far behind. "Well, then, let's get down to work, Tom." He said the name with emphasis. "First departmental briefing is tomorrow at eight in the morning and the subject is 'sensitive cases.' Here's your briefing book to read tonight. They'll need decisions on a number of cases that they've been storing up for you since the election. I've already highlighted the important parts," Alan said matter-of-factly.

Tom didn't realize it, but before he'd come in that morning, Alan had been alone in the EA's office with the pile of briefing books for over two hours, courtesy of the imperious Martha. Short of one quick call to Susan's office to make weekend arrangements, he'd worked non-stop until Baldwin arrived.

Chapter Six

Marcel Gagnon pulled another Gitane from its icy blue package. He reached into a pocket for his lighter and struggled to keep the flame lit against the cool Mediterranean breeze that made Le Petit Nice one of the most pleasant villas in the world that warm day in April.

Looking out over Baie Maldormé with Corniche Kennedy in the background, he could see boats of every size and shape — the white Beneteau sailing yachts with their sleek hulls, powered by nature's breezes, silently slipping through the water, the majestic freighters ploughing through the waves, leaving a trail of smoke curling through the atmosphere (what treasures lay in their noisy holds: wine from Provence, cars from Lyons, foodstuffs from the southwest and perhaps something more sinister from the Far East), and the ugly barges with their black tarpaulins groaning and creaking beneath their stubby little smokestacks, with cargo that even their captains were never sure of.

The mood of reverie was interrupted by a seedy-looking character with an insistent voice: "*Mon Dieu*, Montreal's a bitch of a place to get to. There's no direct flight from Nice and the flights to Paris are fully booked. Best I could get was Air Canada via Heathrow, with an overnight in

London. You'll meet up with your daughter at the Dorchester in London. She'll accompany you to Montreal."

As his sidekick Luc Beaudoin withdrew, unsure that his urgent message had been fully understood, Marcel smiled inwardly in anticipation of once again holding the naked white body of his "daughter" for a solid night of pleasure at the Dorchester. Visions of a sexually aroused Antoinette made Marcel close his eyes and inhale sharply. On opening his eyes, his right eyebrow arched considerably higher than his left. Luc perceived that Marcel somehow did not mind being stuck overnight in London.

The year 1976, when the Olympics came to Montreal, was a magical year for Roger Belair. Life, it seemed, could not get any better. The ugliness of the Second World War was long over. Roger's dangerous liaison work with the French underground in his native France, the clandestine help to Allied paratroopers who had landed near Vichy, his subsequent capture and confinement in a prisoner-of-war camp — these memories had faded with each passing decade. Since the war, Roger had been able to create a stable and comfortable life for himself. In the '50s and '60s, he successfully built up his small trucking business. His wife, Huguette, had given him three healthy children and he owned his own walk-up flat on fashionable Carré St-Louis just off Rue St-Denis.

"Imagine — the 'Big O' less than two miles from here," Roger chuckled to himself. A pity that daughter Suzanne was away for the summer. She was working for a law firm in Toronto (to improve her English, she'd said) before entering McGill Law School. Son Marc was completing his studies at Collège Jean-de-Brébeuf before taking initial vows to become a priest. And the baby Antoinette was still at home trying to figure out what to do with her life.

But the big surprise was the telegram from his wartime

comrade-in-arms Marcel Gagnon. He was coming to Montreal for the opening ceremonies of the Olympic Games and would stay on to see some of the track and field events at the Stade Olympique, the "Big O."

Roger had met the teen-aged Marcel in his work with the French underground. For over two years, they had regularly plotted ways to avoid the tentacles of the German Gestapo. They had grown very close.

Roger and Huguette would never learn that Marcel used his visit in 1976 as a cover to fool Canada Customs and Immigration. The main purpose of his journey had nothing to do with the Olympic Games or personal friendship.

The airport at Nice-Côte d'Azur was crowded that April day in 1984. The terminal was spanking new. In addition to the natural attractions of the French Riviera, many of the French high-tech firms were relocating to Sofia Antipolis, a space-age industrial park near Antibes not far from Cannes that attracted young, clean-cut professionals with their briefcases, doctorates and their American-style ambition.

Marcel Gagnon, with Luc at his side, looked almost out of place. He was too old-world French — the dark blue beret, cigarette drooping from the lip, worn leather valise and rumpled wool jacket. His right eyebrow occasionally arched higher than his left, making him appear interesting but oddly out of balance — like a throwback to an earlier time. Only Marcel's old black leather valise seemed in sync with the mélange of tourists, starlets and technocrats. It was the perfect way to transport his cache of China white, which was much larger than his first shipment eight years before, during the Olympic visit.

The flight to Heathrow was rather pleasant, about two

and a half hours in the air. With only half the seats occupied, Marcel had room to spread out and relax. A glass of red wine helped suppress the thought that, if his North American project succeeded, he might never return to Marseilles and the Côte d'Azur. What made this easier to contemplate was the prospect of ditching the detested Luc, with his foul breath and twitchy nerves. Luc was a rat, he mused. He'd be happy to be rid of him once they arrived in London.

Luc had not smiled since boarding the plane. While his papers were in order and he carried no contraband, Luc knew he looked, smelled and spoke like a drug dealer, and that Her Majesty's customs officers would give him a rough time at Heathrow. Luc made his living from drugs. He had killed more than once, escaped police custody in Italy under an assumed name and nearly lost his life in a shootout in Marseilles. But he was a survivor and had never actually been convicted of anything. Marcel Gagnon had been his boss for almost eight years.

The two had prospered as a team, although Marcel worried constantly about the declining drug market in Europe, the result of stricter law enforcement. He talked incessantly of getting at the lucrative American market through Canada. Antoinette Belair was to be the connection. Luc only hoped that Marcel, from his new "home" in Montreal, would still use him to source heroin from Burma via Marseilles and avoid the temptation of the new, competitive Colombian product that was entering America in record quantities.

"Marcel, we'll be on the ground in a few minutes. The white cliffs of Dover are just below. See the white? Remind you of anything?" he added, carelessly.

The British customs officers took a pretty good run at

both Luc and Marcel. The old valise got a particularly vigorous inspection — even the leather handles were kneaded and poked, as were Marcel's aging body and Luc's jumpy bundle of nerves. The valise was finally opened, and Marcel's French passport and his copies of *Le Figaro* and *Paris Match* were dutifully inspected. The false bottom, which concealed four one-kilo bags of heroin, escaped detection.

Antoinette waited anxiously at the barrier. Marcel saw the long auburn hair first, then the pixie smile and the firm young body beneath the leather bomber jacket. Her arms were around his neck and her tongue in his mouth before Marcel could introduce the objectionable Luc, who seemed all the more sleazy away from his natural habitat in Marseilles.

"It's been a long while, *ma chérie*," Marcel whispered in her ear as she continued to cling to him, like a favorite daughter greeting a father returning from the war.

"Don't ever leave me for so long again, Marcel," she said, almost inaudibly. Even as they exited the terminal, she clung with both hands to his free left arm, not quite believing he would stay with her for long.

Earlier that day, Antoinette had elbowed her way past the Arab guests in their white robes at the Dorchester and booked two rooms. One, for Luc, was on the ground floor. It had a small window opening onto an alleyway, green furniture that must have looked dusty the day it was purchased thirty years ago and a bed so lumpy that it reminded Antoinette of the bunks in some of the cabins at Mont-Tremblant.

Marcel was more fortunate. In addition to the anticipated delights of Antoinette, his suite featured a Victorian anteroom, equipped with a rich ruby-red divan, matching draperies and an ancient fireplace that he imagined once burned coal. The bedroom was more opulent — a high, four-poster bed in brown walnut, sheets of creamy silk, a marble bath with a tub long enough for two and, on the leather-topped table in the alcove, a giant globe of the world as it had seemed to some eighteenth-century cartographer.

Perhaps out of a sense of loyalty for past services, Marcel didn't have the heart to totally abandon Luc right away. He suggested that, after they'd showered and changed, they all convene for dinner in the Grill Room on the main floor of the Dorchester.

After a passable English meal, which included oyster stew, Dover sole, Pouilly-Fuissé and English trifle, Marcel felt he had done his duty to his faithful sidekick of eight years. Under the table he pressed a fat envelope with 490 one-thousand dollar bills into Luc's hand, Luc's promised cut of the initial payment for the heroin shipment. Marcel bade him adieu.

Antoinette had faithfully carried this money — an advance from Gus Bertolini in New York, Marcel's new partner — in the lining of her bomber jacket three days before on the Air Canada flight from Montreal to Heathrow. She had deducted ten thousand dollars as "expenses." The four bags of heroin in the false bottom of Marcel's black valise would net them two million more once delivered and it had a street value of more than four times that. So Marcel was glad to settle up with Luc for less than twenty-five percent of the money still to come.

"*Tu vois?*" Marcel whispered. He drew his index finger away from Antoinette's long hair and traced an imaginary line on the globe from the golden triangle in southeast Asia, through Marseilles and Montreal to New York.

"Marco Polo would be proud."

Antoinette had other things on her mind. She took only a perfunctory look at the globe as her silk robe dropped to the floor and she turned to the more ambitious task of orally rekindling Marcel's desires. It had been over a year since she had seen Marcel and she had genuinely missed him. For her, there was great pleasure in making him feel young again, although there were momentary feelings of revulsion she did not fully understand. He readily responded to her slow, rhythmic stimulation.

"You were only sixteen when we first did this, *ma belle*," Marcel whispered as he began to move towards that unhurried and deliberate orgasmic pleasure that only a physically fit man of his age could experience. At the height, he said nothing, but his right eyebrow arched well above the left.

When it was over, he reminisced. "It was in your father's house, during the Olympic Games. I don't think he ever found out. *Pauvre Roger*. Did he suffer before he died?"

Antoinette slowly came up for air, dreading the thought of providing details of her father's recent death to his wartime friend. "It was a heart attack — it came very suddenly." By lying, she could avoid recalling that distressing time. Her father had suffered for more than four months from a debilitating stroke before finally succumbing in her arms.

Shading the truth was totally in keeping with Antoinette's approach to life. Noble in name and appearance but weak in character and intellect, she had grudgingly completed basic business courses in high school and learned how to type but not much else. Her tastes ran to dancing, shopping for fine clothes and exhibiting her athletic prowess on the ski slopes and in the bunks at Mont-Tremblant. After a brief stint in modeling, she had taken on several bit parts in Canadian films and had eventually found herself in Cannes with an even faster crowd.

Antoinette liked getting high — coke, speed, bennies, even a bit of smack, although she'd never tried white. The buzz she got from drugs helped blot out the intense jealousy she felt towards her siblings and the painful memories of the love-hate relationship with her father. As a bonus, it enhanced her sexual pleasure.

Modeling had been too much like work. Jobs were few and far between. Film work seemed more glamorous except the producers in Montreal tended to write her off as a pretty face with a small mind. As it turned out, Cannes was the ticket. Not far away lay the historic and restive city of Marseilles — the hub of the drug traffic, where East meets West. Not only were users guaranteed a genuine and ready supply, but the huge profits to be gained by those on the ground floor could mean financial security and ultimate freedom.

Strangely enough, with all the exciting young males available to her in Montreal and the south of France, the man who had really caught her fancy was the aging Marcel Gagnon, world-weary veteran of the Marseilles drug trade and her father's old friend. Perhaps it was her need for a father-figure without the pain Roger had caused. Marcel seemed to represent security, wisdom and stability all rolled into one.

Heading for Heathrow in one of those drafty but efficient English taxis, Marcel and Antoinette rehearsed their lines for Canada Customs and Immigration one more time. They had been over all the documents at breakfast that morning. Both had Canadian passports, Quebec health cards, drivers' licenses, assorted credit cards and a small amount of Canadian, American and British cash as well as American Express travelers' checks.

Yes, they had been over to England for a "theater week" — four plays in three days with a small suite at the Dorchester as a treat for the last night. Both were flying to Montreal on the return portion of their Air Canada ticket.

Marcel had mailed his own French passport, assorted European credit cards and French driver's license from the Dorchester to the Belair residence in Montreal. He would drop around to pay his respects to Roger's widow, Huguette, within a few weeks of his arrival, telling her that the envelope with his name on it contained just a few personal things he'd forgotten when he left London. Huguette had no idea that Antoinette had visited London, let alone that she was seeing Marcel.

If nothing else, Antoinette had street smarts. Her plan to bring Marcel and his special cache to Montreal had come together rather nicely. She reminded her lover: "In the customs line at Mirabel, remember not to look surprised when I call you 'papa' and casually explain that this is the first father-and-daughter vacation ever taken by the Belair family."

Marcel knew that Roger would not have been pleased. But he would have respected their audacity.

Chapter Seven

Heading down the Autoroute des Laurentides from Mirabel, the taxi carrying Marcel and Antoinette crossed Rivière des Mille-Îles and Rivière des Prairies, veered west onto the Autoroute Métropolitaine across the top of the city and then turned southbound onto Décarie Boulevard. Marcel tried to recall Montreal in the summer of 1976 and relate it to what he now saw around him — gray overcast skies, dirty snow, roads covered with a messy combination of salt and gravel, and a lot of stony faces reflecting a society ravaged by economic recession, a separatist government and the prospect of several more weeks of cold and slush.

During the summer of 1976, the grass had been green, the trees out in full foliage. Hundreds of thousands of happy visitors had swarmed the streets to watch the events at the Parc Olympique, and Montreal had been decked out in its festive finest.

It was only when they looped into the southern belly of the city and he spied the large, illuminated cross atop Mont Royal (it was the end of the afternoon and the sun was beginning to set) that he felt any twinge of warm familiarity or pleasant recall.

"Remember that midnight walk up to the top of Mont-Royal near the cross the night after we first met, and you later crept into my bedroom on Carré St-Louis?" Marcel recalled softly to a distracted Antoinette.

She had not been paying attention to the familiar sights. Instead she had been wondering what she might do to ensure that Alan Chant did nothing precipitous with the brown attaché case now deposited somewhere in his office. Perhaps she might call his secretary Hélène the next day and tell her she was still mulling over the notaries that Alan had recommended and needed a little more time. She'd ask that Alan continue to hold on to the papers for a while longer. At the very least, she wanted to satisfy herself that they were still there and that the case had not been opened.

Just prior to her departure for England, Antoinette had taken out a month-to-month lease on an apartment on the third floor of 21 Terrace St-Denis. This would be home for her and Marcel for the next little while, at least until he had decided what to do. He could either remain in Montreal as part of a new drug triangle that would include Marseilles and New York, or he could illegally cross into the U.S. and set up a separate identity and address there.

In organizing this temporary new home for Marcel and herself, Antoinette had followed his instructions carefully. "Discontinue service on your old telephone line and have two new lines installed," he had said. "The first line should have a listed number but should only be answered by machine, with instructions in a female voice to 'leave your name, number and time you called, and I'll get back to you.' This line will be our front, our show of legitimacy. The second line should be unlisted, to be used primarily for outgoing calls."

He had gone on to explain that only he, Antoinette and his partner in New York were to know the number. If this phone rang, it had to be one of them. The speaker would begin by saying "This is earth station," followed by twelve digits. This would be the signal to call back from a different location, reversing the twelve digits and dropping the first two to figure out the actual telephone number to be dialed.

Marcel also had Antoinette purchase a third device at the local cellular phone service center. This portable telephone could be used in a car or a briefcase, ensuring mobility. The fact that it was easily intercepted was seen as a virtue as far as Marcel was concerned, because its primary use was to plant false leads and booby traps for the curious, particularly law enforcement officials. Hopefully, they wouldn't be a factor, at least for a while.

Antoinette and Marcel enjoyed their first week setting up house together, their relationship continuing to blossom. One moment he would be the father figure ordering his compliant daughter to move a particular piece of furniture here or a painting there. Another moment, he would be her passionate lover, both of them taking child-like delight in making love on each piece of furniture as it was moved into place — the sofa (relatively easy), a wing-back chair (more difficult), a queen-size bed (easy, of course) and the pine refectory table in the dining room (hard, but sensual). Even the kitchen counter presented exciting and innovative opportunities for this libidinous sixty-one-year-old and his energetic twenty-four-year-old companion.

Their relationship, of course, involved not only love but business as well. As soon as the heroin — now hidden under the floorboards — was delivered in New York, the one and a half million deposit would be unconditionally theirs. When Gus Bertolini had confirmed the quantity and quality of the white, they would receive the remaining two million owed to them. Unfortunately, Bertolini controlled the timing of the whole operation. Until he gave the order to deliver, nothing moved.

The courier's words that day in the hotel lobby, about finding someone with whom to deposit the money "in case, God forbid, you and Marcel don't come through," still haunted Antoinette, even though it had been fairly easy to get Alan Chant to take responsibility for the attaché case. Approaching him in the bar that day had been a spur-of-the-moment attempt to comply with the courier's directive. She had felt some relief when he locked the small case in his bag; until then, she'd carried it with her everywhere, including weekends away. The strategy seemed safer than leaving it at her apartment, and more private than depositing it with a bank or trust company, which would require paperwork and answers to questions.

Now she hoped beyond hope that the money would be safe with Alan and that she'd be able to contact him any time, given his professional standing and what she assumed would be his personal interest in a return bout in bed. She had no particular longing for another night with him but she would do whatever she had to do to get at the money.

Alan certainly seemed dependable. He had called her the next day, the coldest day of 1984, with the names of three Montreal notaries who did successions work — Yvan Corbeil, Harvey Wessenger and Camille Nolan — leaving addresses and telephone and fax numbers for each of them.

She had deliberately delayed making a choice. She preferred to have the papers remain with Alan at his office, knowing full well that he would honor her trust. The attaché case did in fact contain both the money and a mysterious sealed envelope addressed to the Belair family priest. In broken handwriting, Roger had scratched out its contents on a wrinkled piece of paper only hours before he died, stuffing it awkwardly with a shaking hand into the envelope and solemnly pledging Antoinette to deliver it to Father Péloquin "at least one year after I go — when you feel the time is right." Partly out of convenience, she had simply put the envelope with the money the courier gave her several weeks later to keep them both safe and hidden for a while.

Antoinette's plan was to tell Bertolini and his people that the deposit was being held by a trusted lawyer in Old Montreal. Once the white had been delivered, she would simply give Chant a phone call telling him to send the attaché case to her apartment or some other location, or she would go to his office and pick it up. With any luck, she would not have to disclose Chant's name or the location of his office.

Gus Bertolini would not be pleased with these custodial arrangements. He would no doubt prefer the money to be stashed with someone she knew well. But that was his problem. Technically, her solution complied with his "deposit" requirement. Antoinette knew from something Susan had told her when her sister was in law school that it was Chant's professional duty to safeguard the attaché case even if he later discovered what it contained. Besides, as far as he knew, Antoinette had committed no crime nor engaged in any wrongdoing, so he would be under no obligation to report her to the police or other authorities.

The big problem would be Marcel. But she would try to convince him that the story about her father's papers as a cover for leaving the money with Chant was the best way to avoid being double-crossed by Bertolini and his thugs once delivery was completed.

Antoinette had done a good job in selecting the flat at 21 Terrace St-Denis. Not only did it have the warmth and charm befitting this seventy-year-old neighborhood, but it had a doorman stationed at the entrance from noon to midnight each day. René Séguin made it his business to know the intimate details of the life of each of the tenants. "Far easier to provide security that way," he reasoned, with a somewhat wicked grin.

Watching Antoinette in the two weeks before she departed for Europe, René had concluded that she was a high-priced hooker with fabulous looks and great promise. Amazed that she had so few visitors in those fourteen days, he wondered how she made a living, particularly since she had rewarded him with a crisp twenty-dollar bill every Monday morning, accompanied by a peck on the cheek and a full squeeze of the upper arm.

When Marcel arrived on the scene after her return from Europe, René figured him to be some permanent sugar daddy, although he looked too weather-beaten and tired for the role and certainly didn't dress as a man of wealth. He soon learned otherwise. René was good at working both sides of the street.

"I'm going to keep an eye on this pair," the observant René thought to himself as he watched them leave the building each Friday morning that spring to go shopping. For one thing, their age difference made him suspicious. He figured his good friends in the RCMP might be interested in these two when he paid his monthly visit to sell neighborhood gossip.

One noteworthy feature of this charming neighborhood

was the corner grocery store and delicatessen of Mamma Leonardo. This old-fashioned store on the corner of St-Denis and Rigaud, a very un-Italian neighborhood just north of Sherbrooke, catered to the professionals in that part of town. It stocked high quality fruits, fine cut meats, fresh fish, and breads, brioches and croissants baked fresh each morning. Its shelves overflowed with specialty items including spices, antipasti, sauces, exotic coffees, teas and a famous lasagna made by Mamma Leonardo herself early each day. No credit cards were accepted at this fascinating shop, but all the customers who came to know Mamma Leonardo were extended generous terms of credit. She knew from her days of running a grocery and delicatessen in Palermo that her clientele would buy more, particularly higher-priced items, if they could buy on credit. No one would ever think of defaulting on Mamma. Her sons Bruno and Luigi were known to have mastered Sicilian techniques of ensuring payment of debts, and no one in this unique Montreal neighborhood wanted to test the system.

Within a week of their arrival from England that cold, gray April, Marcel and Antoinette had decided that shopping at Mamma Leonardo's was to their liking. While the quality of the food, the service and the home delivery were key features, most important was the fact that she agreed to let them defer payment of their weekly account for up to six months in return for a premium.

Antoinette dialed the Chant & Doucet office number. "Alan Chant, please."

"I'm sorry, he's not in," replied Hélène, politely. "May I say who called and have him get back to you?"

"Tell him it's Antoinette Belair. I just want to make sure that he's still holding onto the papers from my father's estate. I still haven't chosen which notary I want to do that work. It'll take me a little bit longer to deal with this, so if he can be patient and just hold on to them, we can sort it out soon."

"Don't worry," replied Hélène in soothing tones. "I know where the papers are. They're in a locked brown attaché case in the pending file drawer of his inner office, and they won't be going anywhere. Can I have him call you?"

"Yes." Antoinette tried to think things through carefully. "Have him call 748-7185." She had memorized the first number, which was always hooked up to the answering machine and would allow her to call back on her own time. This would be a good test of the system that she and Marcel had set up.

"God knows this is important since he's holding our money," she whispered to Marcel, who had approached from behind and was kissing her tenderly on the cheek. Suddenly he grabbed her wrists tightly till they hurt. "You know I'm not happy about where you deposited that money," he said between clenched teeth. "I'd have preferred someone that you've known for a while. Maybe a relative. You'd better stay close to that young lawyer or we're both in serious trouble."

Bertolini's people apparently had similar concerns. Thanks to their own wiretap, they overheard Antoinette's call to Alan's office. By the next day, both Alan and the offices of Chant & Doucet had come under twenty-four-hour surveillance by Bruno and Luigi Leonardo.

Chapter Eight

At Heathrow, British Customs and Scotland Yard had not known that Marcel Gagnon was carrying a large cache of heroin when he and Luc Beaudoin had disembarked from Nice in April. Marcel was experienced enough not to pick a supplier known to the U.S. Drug Enforcement Authority. His purchase and transport of product to England had been achieved without detection.

For Antoinette Belair, it had been a different story. Her rendezvous in late January at Le Quatre Saisons Hotel in Montreal with Bertolini's guy from New York had been observed by both the RCMP and the DEA.

They had actually seen the two million dollars change hands. Moreover, a hidden parabolic microphone had picked up the courier's instructions about withholding a quarter of the money and depositing the remainder with a reliable contact.

Ever since that cold day, the RCMP had had a man tailing Antoinette, at least to the extent that was possible given her lifestyle. The Mounties were able to trace her movements, including the weekend ski trips to Mont-Tremblant. But they were never able to pin down the identity of her companions (let alone what she might say to them) unless she rode in a car, in which case they could record the license number.

The telephone at her old apartment on Avenue Laval had been tapped with the assistance of a judge's warrant and Bell Canada. Both the listed and unlisted phone lines at 21 Terrace St-Denis were tapped shortly after she moved there in April.

RCMP surveillance had observed her purchasing airline tickets from the Air Canada office on Sherbrooke Street. Polite questioning of the Air Canada ticket agent disclosed that she had bought two executive class tickets to London, England, for A. Belair and R. Belair. Since they had already determined her name through discussions with René Séguin, her doorman (who was now drawing cash payments from both Antoinette and the RMCP), they had reckoned that "R. Belair" was her accomplice in making payment and taking delivery in London.

When Antoinette headed for Mirabel Airport in a Murray Hill limousine that April morning, she was being closely observed. But to the surprise of RCMP and DEA surveillance officers following her, no accomplice showed up to join her when it came time to board. They assumed that she had a quarter of whatever sum had been given to her at Le Quatre Saisons sewn somewhere into her clothing. They also suspected that her movements in England might well help establish links between the foreign source of supply and Gus Bertolini, the notorious New York distributor who had been the object of DEA surveillance for over two years.

In fact, the DEA had reason to believe that Bertolini was behind several huge transactions throughout the western hemisphere. They desperately needed to collect evidence regarding large transfers of product in return for payment. The retail sale of pure China white within the United States by Bertolini and his people was already well documented, but the DEA wanted to find out the wholesale sources before pouncing.

↑ ↓

Antoinette stretched out in the empty seat beside her and closed her eyes as the plane lifted off the ground from Mirabel, circled Montreal to the south and headed down the Gulf of St. Lawrence towards the Atlantic. Before falling asleep, she savored the prospect of two days of shopping on Regent Street and in Soho before Marcel arrived.

To her, the British used to seem so dowdy. But Lady Diana, Rod Stewart and Mick Jagger had spawned a more modern and trendy approach to clothes and life in general. This appealed to Antoinette's sense of adventure. She reckoned that she could lavish up to three thousand dollars on herself before Marcel arrived, having already spent about two thousand on the air tickets. After the $490,000 "delivery commission" to Marcel's accomplice, that left about five thousand dollars for hotel, theater tickets and some basic set-up costs at 21 Terrace St-Denis, where she and Marcel would return three days later.

Before she fell asleep, her thoughts wandered to the two men on whom her future now depended. She eagerly looked forward to her reunion with Marcel once he cleared customs at Heathrow following his flight from Nice. She would try to book a particularly nice room for the two of them at the Dorchester. That's where he'd asked to stay. On their two previous meetings in Cannes, he'd already proved to her that atmosphere and ambiance were central to his sexual prowess.

She had many pleasant memories of her times with

Marcel because with him, unlike most things in her life, she was always in control — of the circumstances, the pace, the climax. She knew she made him happy when they were together, rekindling his old desires and releasing untapped sources of energy. They would be great partners.

Then there was Alan Chant. Not that *he'd* been a spectacular partner that night in his room at Mont-Tremblant. In fact, he had been like so many of the other good-looking studs that she seemed to attract — demanding, short on tenderness and always in a hurry, particularly when it was over.

In a strange way, she equated this approach with the offhand and occasionally abusive treatment afforded by her late father. Roger Belair had seemed more interested in getting on with his trucking business or reveling in the academic successes of her older siblings, Susan and Marc, than providing fatherly love, care and affection for an uncertain youngest daughter still unable to figure out how to get along in the world.

"Here she comes, mates. Be prepared to move quickly," the small wiry bespectacled surveillance officer from Scotland Yard breathed into his pocket microphone. Joining him in watching Antoinette come down the arrivals ramp at Heathrow's Terminal Three were his two plainclothes companions, one from the DEA and the other from the London constabulary.

She looked older and more obvious than they had imagined. But that might have been the result of only a few hours' sleep on board. It was only three in the morning Montreal time. As well, Antoinette's high-fashion leather bomber jacket was more appropriate for the corner of Sherbrooke and St-Denis than Regent Street.

The DEA had spared no expense on this assignment. The three plainclothes surveillants, from different vantage points in the arrivals terminal, watched Antoinette gather her luggage, load it on a cart and move towards the exit where taxis waited. They had rented a gray Jaguar for this assignment, and it was parked only fifty feet from the taxi line-up, in a special "no parking" zone reserved for the use of police and security officers.

It never crossed Antoinette's mind that she would have even one surveillance officer, never mind a trio of experienced ones representing three separate law enforcement agencies tailing her around London on a shopping spree for two days.

She took a small room for two nights at the Royal Garden Hotel, a medium-priced, unimpressive establishment near Buckingham Palace, since she wanted to play tourist in addition to shopping. Like thousands of others, she craned her neck to watch, over the barrier, the changing of the guard at eleven o'clock that first morning. Scotland Yard had managed to install a tap on the phone and a bug in the room at the Royal Garden within two hours of her checking in, but there were no calls or visitors during her brief stay.

After two days of tailing Antoinette through Fortnum and Mason, Marks and Spencer, Harrods and about twenty specialty shops in Knightsbridge and Soho, dutifully noting all the purchases that she carried back to her small hotel room at the Royal Garden, the surveillants began to despair that this expensive operation would produce anything of value.

"Good thing the Yanks are paying for this one," the

Scotland Yard officer said quietly to his colleague from the London constabulary while the DEA officer soldiered on glumly.

Finally, on the afternoon of the third day, when they observed Antoinette checking out of the Royal Garden and taking a taxi to the Dorchester just off Hyde Park, they sensed that something significant was about to happen. Within an hour of Antoinette having reserved the small suite and single room at the Dorchester, Scotland Yard had tapped the phones.

"None of this judicial warrant stuff in England, matey," the two British police officers had noted, for the benefit of their American counterpart.

While the taps were being installed, the three surveillants in their gray Jaguar followed Antoinette's taxi as it headed for Heathrow. She stopped at Terminal Two, which serviced flights to and from Europe. They followed her to Gate 14 where the Air France flight from Nice was scheduled to arrive that afternoon at five past five.

Neither Marcel nor Luc were known to the three when Antoinette greeted them at the gate. But the information obtained from the listening devices that evening at the Dorchester launched them on their task of identifying Marcel. Within hours, Scotland Yard sent out protected communications to the Police de Sécurité in Paris. They in turn contacted their southern region office located in Nice, which covered Marseilles.

Profiles on ten known drug dealers and intermediaries operating in southern France appeared on the protected fax system at Scotland Yard headquarters by noon the next day, approximately one hour before Antoinette and Marcel, now traveling as Roger Belair, were set to leave Heathrow for Montreal.

A description of Marcel Gagnon, complete with photograph showing the elevated right eyebrow, was included among the ten profiles. This was immediately handed to the three surveillants, who had been waiting anxiously at Scotland Yard headquarters near Victoria Station.

Navigating the Jaguar towards Heathrow at high speeds through heavy traffic, they arrived at Terminal Four just ten minutes prior to departure — not with a view to apprehending Marcel and Antoinette, since that would have been of little assistance to the DEA. They wanted simply to ensure that the male individual traveling to Montreal on an Air Canada ticket issued in the name of Roger Belair was, in fact, the "Marcel Gagnon" described in the protected fax received at Scotland Yard headquarters.

They caught only a glimpse of Antoinette and Marcel as they entered the gate and walked down the ramp leading to the aircraft. Marcel now sported a beard, which he hadn't in the faxed photo. In the end, it was his right eyebrow that gave him away. The police felt reasonably certain that this was their man, which justified communication to the RCMP in Ottawa.

Luc Beaudoin was another story. Somehow, nothing that had been received from the Police de Sécurité bore any resemblance to Luc; he had radically changed his appearance by shaving his beard and cropping and dyeing his hair. There were no conversations or calls to his room at the Dorchester, and the three surveillants somehow missed the under-the-table transfer of the $490,000 to Luc in the Grill Room of the Dorchester that evening. There was no basis for apprehending him when he departed Heathrow for Nice on the flight at two o'clock the next afternoon.

At RCMP regional headquarters in downtown Montreal, an animated conversation was taking place as Antoinette and Marcel winged their way across the Atlantic. The RCMP director of drug enforcement, Bert Kaufman, a slim, middle-aged man in aviator glasses, and his deputy director Mario Gingras were on the protected speaker phone from Ottawa. So were a senior DEA official and his assistant from Washington.

"Listen, we have to nab these two at Mirabel and put them through the wringer!" shouted Jean Thibault, the Montreal RCMP regional director. His right fist drew circles in the air as if to illustrate his intentions. Thibault, a tall, charismatic man, tended to gesture dramatically when he became impatient, which was often. "One of them has got to be carrying a large quantity of heroin. Why else would she have gone to all that trouble? He's seeking entry into Canada under a phony passport, so we'll have no trouble stopping him at immigration and that'll give us an excuse to go through all their possessions."

"Is this really what we want?" the DEA officer responded, with a touch of condescension apparent even over the telephone. "Given what we know and what we don't know" — he was still annoyed that Luc Beaudoin had not been properly tracked down — "isn't it better to let them come in innocently? We've got their apartment and their neighborhood covered. We can then obtain direct evidence of transferring product to our friends in New York. Confiscating one cache of heroin and sidelining one European supplier and his young Canadian girlfriend is not going to accomplish very much for us, gentlemen."

Although Bert Kaufman was uncomfortable with this suggested strategy, he knew he would have to make the decision. He looked across the desk at Gingras and frowned. Letting a known European drug dealer into Canada using a phony passport and probably carrying a bag of heroin was a serious matter indeed. Political shit would hit the fan if anyone ever found out. His boss, the RCMP commissioner, would be hauled before the solicitor general, whose own reputation would be on the line.

Yet there was indeed a larger objective involved: shutting down the heroin trade. Canada had an important role to play in identifying links between the major U.S. distribution centers and European and South American sources of supply.

Canada had its share of drug problems in the big urban centers of Montreal, Toronto and Vancouver. But it was nothing compared to the situation in New York, Chicago and Los Angeles. Marcel Gagnon and his girlfriend, while important suspects, appeared to be small players. There was more to be gained in the long term by keeping them under surveillance from their Montreal base than by blowing them out of the water at Mirabel.

The Yanks were right. Running a hand through his thinning dark hair, Kaufman took a deep breath. "Gentlemen, we're going to go along with the DEA on this one. We've worked well together so far in Montreal in observing the transfer of money, establishing surveillance and wiring the apartment. And we've worked well with our British friends in bringing Marcel Gagnon into the loop. Let's see where this leads us over the next couple of months. Lay off at Mirabel and let's hope that customs and immigration don't do their job too well."

He finished his remarks almost as a judicial pronouncement, and then looked inquisitively at Gingras. Even though they had only voices to judge by, they could both sense the sigh of relief from Washington and the controlled anger from Montreal. "Good luck, Jean, to you and your guys. You've been doing a good job so far. I want you to know that we appreciate it here in Ottawa, just as I'm sure they do down in Washington."

Thibault was far from placated. But by then, he was already beginning in his own mind to plan the surveillance of Marcel Gagnon and Antoinette Belair for the balance of the year. An experienced investigator, he knew that these types of operations took far more time and money to carry out than anyone could reasonably imagine.

Chapter Nine

When Alan first received a call from Savard to go up to Ottawa in June, he tried to make a clean breast of things at the office of Chant & Doucet. He knew there was no point in trying to keep his end of the practice going because of the potential for conflict. From this point on, Guy Doucet would carry on the practice in his own name.

Besides, he would not have the time to provide the sort of hands-on service that his type of clients usually demanded. Inattention to client affairs could blossom into allegations of professional misconduct if he wasn't careful.

Within days of making his decision, he sent out a formal notice to clients that he would be taking up the position of senior policy advisor to the leader of the Opposition in Ottawa and that the partnership of Chant & Doucet would be dissolved, effective June 30, 1984. That left him only ten days to try to clean up and assign old files at the office.

It was a difficult and unpleasant task, deciding what to throw out and what to keep. So much of it was like reliving the past three years of his professional life. In some ways, it reminded him of the agony of reviewing his examination paper in criminal law with his professor at McGill, a subject that he loved but on which he had not scored particularly well.

The active files requiring immediate attention, such as the Russo matter, were easy. For each he dictated a memo, to be typed by Hélène, explaining to Guy what had been done, together with a recommended strategy for future action, noting fees and disbursements received or owing. If there had been an agreement with the client as to fees in the future, he noted this too, although he knew Guy well enough to suspect that he would try to weasel out of any agreement if he thought the client was capable of paying more.

In fact, he worried that Guy, being senior to Alan at the bar, would charge his clients a higher hourly rate, possibly leading to a bigger fee. Guy would argue that he could do the work more efficiently because of his experience and that in the end the fee might be lower, although Alan didn't believe that.

With a few files, such as those involving matrimonial causes, he decided that they should be referred to another firm. Guy didn't like to do that kind of work and would only take on such cases if a current good client of his insisted. Alan had worked hard to develop this side of his practice, particularly among the spouses of wealthy professionals, and he wanted to be very careful not to let them down or give the appearance of steering them to his ambivalent partner.

Alan would give each of these clients the names of three qualified matrimonial lawyers, together with background résumés, which he kept on file, and suggest that they choose the one best suited to their circumstances. He felt that this ethical approach would protect him if anything ever went wrong on the file as a result of some action done by the new lawyer. It also left a good impression with the clients that might pay dividends when Alan returned to private practice. That was the same approach he'd taken with Antoinette Belair when she'd asked him five months earlier to help her look after her late father's estate.

In the process of closing down his practice, Alan was astounded at all the junk he'd accumulated over three short years. In addition to his old law school notes and summaries issued by the École du Barreau (which he couldn't bring himself to throw out, even though he hadn't consulted them once since his call to the bar), there were conference materials, law journal articles, court judgments, legislative updates, law firm brochures, annual reports of government departments and agencies, and law firm management materials.

It was amazing the stuff that he'd stored away, thinking that somehow these papers could be relevant to giving him that extra jump in serving clients and staying ahead of competitors. He'd been a veritable pack rat, slave to the written word, not quite trusting electronic storage.

He'd have kept the stuff but Guy needed the space. A young junior was starting in mid-July, and Alan could not envisage boxing up and carting all this material off to the small pied-à-terre he'd rented. It would simply be overrun with paper. So he'd screwed up his courage and thrown most of it out.

Other files and folders, some personal in nature, some professional, he had to keep. Income tax returns, RRSP contributions, law society filings, frequent flyer statements, credit card information, insurance policies, personal correspondence — all these had been bundled up and boxed, ready to go into the trunk of the BMW.

Alan had also taken great delight in creating a new personal file containing the formal job offer from the office of the leader of the official Opposition, which he labeled "Ottawa Employment."

He'd decided to give up his two-bedroom apartment on Rue Chomedy to save money since he would need a place in Montreal only one or two nights a week, given the forthcoming election campaign. Also, he'd begun to see Susan on a regular basis and the prospect of moving in with her lock, stock and barrel had already crossed his mind.

The pied-à-terre at 3509 Peel Street was on the second floor of a once magnificent, three-story Victorian house. Built by the youngest son of a wealthy St. James Street sugar merchant, it was adorned with opulent French windows and a mansard roof shingled in timeless gray slate. Its current owner, a small developer, had done a minimum amount of maintenance and hoped to tear the building down to replace it with a highrise once he'd overcome city and university opposition. To cover taxes and interim carrying costs, he had carved it up to provide temporary student and faculty housing close to the university.

The building suited Alan well. It offered lots of charm and privacy and a spot to store his clothes, recreational gear and personal files. A huge walk-in closet would hold all his boxes from the office and maybe a couple of filing cabinets; its door could be shut when he had visitors. Centrally located near the law school and the main campus of McGill, the apartment was a five-minute walk to downtown Montreal and about a ten-minute drive from Susan's larger and more modern apartment on Côte-des-Neiges.

The last category of files he encountered that June afternoon was the most problematic. Some may have originated as client matters that never materialized. Others may have involved a prospective case or legal event that had not yet occurred or even been scheduled. They all involved situations where the client wanted Alan, and no one else, to look after the situation.

He kept these materials close by in a separate drawer in his office credenza, and called them his "wannabe" files. They were always ready to be pulled out on short notice if the "wannabe" client called to advise of a new development or wanting Alan's offhand opinion (typically, they would start by saying, "now don't turn on your meter, I just want to get your off-the-cuff reaction").

None of these "wannabe" clients had paid Alan anything. He wasn't even sure they were "clients" in the formal sense of the word. But all these files involved situations where he felt people were relying on him to look after their interests and it was far too early to open an official file, let alone send them a bill.

He added the small brown attaché case containing the estate papers of Antoinette Belair's father to his "wannabe" drawer that cold February morning following his drive south from Mont-Tremblant. He had dutifully called her that afternoon with the names of three qualified notaries, leaving the information on her answering machine. Two days later she had phoned to thank him, saying, "I can't make up my mind — the situation regarding my life is changing so fast. Please hold on to the attaché case for a while longer."

Feeling somewhat embarrassed about the one-night stand and not particularly wanting to pursue Antoinette, he had done nothing. Later, in May, he'd received one or two messages from her on the answering machine at Chant & Doucet saying that her life was still uncertain and that he should continue to hold on to the papers until she could figure out what to do.

Alan decided, that hot June afternoon, that none of the "wannabe" files could realistically be transferred to Guy Doucet. They were just too personal. For that matter, none of the files had really materialized to the point of warranting transfer to any other professional.

Alan simply slapped all of them, including the attaché case, into brown cardboard file boxes marked "Wannabe" — to join the other personal papers in the trunk of his car.

"God, I wonder when I'll ever have the time to follow up on these 'wannabe' files?" Alan said to Hélène as he left the premises of Chant & Doucet, bound for Peel Street.

"Weren't there any that you could have let Guy look after?" Hélène inquired, knowing full well how jealously he had guarded these files during the two years they had worked together. He'd sighed and, just for a second, wondered whether he'd made the right decision to leave the practice of law, abandon his clients and go to Ottawa without fully appreciating what lay ahead.

"Most of those folks'll be able to sort out their own problems, and a lot of this paper'll become irrelevant," he rationalized, as he loaded the boxes onto the dolly for transport to his car.

"You're wrong, Alan," Hélène said quietly. "Most of those people were counting on you. If you can help some of them from Ottawa, do it."

Alan tried hard to hide his feelings of guilt. He kissed Hélène gently on the cheek, something he'd never done before. As he drove off with the boxes of files securely packed in his trunk, he wondered if he would ever make it back to private practice.

Chapter Ten

"What the hell is this guy doin'?" Bruno Leonardo said to his brother Luigi. Bruno, the elder of the two, was shorter and paunchier than his brother, which irritated him almost as much as the fact that he was quickly balding while Luigi showed no signs of losing his thick black curls. They had just seen Alan Chant outside the offices of Chant & Doucet that hot June afternoon, loading eight boxes into the trunk of his black BMW before driving off to the north.

"We better follow him," Luigi hollered as he raced down the street and hopped into his red Alfa Romeo.

"No problem, we'll get it out of the secretary," Bruno said to no one in particular. "She cooperated before when Bertolini first put us onto this job. No trouble at all."

Luigi returned in about ten minutes. He screeched to a stop in front of Bruno, who was standing across the street from the offices of Chant & Doucet. "Son of a bitch! Lost him. Traffic too heavy. Those one-way streets are killers!" Bruno got into the car. He had a habit of rubbing the thin, two-inch scar on his left cheek when confronted by a problem. He was rubbing it now.

"Don' worry. He's probably just doin' some housecleaning. I doubt he'd be usin' the trunk of his car in broad daylight to move a million and a half bucks," Bruno responded nonchalantly, trying to convince himself, as the more experienced brother, that nothing was amiss.

"Call his secretary again," Luigi nervously reminded his brother. He'd already spoken to Hélène about a month ago to confirm Alan Chant's mailing address. He'd also inquired whether the firm had any facilities on the premises for safekeeping client valuables.

Hélène had found that call mysterious, to say the least. After confirming the address and the correct spelling of Alan's name, she'd said, "We advise most clients these days to keep their valuables with a bank, trust company or caisse populaire in a safety deposit box. We can make such arrangements for clients at the Royal Bank or the National Bank of Canada, which are the two institutions we use." There was no way Hélène was going to tell a stranger about Alan's "wannabe" files.

Feeling just a little panicky, the image of the BMW's trunk full of boxes flashing against his eyelids whenever he blinked, Bruno dialed Alan's number from his cellular phone.

"Hello, Doucet law offices, may I help you?" Hélène responded.

"I'd like to speak to Alan Chant — he one of your lawyers there?" Bruno said, trying desperately to muster his best English.

"Sorry, he no longer works here. He's gone to Ottawa on a leave of absence to work on a special assignment. Can I put you through to the other partner, Guy Doucet, who's taken over most of Mr. Chant's files?"

"Nah, that's okay, I really wanted to talk wit' Alan Chant — d'you have a number or address where I could find him?" Bruno said, trying not to sound disappointed. He fingered his scar.

"Yes, he'll be working with Jacques Savard, leader of the Opposition in Ottawa, telephone 613-996-6740. He starts work July third."

"Any way I can find him before then?" Bruno asked.

"Don't know — he's in the middle of moving. I don't have an address or a phone number for him," Hélène lied, protecting Alan's privacy. She'd been instructed to give his new local phone number and address only to the "inner circle" — Guy Doucet, his parents Sam and Laura, and his new girlfriend Susan Belair.

"Sorry to have troubled you, *madame*." Bruno was careful not to slam the phone down. "Shit, the bastard was clearing out his office. I'll bet the money *was* in those boxes."

"What the Christ we gonna tell Bertolini's guys?" Luigi was incredulous.

Bruno had already thought ahead. "Give it a few days. We'll find out where he's living from his Ottawa office. Don' worry, shithead," Bruno reassured his agitated brother. "And if that don't work, we zero in on the girlfriend. We already know where she lives."

Jean Thibault and his men at RCMP regional headquarters on Sherbrooke were doing a slow burn. It was almost three months since Marcel Gagnon and Antoinette Belair had arrived at Dorval with their China white. Not only had they been behaving as perfectly normal residents of Montreal, but the phone taps at 21 Terrace St-Denis had yielded nothing but the usual sort of calls between two lovers, disparate in age, living together for the first time.

To make matters worse, Thibault was convinced that

the two DEA operatives, Eric Bourne and Carl Swayze, were both incompetent. They followed Antoinette and Marcel brazenly wherever they went, risking detection of the entire surveillance operation.

At one point, Bourne and Swayze had wanted to break into the apartment and search for the heroin. They had finally been persuaded by Thibault that this would have guaranteed failure of the whole operation.

Ever since early February, when Antoinette had been spotted by Bourne and Swayze at Le Quatre Saisons, both the RCMP and DEA operatives had spent literally hundreds of hours trying to figure out how Antoinette had complied with the New York courier's instructions. With whom had she stashed the money?

Their first thought had been Antoinette's mother Huguette, who still maintained the family home on Carré St-Louis, just off St-Denis. Through investigation of public records, they had learned that Antoinette's father had died in January, a month before the money transfer, and that Antoinette was with him when he finally succumbed to a stroke suffered the previous fall.

Yet, as they had discovered from Huguette's neighbors, Antoinette had not really lived at home for over five years. She had flitted from apartment to apartment, sometimes alone, sometimes with a young man, as she worked her way through the Montreal film crowd. In fact, it was only the stroke that brought Antoinette back to her father and anywhere near Huguette.

The two older children had been off doing other things, Marc at the seminary and Susan starting her own law practice on Park Avenue.

"*Bonjour*, Madame Belair, my name's Thibault from the RCMP

regional office here in Montreal. We've found a wallet that appears to belong to your daughter Antoinette. There's no one home at the address on the driver's license in the wallet so we thought we'd check here. Your name and address are listed on the identification card as next of kin."

The RCMP had taken the wallet from Antoinette's room at Mont-Tremblant, hoping it would yield some clue to the intended depository for the cash. This had been their way of returning it and at the same time seeing what additional information they could pick up.

"Let me see." Huguette Belair frowned slightly as she took the wallet and examined the driver's license. "That's Antoinette's old address. I think she's moved a couple of times since then. She's doesn't come home much since her father died. I've always had trouble keeping up with her, but I'll give her the wallet when she next comes to visit," she said, apologetically. Then, somewhat embarrassed, Huguette added, "I don't even have Antoinette's telephone number. But I know she's never home, what with skiing, films and all her boyfriends. *Pardon*."

The RCMP had kept the Belair residence under surveillance for about a week. But no one came to visit so the operation was canceled. Antoinette had dropped in on her mother the Wednesday before departing for England to meet Marcel and had been glad to have the wallet back before her trip abroad. It never dawned on her, or on her mother for that matter, that it was unusual for the regional office of the RCMP to engage in the business of returning lost wallets.

The RCMP and DEA had also investigated other possible locations for the depository. Through another of Antoinette's Mont-Tremblant male acquaintances, they ascertained that for about two months Antoinette had lived in a small furnished bachelorette on Avenue Laval. She had given this up when she took on the larger flat at 21 Terrace St-Denis. The friendly landlord on Avenue Laval had permitted a search with no questions asked, but nothing had turned up.

Other locations were considered — a safety deposit box in some bank or trust company, or a storage locker at Central Station or Windsor Station, the airport terminals at Dorval or Mirabel or the bus terminal. But this exercise turned up nothing since Antoinette frequented none of these places.

The RCMP had also developed a list of names derived from license plates of vehicles in which Antoinette had ridden around town or to and from Mont-Tremblant before the trip to England. So far there were eight names, all dashing young skiers, usually stockbrokers or lawyers. Alan Chant was one of them.

Up at RCMP headquarters in Ottawa, all this information had been fed into the giant Canadian Police Information Center (CPIC) computer, which was connected to the DEA's huge CRAY computer in Washington.

As Antoinette winged her way to England, all Bert Kaufman and his men in drug enforcement at RCMP headquarters in Ottawa had been able to do was to shake their heads in disbelief.

"After chasing down every lead, after checking every cross-reference kicked up by the computers in both Ottawa and Washington, after blanket surveillance of this silly bitch for over two months — our guys in Montreal still don't know where the hell the money is stashed," Kaufman had complained to his deputy Mario Gingras. "The DEA will be on our tail if we don't sharpen up."

"*Maudite affaire*, after almost seven months of screwing around, spending a lot of our time and money, and allowing those goddamn bureaucrats from Ottawa and Washington to slow us down, we're still not much further ahead," a frustrated and impatient Thibault blurted out to his deputy Claude Pilon that humid September day in Montreal as he leafed through the Antoinette Belair/Marcel Gagnon file. Pilon, round-faced and overweight, was as stolid as his boss was volatile. He took a chocolate-glazed doughnut from the box on his desk and munched impassively as Thibault continued to fume. "All we've got is a recording of the handoff last February full of gaps and static, a list of the guys this girl slept with last winter, a whole lot of heavy breathing with the old Frenchman at Terrace St-Denis and a detailed profile on the neighborhood." He slammed his hand down on his deputy's desk. The doughnut box leapt six inches.

"Hey, if you want, our guys could go in any time and pick up the dope, that'd be easy," Pilon tried to assure Thibault, who now looked pensive. "But the tapes we have from the phone are mostly shit. Not one call anywhere outside Canada since they set up house. So we can't prove any connection with the Bertolinis in New York, which is what the DEA and Kaufman need. We've discovered a second line and got a tap on it, but it's almost never used. *Tu veux?*" Pilon proffered doughnuts to Thibault, who shook his head. "The only thing we've found that's the least bit interesting is the girl's several attempts to call a law firm in Old Montreal, by the name Chant & Doucet. Seems that one of the partners, Alan Chant, is one of the guys she shacked up with at Tremblant last winter."

"She still seeing him?"

"No, I don't think she's seen him since, and her few telephone calls to him don't make much sense. They're mostly with his secretary, and concern some legal work involving her late father's estate." He brushed some chocolate icing from his striped tie, which had already seen more than its share of doughnut crumbs. "Only thing is, we can't locate the lawyer — seems he left the firm at the end of June and we haven't been able to find out where he's gone or where he's living. But we'll try to stay on top of it."

"What do you mean you can't find out where he's gone? Who's in charge of that?"

Pilon's large forehead creased as he tried to remember. Details were not his strong suit. "I'll have to check on that, sir."

"*Sacrement!*" Thibault threw up his hands in disgust. He wondered yet again what he'd done to deserve such incompetence. "What about the money? Haven't our guys got any leads yet where she might have stashed it? We've got to keep track of it so we can prove the connection between the handoff at Le Quatre Saisons and any attempt to deliver the white stateside."

"We're working on it, Jean. We're pretty sure it's not at 21 Terrace St-Denis. Our guys went through the place pretty carefully when she and the Frenchman went off on a little weekend trip to the Eastern Townships last month. They've hidden the white beneath the floorboards, but there's no sign of the money." Claude Pilon reached for the last doughnut, then, seeing Thibault's scowl, thought the better of it. "We'll just have to continue watching her closely to see where she goes or who she contacts to look for clues where it might be. Might have some connection with the lawyer Chant, but we're not sure."

"I don't want to hear the words 'not sure' or 'we'll try to stay on top of it' again," Thibault exploded at his startled deputy. His anger made his brown eyes appear black. "For chrissakes, let's get some certainty into this operation. Bourne and Swayze are gonna be laughing at us if we don't pin things down a little tighter around here. Even though they're assholes, they're the ones who gave us the details of the handoff from Bertolini last February. Kaufman, Gingras and his gang in Ottawa are going to be mad as hell if the Frenchman decides to deliver the white before we're able to establish the link."

"You're absolutely right. We'll get on it."

"Don't just get on it. Get it done. Do whatever you have to do to find the goddamn money!"

Chapter Eleven

"Tom, you've got a bee in your bonnet." Carolyn peered out from beneath the covers. A pretty woman with pale blue eyes and dark blond hair, she watched her husband straighten his bow tie and search for the clothes brush to apply the last finishing touch to his carefully groomed appearance. It was barely six in the morning, and Tom had already been up for almost an hour. He had shaved, showered, read the Globe and Mail and had breakfast.

Carolyn remembered that it was after midnight the previous evening before Tom had returned home. He had chosen to stay at the office poring over the most urgent departmental briefing memoranda and trying unsuccessfully to work his way through the mound of green correspondence books. They had begun piling up on the small conference table in his office the day after his swearing-in. That was a long three weeks ago, and there were less than two weeks before the House of Commons adjourned for Christmas break on December 14th.

The briefing books required his full concentration. They contained carefully crafted policy position papers requiring his approval on such diverse topics as conditions of entry for entrepreneurs, criteria for deciding hardship cases on humanitarian grounds, refugee claim determination and special conditions applicable to domestic workers.

Each letter in the correspondence books involved some intractable problem for which some official had decided that a routine letter from a faceless bureaucrat was insufficient. To make the problem go away, a letter bearing the minister's signature on specially embossed, cream-colored stationery with gold lettering was needed.

Typically, such a letter would have a brief note attached to it providing background information. It would invariably conclude "Minister, attached letter is for your signature, if you agree." After a few days on the job, Tom had decided that there would be at least one letter in each correspondence book to which he would *not* agree, just to remind the department who was in charge.

"Is it always going to be like this, Tom?" Carolyn asked gently, thinking about the three previous evenings she had spent alone watching TV in the Park Lane, their small Ottawa apartment hotel. Her only previous trip to Ottawa, other than a family excursion in the '60s, had been a brief visit three weeks previously for the swearing-in and a celebratory dinner with close Regina friends, now living in Ottawa and working for the government.

"Carolyn, it's rough at the beginning. They told us that at the PMO briefing two days ago. Long hours really can't be avoided. A minister has to stay on top of his department, otherwise the bureaucrats will run away with it, and we lose control . . ."

"That's not what I mean, honey," Carolyn chose her words carefully. "It's not the long hours. I'm used to that. You used to leave for the hospital at five-thirty in the morning, and you'd have emergencies that kept you out to all hours. It's . . . well, you're so uptight. You didn't kiss me when you came to bed. It was as if I didn't even exist

— you were so absorbed in whatever was running through your head."

Tom looked contrite. "I'm sorry," he murmured. Encouraged, Carolyn ploughed on.

"You must have had an intense moment or two yesterday that you dreamt about. Just after two, you tossed and turned and said 'I won't do that — it's not right.' When I tried to snuggle up, you said 'no way' and rolled over with your back to me. Are you sure you want me here in Ottawa, Tom?"

Carolyn was now sitting upright in bed, eyes wide open. She had dreaded asking that question, but knew it had to come. Ever since election night she wondered what would become of their comfortable lifestyle in suburban Regina. She'd been relieved to learn that MPs and their spouses had generous travel subsidies to and from their constituencies and that she'd be able to be with Tom in Ottawa fairly often when the House was in session. They'd be able to keep their Regina house, and Tom would try to get home most weekends.

Carolyn Baldwin was no slouch. Her achievements and her personal skills had been a great asset during Tom's election campaign in Regina East. Born Carolyn Thorvaldsen in Leroy, Saskatchewan, she'd graduated with an honors English degree from the University of Saskatchewan in Saskatoon, where she'd met Tom. After earning a second degree in education, Carolyn joined the English department at Campbell Collegiate in Regina. She and Tom had wanted a family, but that dream turned out not to be in the cards. The end of the baby boom and shrinking enrollment eliminated her job five years later just as Tom's career at the hospital bloomed.

Unfazed, Carolyn had plunged into volunteer work in Regina. She was elected president of the local chapter of the Imperial Order of the Daughters of the Empire, an organization that supported worthwhile causes throughout the community. And she had played a major role in reviving the women's auxiliary at Tom's hospital, which had grown moribund over the years.

An energetic woman who was used to keeping busy, she wasn't at all certain that the role of politician's wife suited her. Carolyn was not enamored with Ottawa after the last four days, the damp cold that seemed to characterize both the weather and the personality of the people. Neither did the cramped, antiseptic one-bedroom apartment at the Park Lane appeal to her as a place to spend time when Tom was held up at the department, attended cabinet meetings or did House duty. You couldn't even see the Peace Tower from their tiny balcony.

"Of course I want you here, Carolyn. I'll try not to leave you stranded if I can help it. If you don't mind it and I can convince the security people, I'll bring home some of the briefing and correspondence books and beaver away here. That way you'll have at least a part of me." Tom went over to the bed and sat down beside her. "I forgot to tell you that I lucked in to a pretty good executive assistant last week, sent over by the PMO. His name's Alan Chant. He's young, but he's mature and smart too, a lawyer from Montreal who's fully bilingual as far as I can see. He's been working for Savard here in Ottawa since last summer so he knows his way around. Also, he seems to have a pretty good handle on how to deal with some of these tough immigration cases, the ones that really get my goat, if last night was any example."

Carolyn now had an inkling as to why Tom was uptight. "Couldn't this new EA — what's his name — Alan Chant — take some of this load off you?" That struck a familiar chord. He recalled the previous evening and the ordeal of working through those interminable letters written in bureaucratese, each requiring his personal signature "Minister . . . if you agree." "*If you agree*" — there had to be a better way. "Chant's going to be able to take on more and more as he gets into it, that's for sure," Tom acknowledged. "But he hasn't even got his security clearance yet. That may take a while. Carolyn, you've got to remember that it's the minister who carries the can on each file reviewed, on each decision made, so I'm going to try to stay on top of everything. I'm going to run the department, the department's not going to run me." Tom chopped the air for emphasis.

Carolyn winced at Tom's naivete, but still admired and respected his principles and sense of responsibility. "Look, if you trust your new EA, give him as much rope as you can. If he's worked for Savard for six months, he's not going to get *you* into trouble, let alone damage his own career and hurt the PM." She touched his shoulder reassuringly.

"We'll see," Tom said cautiously. "We're having our first review of sensitive cases with officials starting in less than two hours. I did the prep last night. There are some real doozers. I have no idea how Chant works face-to-face, but he certainly highlighted well for me, and his recommendations seem basically sound." Tom looked away, his mind already on the meeting ahead. Carolyn gently took his chin in her hands and turned his face towards her.

"Just remember," she said, looking directly into his eyes, "the voters of Regina East aren't going to reward you on the basis of how many individual cases you review and decide in a day. The only thing they want is for you to manage the system properly and not screw up. If you think Chant's a decent guy and has similar instincts to you, let him have his head. I want part of you for myself, even though I know it'll be much smaller than in the past."

Tom hugged Carolyn for a long minute in his first genuine display of affection since the swearing-in. "We can work this out, sweetheart. Give me a few days," he whispered as the intercom rang, gently, for the second time. The ministerial driver, Denis Forget, was signaling polite impatience from the lobby below. Alan had told Denis he had to have the Minister at the office by seven-fifteen sharp.

Chapter Twelve

Each summer for seven years during the '60s and early '70s, Alan had escaped Montreal to attend Camp Hurontario in Georgian Bay. This camp, nestled in the 30,000 islands running all the way from Honey Harbor in the south to the French River in the north, was known for developing leadership qualities in its young campers. With its extensive sailing and nature programs, arts and crafts, and, especially, canoe trips throughout the bay and the surrounding rivers, Sam knew it would broaden his son's horizons beyond Selwyn House and Westmount. By his seventh year, the gangling seventeen-year-old had become program director.

Alan remembered it clearly. That first morning, with all campers on hand, demanded organization, preparedness and enthusiasm. The sagacious camp director was getting on in years. When he stood to deliver the opening remarks of welcome and to outline the day's program, Alan handed him the newly written schedule, each event clearly marked in chronological order, all the team leaders listed alongside their respective sport or activity, nothing left to guess-work or uncertainty. Campers and staff alike marveled that the old camp director got everything right that year.

At the closing campfire towards the end of August, Alan stood off to the side, smiling and satisfied. This was his last year at camp, maybe his best. At times, he had been the one running the place even though it had never been formally acknowledged.

"Minister, in the absence of the deputy, who's tied up at a meeting today, let me introduce you to our presenters. They've been itching to get at you since the election because they're holding some files that are burning holes in their hands." Alan tried to break the ice gently. "First, let me introduce Mr. Bev Callen, Associate Deputy Minister of Immigration. He's in charge of the agenda today."

Callen was tall, well dressed and understated, with spectacles befitting an Oxford don. He was the second-highest ranking officer in the department, but Alan didn't need to make this point since Callen's demeanor and his position in the middle of the solemn group of officials opposite Baldwin at the conference table said it all.

"Minister, you'll be seeing Mr. Callen on a weekly basis at the very least," added Alan. Callen stood up but avoided eye contact with his new minister. Tom invoked his Regina physician's "warm and friendly" approach and tried to disarm him.

"Glad to have you on my team, Bev. You've been a real leader in this department, I understand." Tom may have exaggerated a little, but Alan had suggested at a pre-briefing meeting that some first-name familiarity and ego-stroking was necessary for these hard-working officials who had been inconvenienced by the election and the change of government.

Alan continued. "Second, we have Bill Kirke, Executive Director of Immigration Operations and Case Management." Kirke was a small, wiry, nervous man who looked as though he never slept, and his rumpled suit reflected that condition. Alan had already identified him as the detail man the minister's staff would call in the middle of the night when things started to run amuck.

"Third, meet Joe Bédard, Director General of Enforcement," Alan soldiered on. "Minister, he's our chief of police. You may have seen him quoted in the media from time to time on various high-profile deportation cases."

Bédard was balding, gray at the temples, and smoked a pipe, or at least appeared to, though there was never any smoke coming from the bowl. The minister was a virulent anti-smoker but had not yet got around to issuing instructions throughout the office. He made a note to speak to Alan about this. He already suspected his secretary was a furtive smoker. Why else would she take so many breaks, leaving the reception desk unattended?

"Also joining our group today is Frank Legault, Director of Control and Intelligence." Legault, a tall ramrod of a man with a stiff mustache, stood up smartly to shake the minister's hand across the table, but said nothing as he fixed his steady gaze on Baldwin.

Alan had already sized up Legault in an encounter at the PMO a few days before coming over to Baldwin's office and disliked him intensely. He had been a member of the security intelligence briefing team put together to sensitize the prime minister elect to security issues, four days after the election. Legault was a man of few words. When he spoke, it sounded more like a typed memorandum than natural speech, which reflected his background as an RCMP officer. It was rumored that Legault couldn't avoid using the word "suspect" when he first joined immigration, and that no one had the courage to tell him to stop.

Quietly observing the pleasantries at the far end of the table was a well-dressed, attractive woman who looked slightly out of place. Her lustrous dark hair was cut in a short, smooth cap and her large, brown eyes highlighted an otherwise expressionless face. Alan had asked that she be included as part of this first briefing because of a couple of difficult cases to be discussed. "Francine Côté, Director General of Counterintelligence with the Canadian Security Intelligence Service," Alan announced.

She stood up and politely acknowledged the minister, but was obviously uncomfortable being included in these immigration department introductions. Her eyes gave the impression that she had more important things to do than attend this initial meeting with a neophyte minister, a point Baldwin didn't miss. Nevertheless, he was intrigued and made a quick mental note to find out more from Alan.

"Finally, Minister, you have not yet had the pleasure of meeting Dominique Rodriguez, Senior Policy Advisor for Immigration, seconded to your ministerial staff." Alan had almost finished the introductions. "Her job is to protect you from the day-to-day immigration matters that literally pour into this office each day from MPs and their staff, lawyers from across the country and ordinary citizens. She can manage a case load like no one else on the Hill — speaks four languages, and there's nothing in the major immigrant communities in Montreal, Toronto and Vancouver that she's not familiar with."

Dominique beamed confidently. A large woman given to wearing flower-print dresses, she had a gentle, heart-shaped face animated by intelligent gray eyes. Baldwin sensed she would be important to him. Alan had already heard about Dominique from Susan when he first learned that he was being posted as an EA to the minister of immigration. Susan had often used Dominique as a conduit to get through to the appropriate departmental official in Ottawa when the system was throwing up a brick wall in Montreal. Even though Dominique had worked for the immigration minister in the previous government, she was clearly a non-partisan whom Alan had identified as a "keeper." The political loyalty test would have to come later.

"Minister, this morning we have two objectives." Callen began the formal part of the briefing without looking up. He was trying hard not to show displeasure at young Chant's presumptuousness in having introduced the officials present, a task usually reserved for the most senior public servant in attendance. "The first is to give you an initial exposure to what we call 'sensitive cases' — cases the department cannot or will not resolve without direct input from the minister because of one or more of the following: a) their high political profile as a result of credible representations received, b) their potential threat to the security of Canada, or c) conflict with another minister or department."

The mention of departmental conflict startled Tom. He had received a call at the office from Forrester the previous evening, asking how things were going after the first day on the job. "Not bad," he'd responded, knowing full well that he really wasn't into it yet.

"It's fascinating here at justice, Tom. The media thought I'd been demoted, but I'm really enjoying it — good juicy legal issues. Got a few with your department — maybe we'll get a chance to spar real soon," she had added, provocatively. Tom now wondered if the sparring was about to begin that morning, and he wasn't sure he was looking forward to it.

"The second objective," continued Callen, "is to begin to put a dint in the large backlog of sensitive cases that have accumulated since the election was called. Minister, your predecessor, against our advice, refused to take any of the hard decisions once the election campaign began, preferring to pass any decisions along to whomever would be minister after the election."

Callen appeared to be trying to sound scrupulously objective. He cleared his throat, made a minute adjustment to his spectacles, and went on. "Today, we've picked out three key ones, probably our most pressing. We need the minister's decision on all of these, if possible." Callen looked around the table at all the players. "Now let's get started. We should try to finish by ten o'clock since I know the minister is scheduled to meet the deputy minister about that time."

Tom didn't know that a meeting with his deputy minister was scheduled. Alan had actually set up the meeting the previous evening, calling Douglas Morrison, the austere and experienced deputy minister, on his unlisted number at his home. Just to make a point, he had introduced himself as the minister's new executive assistant, formerly of Mr. Savard's office.

Callen detailed the first case. A Chilean sailor, Juan Barcelona, had jumped ship in Vancouver. He claimed to be a pro-Allende activist threatened by the current Chilean regime. He had become a west coast media target and had gained the support of and legal representation provided by the B.C. Civil Liberties Association.

Kirke pointed out that while Barcelona might normally qualify as a refugee he had not yet formally filed a claim for refugee status and had provided conflicting information to immigration officials. Somehow this had leaked out. A backlash appeared to be developing, he explained, not only against Barcelona but against the refugee determination system in general, which some on the right saw as too generous and too easily abused.

Bill Kirke nervously twisted his pen. "Our best information is that Barcelona will be under no physical threat to his safety if he rejoins the crew on the *s.s. Valparaiso*, which is currently tied up in Vancouver harbor, and returns to Chile. But we know that others in the community will protest and the matter will probably be raised in the House, since at least two Vancouver-area MPs in the opposition have taken up his cause." Kirke appeared to have good information, and both Tom and Alan appreciated his political candor.

Bédard, the director general of enforcement, pointed out that Baldwin could instruct officials to take the man back to the ship before it departed for Santiago the next morning or grant him admission on a minister's permit on compassionate and humanitarian grounds. He could also delay making any decision for a week.

"This last option," warned Bédard, "would throw him into the refugee determination process, which would buy him at least three to four years in Canada until he exhausts all levels of appeal. By that time, the department would be faced with an extremely difficult enforcement situation. Your call, Minister," said Bédard, looking first at Baldwin, then at Chant.

"Is there any more information other than what was in the briefing note?" Baldwin tried to sound thoughtful and responsible as he searched the faces around the conference table.

At that point, Dominique Rodriguez interrupted with a practical suggestion. "Why don't you talk to the two Vancouver MPs? Their perspective may be helpful. For example, I heard one rumor that the reason Barcelona left his ship was not out of fear of persecution back home for his political views but out of fear for his safety because his shipmates had found out he was gay and were threatening violence. The politics are obviously tricky here."

Alan was not ready for this. He was appalled that the senior policy advisor would feed in this kind of rumor and recommend consulting with two people so different politically from Savard and Baldwin. After all, hadn't Savard's party been elected to take a tougher stand on these kinds of issues compared to the previous administration?

Lacking Alan's partisan experience gained working in Savard's office for the previous six months, Baldwin followed his instincts. "Seems like a good idea," he said, believing in his responsibility to be fair, regardless of party politics. "Let's call them later. Once I hear their story, I should be able to give you my decision by tonight."

The immigration officials were not happy. Kirke looked particularly glum. Apparently, this doctor was going to approach these decisions as he would a consultation on a medical diagnosis at Regina General Hospital. With this kind of dithering, it could take days, weeks, even months to get decisions out of him. Alan saw it more positively. He would call the two MPs, find out what they knew, and then try to steer Baldwin to either of the first two options. Besides, the fact that Baldwin had taken this extra step of consulting the two most vocal opposition members of Parliament could be turned into a virtue. "The thoughtful but decisive minister," Alan mused as he ambled towards the end of the room to refill his coffee mug.

Alan knew a lot more about the next case. Professor David Firestone of Concordia University was a client of Susan Belair. Callen summarized the briefing note. Firestone was an American who had been allowed into Canada four years previously by a benevolent minister of immigration to fill a vital hole in Concordia's history department. He had held successive minister's permits, and his last one would expire within the next thirty days.

His appointment at Concordia had caused public concern at the time, not so much because he was an avowed Marxist (he'd been investigated three times by Senator McCarthy's Committee on Un-American Activities), but because many of the younger academics at Concordia strongly believed that the post should have been filled by a qualified Canadian. But the Canadian academics' concerns generally subsided because Firestone turned out to be a talented and popular professor. A fifth minister's permit would normally have been issued in due course, to be followed by landed immigrant status, but a new complication had developed.

This time, Francine Côté of CSIS took the lead. "We have reason to believe that Professor Firestone is on the payroll of the Cuban government as an intelligence officer. For the past year, he's been observed twice a month at the Cuban consulate in Montreal. Intelligence that we've received suggests that Firestone has been providing detailed information on certain Cuban students enrolled at Concordia, particularly those who might be sympathetic to exiled Cuban organizations headquartered in Miami and opposed to the Castro regime. By using threats, blackmail or hard cash, the Cubans could probably persuade some of these students to infiltrate these organizations. Firestone's efforts are an important first step towards their recruitment by the Cubans." Her large brown eyes lifted from the page she was reading and looked squarely at Tom, who was already feeling out of his depth. Was this something right out of a spy novel or was this for real?

"CSIS would like you and the immigration department

simply not to renew his minister's permit next month, which would force him to return to the States without requiring a formal expulsion and perhaps endangering our information source at the Cuban consulate." The representative from CSIS, expressionless throughout her initial presentation, allowed just a hint of a smile as she sat down.

"The trouble is," countered Kirke, who seemed to resent the CSIS position, "this appears to be a relatively straightforward, routine case where a minister's permit would be renewed, followed by landing. Professor Firestone has strong support from the Canadian Civil Liberties Association and he's retained a prominent Montreal immigration lawyer who has already made formal representations on his behalf." Kirke paused and glanced edgily at Côté.

Alan was pleased by the respect they seemed to have for Susan, his lover and regular weekend companion. He wondered if their relationship — it had already been six months — might eventually lead to professional conflict and force him to declare his interest or even remove himself from the discussion when her cases came up for review. They weren't at that point just yet, but it was not without worry. He forced himself to re-focus on what Kirke was saying.

"If there's even a hint of CSIS involvement causing a negative decision, the CCLA will scream blue murder. Trust me. They'll argue that CSIS surveillance of an academic is totally inappropriate, that it's an infringement of academic freedom." Kirke watched Côté for a reaction. Though her face remained impassive, he thought he saw her eyes narrow for a second as she sipped her coffee.

"There is nothing that took place on any university campus," she interjected. "We tracked this bird through surveillance at the Cuban consulate. The fact that he's a university professor doesn't give him special status. In any event, a written ministerial directive from the solicitor general in the previous government allows CSIS to carry out activities on a campus where there are —" she rifled through her notes and then read, "'objective indications that one or more individuals may be involved in activities prejudicial to Canada.'" Côté put down her papers and looked around the table. "This situation surely qualifies. And the new solicitor general, the minister's colleague, has confirmed this written directive and is aware of our surveillance operations."

Kirke now knew he was in deep water. The new immigration minister was unlikely to want to take on the solicitor general, an experienced parliamentarian and once a distinguished trial lawyer from Edmonton. But he felt compelled to challenge Côté as to how much the new "SolGen" had been told about this operation. "Are you telling us, Ms. Côté, that the SolGen has specifically authorized CSIS to carry out surveillance of Firestone on the Concordia campus?"

"Well, not quite. CSIS believes that it's surveillance of Firestone at Concordia is within the written directive of the previous government, which the new SolGen has confirmed. He's not aware of the surveillance of this particular person at this specific university. I'll concede that."

Kirke briefly savored his moment of minor triumph, but Côté quickly went back on the attack. "Look, as a senior professor, Firestone abused his position of special trust and subverted young Cuban students. This gives us all the more reason to gently put him out of business. Minister, we could recommend to the solicitor general and the secretary of state for external affairs that they PNG his Cuban friends at the consulate. But that could cause a diplomatic uproar. The immigration route's easier," Côté concluded, with a touch of finality.

Tom and Alan, with detached amusement, watched this sparring match conducted for their benefit. In a quiet whisper, Tom asked Alan the meaning of the term "PNG." Alan explained that it was an acronym for "*persona non grata*," the device used by a host government to formally expel a foreign diplomat or other functionary for inappropriate activities.

To Alan, the CSIS position seemed sounder, provided the information was solid. He was too fresh from law school not to be influenced adversely by the thought of this part-time spy using his academic position to subvert the free speech rights of a minority student group.

In the briefing notes, Alan had signaled Baldwin to agree with the CSIS position and refuse to renew the minister's permit. Baldwin went along without fully understanding Alan's reasoning. He assumed, wrongly, that they were simply siding with the group that could potentially scream the loudest and cause the greatest uproar. If the student political movement got wind of this, thought Tom, they could cause more trouble than the civil libertarians in the CCLA, who seemed to be growing old and out of touch with reality.

In fact, Alan's recommendation was based more on principle than pragmatism. It didn't really bother him that Susan's client was the loser. All the better to have it as a precedent should the conflict question ever come up, he thought to himself.

Neither Alan nor Tom had stopped to consider the prospect of CSIS advancing specious information simply to help their buddies at the FBI settle an old score with this aging communist. After all, wasn't it considered gospel within CSIS that Canada generally gets more information than it gives from allied services like the FBI, and that no opportunity should be lost to even up?

Baldwin suggested a five-minute break for trips to the washroom and a chance to get more coffee or juice. Privately, he wanted to give everyone a chance to cool down.

The third case that day was also not new to Alan. Frank Russo had drawn it to his attention when Alan was working in Savard's office before the election. The nervous Bill Kirke, in charge of case management, would have preferred that Professor Firestone's minister's permit be renewed, to get the CCLA and Firestone's lawyer off his back. So, with renewed aggression, he took the lead on case number three, backed up by Frank Legault, Director of Control and Intelligence.

"Fred Milanowski was brought to Canada from the U.S. eight years ago by the RCMP to crack an apparently insoluble case of commercial fraud. Milanowski's a U.S. citizen. He'd served two years in Joliet Federal Prison, south of Chicago. That was for theft and fraud in a complex set of transactions on the Chicago Board of Trade and the Chicago Mercantile Exchange."

Kirke explained that things could have gone a lot worse for Milanowski, but he and his lawyers made a deal with the FBI. In exchange for a guilty plea and a plea bargain on sentence, Milanowski gave evidence that sent seven people involved in the transactions to jail. When it came time for Milanowski to be released from prison, the FBI, as part of their bargain, scouted around for the best situation in which to set Milanowski up with a new identity.

Frank Legault, sitting up as straight and rigid as a board, picked up the story at this point. "The FBI's close liaison with the RCMP turned up the possibility of his moving to Winnipeg with the prospect of landed immigrant status after three years. It seems that the Commercial Crime Division of the RCMP Western Region had uncovered some form of scam connected to the Winnipeg Commodities Exchange, but had been unable to make much progress because the alleged participants were real pros and didn't use phones susceptible to wire taps. The Mounties were having trouble recruiting an insider at a sufficiently high level, notwithstanding generous cash offers."

Legault ran a finger stiffly over his mustache. Tom wondered if the man ever relaxed. Legault continued. "The RCMP liked the thought of Milanowski — that's his new name — complete with an official make-over and a freshly trimmed beard, setting up business in Winnipeg and infiltrating their primary targets. They did a deal with the FBI. Milanowski was given a modest house in Winnipeg purchased with FBI funds, and the RCMP agreed to help him set up a small commodities business in downtown Winnipeg. Milanowski was given an employment authorization by Canadian immigration for a period of three years, following which he would be landed, on condition that he continue to provide useful information to assist the RCMP in their ongoing investigation."

"The issue for you, Minister," said Bill Kirke, intervening politely, "is whether Milanowski, a convicted criminal in the U.S., kept his part of the bargain that would justify your landing him."

Frank Legault chimed in. "We — I mean, those on the control and intelligence side of the situation, including the RCMP, feel that Milanowski didn't do what he was asked to and, therefore, you owe him nothing!"

In the center of the room, the senior immigration official, Bev Callen, began to stir. "Well, it's really not that simple. Milanowski may have let down the RCMP in moving along their floundering investigation. But he did alert the government to a new problem involving a particular Canadian senator who had been allegedly taking kickbacks on awarding concessions by Transport Canada at Winnipeg International Airport. Surely the fact that Senator Joe Semeniuk has been charged as a result of a tip from Milanowski justifies immigration keeping its part of the bargain."

The mention of Senator Semeniuk immediately set off alarm bells in Alan's mind. The previous day, he'd received a call from the PMO to keep an eye on the immigration case of the FBI transplant who was trying to blow the whistle on the PM's friend in the senate.

"At the best of times, we don't like our immigration process being used by other government departments for their own particular objectives," Callen philosophized. "But this situation seems to warrant discretion in Milanowski's favor."

"But, guys, can you imagine the cynicism?" asked Joe Bédard testily. "Imagine if this one leaks out and every potential deportee says 'Waive my transgression if I go out and turn in some big shot.'"

Russo had called Alan on this case just after he had started in Savard's office the previous summer. Russo had known little of the background. He'd met Milanowski on only a couple of occasions when the up-and-coming Winnipeg broker was thinking of starting a business on the Montreal exchange. Milanowski had told Russo that he was having problems with immigration. Russo had offered to call his former lawyer, Alan Chant, who was now working in Ottawa for the man likely to be the next prime minister.

Alan had looked into the matter briefly at the time and had called Dominique Rodriguez, the minister's senior advisor, whose name he had got from Susan. Dominique had reported back that immigration didn't know what the complication was. Somehow it was in the hands of the RCMP, and Alan might want to call Corporal Rivers in the Winnipeg regional office. Rivers told Alan it was unlikely Milanowski would be allowed to stay in Canada. The RCMP had discovered he was a convicted criminal who had entered Canada under false pretenses and was living here under an assumed name.

What Alan didn't know then, but had since discovered, was that Milanowski had fallen out of favor with the Mounties because he had messed up their investigation of the Winnipeg airport concession situation by revealing the senator's involvement. Not that they were supporters of the senator. But they had bigger fish to fry, and they would have rather excluded the senator from any public exposure, given his close ties with the Savard people.

Given his prior knowledge, Alan had fretted about this case when he first read the briefing note. And that was before the call from the PMO. For Baldwin, it was probably a no-win situation. If he didn't land Milanowski and the story ever got out, the public might see this as reneging on a deal that had legitimate law enforcement objectives. If he did land Milanowski, the RCMP would be unhappy and would not forget.

Ministers usually like to have the RCMP on their side. The Mounties had been known to run to the prime minister regarding any minister who stepped out of line, often with the flimsiest evidence related to some personal peccadillo or misconduct. Still, Alan had decided to let Baldwin have his head on this one and had scribbled in the margin of the briefing note "Too close to call — you decide."

"Well, ladies and gentlemen, this is indeed a tough one," Baldwin began. "Where I come from, a deal is a deal, no matter how unsavory the participants or how changed the circumstances. Milanowski has no life back in the States. He came here to get a fresh start, and the Canadian government helped him, in return for his help. The kind of help he delivered may not have been to everyone's liking but it certainly wasn't something that Joe Q. Public would regard as improper. I'm sorry that the RCMP is so unhappy with Milanowski, but I really have no choice but to land him."

Alan expressed no emotion but was inwardly troubled. No doubt the PMO would be calling again. Dominique was pleasantly surprised that her new boss would stand up to the Mounties. "Should be interesting," she whispered to Alan.

It was five to ten. Baldwin stood up. "Thank you for a very interesting morning, ladies and gentlemen. Now Mr. Chant and I are going to get ready to meet the deputy." Baldwin walked to the door and opened it, signaling that the meeting was now over.

The room cleared quickly. Alan and Tom had only a moment together before Douglas Morrison, the deputy minister, entered. "Well, how'd I do?" Baldwin asked as he gazed out the window at the Peace Tower on Parliament Hill, across the Ottawa River.

"Not bad at all, Minister. One in immediately, one out immediately and one deferred while you consult two opposition MPs," summarized Alan glibly.

"Well, that wasn't too difficult for the first day in the hot seat. I've had worse mornings in the operating room at the hospital." Baldwin shifted his gaze to look directly at Alan and smiled his warm doctor's smile. "We're going to get along just fine!"

"Minister, don't get too self-satisfied on these three cases just yet. Some of these decisions may come back to bite you. And there are more difficult ones to come."

Baldwin missed the warning because the door was opening, and the omnipotent Douglas Morrison was about to enter.

Chapter Thirteen

N

ot surprisingly, the extensive RCMP investigation of Antoinette Belair resulted in a minor glitch in Alan Chant's background check when it came time to have him cleared for work as executive assistant to a federal minister in Ottawa.

Prime Minister Savard and his advisors had wanted to have all executive assistants selected and posted to their new ministers immediately following the swearing-in of the new cabinet on November 12th. "Top secret" security clearances were required for all EAs to ministers, with no exceptions. The PMO conceded, though, that the mandatory personal interview to be conducted by CSIS (according to Cabinet Document 35) could be undertaken after an EA had actually started on the job so that the transition would proceed quickly and smoothly. Any problems identified could be dealt with subsequently.

Under CD 35, an EA or any public servant requiring a top-secret clearance could be rejected for unreliability as well as disloyalty. The term "unreliability" was never clearly defined but was generally understood to mean that the individual, in the opinion of CSIS, might be inclined to disclose classified information. A disclosure might result, for example, from careless talk with friends outside the government, or from the threat of blackmail related to undeclared indebtedness, adultery or sexual orientation. Dubious habits, such as drinking or drug use, could also result in the unintentional spilling of classified information.

When CSIS believes that an EA is inclined to be "unreliable," the decision whether to dismiss, demote or transfer is usually left with the minister, with or without consultation with the PMO. This is an exception, made because of the political nature of the hiring and day-to-day duties of ministerial staff. Usually, when senior public servants are found to be unreliable, it is the deputy minister who is accountable for security within the department and decides what to do.

Alan's CSIS interview was not the first among the new EAs appointed by Savard. Owing to a backlog in the screening process — typical of the early days of a new government — it was not scheduled until mid-December, over a month after the government was sworn in. At the interview, he was asked point blank whether he'd had an affair at Mont-Tremblant in February 1984 with one Antoinette Belair, and whether she had been his passenger that Sunday traveling from Tremblant to Montreal.

Alan had spent enough time around Ottawa by that point to know that the PMO took CSIS security clearances seriously, so he readily acknowledged his weekend escapade. He also added that this was a one-night stand and that he had not seen her since. After extensive probing about his relationship with Antoinette, including questions about her alleged drug use and relationships with known criminals, the CSIS officials seemed satisfied that this was a casual, one-time-only affair. They accepted Alan's assertion that he knew nothing and was not involved with her on an ongoing basis.

He was not asked, and did not feel it necessary to disclose, that he'd agreed to hold on to the estate papers of Antoinette's deceased father until they could be properly disposed of. Or that he was now seeing Antoinette's sister Susan on a regular basis during his weekends at home in Montreal.

Alan's top-secret security clearance came through exactly one week before Christmas. He learned of it only from Tom Baldwin's handwritten note left inside one of the confidential briefing books just before the minister's departure for the holiday season in Regina.

As summer turned into fall, Marcel and Antoinette actually began to enjoy life at 21 Terrace St-Denis. Strolls in the park, visits to the art gallery, shopping at Mamma Leonardo's and the occasional trip out into the country in the eastern townships or the Laurentians suited them both rather well.

Ever since late April, Antoinette had been regularly calling the firm of Chant & Doucet to be reassured by Hélène that Mr. Chant still had the attaché case containing her father's estate papers. Antoinette missed the subtle change when Hélène began to answer the phone with "Doucet law offices" at the end of June. The soothing voice of Hélène provided all the comfort she needed.

Even though Hélène suspected that the attaché case was with the files that Alan had moved to the pied-à-terre on Peel Street, she had not felt the need to tell Antoinette. She believed that Alan could look after the matter from Ottawa once Antoinette chose a notary.

Secretly, Hélène had hoped that Savard might lose the general election. Then Alan would be back at Rue St-

Pierre, business as usual. Hélène remembered vividly Alan's instructions when he'd dropped into the office in late August just before the start of the election campaign. "Don't tell anyone my Peel Street address. If anyone calls wanting to talk to me personally, refer them to Savard's office in Ottawa. If it's a weekend emergency, contact Susan Belair at her apartment at Côte-des-Neiges or her office on Park; she'll know how to reach me."

Alan had known that this might deter Antoinette from contacting him. He'd also picked up enough from Susan to know that the relationship between the two sisters was not close, and that Antoinette would almost certainly keep her distance. Sooner or later he would have to deal with Antoinette and her damn estate papers, but there was no time now with the election approaching. And he sure didn't want to bring Susan into the loop — at least not yet.

It wasn't until Savard won the election in late October and it looked like Alan would be in Ottawa for a long stay that Hélène had begun to worry about Alan's unfinished business. Should she confront Alan about continuing to hold on to Antoinette's attaché case at his apartment while this strange woman dragged her feet about making a decision? Or should she should deal with Antoinette directly and give her a deadline? Maybe Susan could help sort things out — except that Alan had specifically asked that she not become involved.

The call to Hélène from the CSIS official in mid-November, wanting to schedule a personal interview to discuss what she knew about Alan Chant's personal background, did nothing to dispel her anxiety. She mentioned the impending CSIS visit to Guy Doucet. He summarily dismissed it as nothing more than the product of a careful bureaucracy in Ottawa preparing for change-over to the new government.

"Hélène, don't worry about it. The fact that they're requiring Alan to have top-secret clearance tells me that he's destined for something big. You and I know that he's 'Mr. Clean.' When they come, don't be afraid to be up front with them and tell them everything you know. The only thing you should hold back on are client confidences or privileged information. You've had enough experience to know what that's all about. But if you have any doubts, call me in."

With that general guidance, Hélène did not feel obliged to say that she knew anything about Antoinette when the CSIS investigator posed the question later that week. Aside from acknowledging his occasional dalliance with young women and his new, more regular love interest Susan Belair, the immigration lawyer whose office was on Park Avenue, Hélène gave Alan what she thought was a clean bill of health.

Within hours of the CSIS investigator leaving the office of Chant & Doucet and passing the information back to higher-ups in Ottawa on the protected line, the name Susan Belair was carefully added to Alan's CSIS file and specific instructions went out to obtain more background information on this Montreal lawyer.

Chapter Fourteen

Susan liked Monday mornings the least. The alarm would ring at five-fifteen, and Alan would bound out of bed, throw cold water on his face, go into his exercise routine of forty sit-ups (to firm the belly) and forty push-ups (to firm the arms and shoulders). Then he'd shave and shower, gulp down orange juice and coffee, blow her a kiss and head for Central Station to catch the train for Ottawa. This had been his routine for almost a month following the election.

On weeks when Alan had a lot of personal running around to do, he'd drive his car to Ottawa. But he preferred to take the train. This meant that by catching the six-fifteen back to Ottawa on Monday morning, he'd have time to read *The Globe and Mail*, *The Gazette*, *The Ottawa Citizen*, *La Presse* and *Le Devoir* as well as finishing two more cups of coffee before he arrived in the nation's capital. Denis Forget, Baldwin's driver, would meet him at the Ottawa train station and hand him a green correspondence book, which Alan would race through voraciously on the drive through rush-hour traffic to the minister's offices in Hull. The book usually contained key ministerial communications that had come in over the weekend. It would have been organized by the early morning secretary and then given to Denis for delivery to Alan on arrival in

Ottawa. He would reach Baldwin's office by eight-forty-five at the latest, ready to take on the world for another week. The office of Chant & Doucet on Rue St-Pierre seemed light years away.

Since the election, Susan had tried to share vicariously in the excitement of his powerful position in Ottawa. She was even slightly envious. After all, wasn't he virtually running the immigration department in Ottawa? Who wouldn't be excited about going to work in the morning?

By comparison her Monday mornings were dull. She would try to go back to sleep after Alan left, then drag herself out of bed about eight o'clock and walk briskly across Outremont to her modest three-room office on Park Avenue, arriving in less than an hour. On bad-weather days, she would take the bus along Côte-Ste-Catherine and then along Laurier to Park.

By nine-thirty, her waiting room would be filled with desperate-looking people — mostly refugees and illegals — only some of whom had appointments.

Her assistant Andreina would inevitably have another two or three urgent cases to discuss — people who had been placed in detention over the weekend at the immigration wing of the Holiday Inn on Côte-de-Liesse in Ville St-Laurent, or who were facing a deportation inquiry at Dorval Airport scheduled to proceed later that day.

It was never the same, yet it was always the same. After almost three years of practice, she was beginning to feel a bit jaded, even cynical about her work as an immigration lawyer on the front lines. Alan's horizons were limitless. Hers were confining. The contrast was stifling.

Sure, they enjoyed their weekends together. Ever since Alan started going to Ottawa to work in Savard's office the previous summer, he had camped out at her place on Côte-des-Neiges for at least part of the weekend. Since the election, they'd fallen into more of a routine. They'd have a late Friday night dinner by candlelight with her favorites, James Taylor, Charles Aznavour or Edith Piaf playing in the background. After sharing war stories about their experiences of the previous few days, the discussion would inevitably turn to politics. At first, they talked about the prospects of the Opposition under Savard upsetting the government once the detested prime minister had the guts to call the election. After the election, their conversation was more a candid assessment of how Savard and his new ministers were doing, particularly Alan's boss, Tom Baldwin.

While both of them knew it was dangerous ground, they couldn't resist discussing high-profile cases of Susan's that had come to the attention of the minister or in which Alan had become involved.

"You guys really did it to poor old Professor Firestone, the one you alleged was helping out the Cuban consulate," she said one Saturday, with a touch of bitterness. "Four days after he received the departure notice authorized by your compassionate minister, he suffered a fatal heart attack." Alan had looked rather uncomfortable, but let her continue. "Guess it solved *your* problem," she'd noted cynically. "But the president of Concordia University will be paying your minister a little visit. Seems the university community is a bit upset. The president will be demanding a public apology. If he doesn't get one, he'll probably resign as chairman of the Advisory Council on Science and Technology. You'll remember that he was appointed by Savard's office with a big splash just last week." Susan was clearly an insider to this strategy and was sending Alan a message.

"I hear you, love. Just remember that there's more to this story than meets the eye. I'll take it up with Baldwin to see if there's anything we can do to make amends. But don't lay this guilt trip on us. I'm sorry about the heart attack."

She only raised her cases with Alan one at a time, taking care not to overuse her privileged access.

Of course, their relationship was not all business. Occasionally, she'd rent a movie to watch on the VCR, located conveniently in the corner of her bedroom. More often that not, they would start the video and then become distracted by the warm sensuality of each other's presence. Clothes out of the way, Alan's favorite technique was to have Susan lie face down on the bed. With his index and third fingers he'd start at the nape of her neck and gently move down her spine to the top of her buttocks. With circular motions, he'd slowly massage both sides of her back at the same time and then move the palms of his hands back to her neck and start over.

After two or three repetitions of this maneuver, Susan's hips would inevitably begin to undulate, and soon they would be making love. Eventually they would fall asleep with arms and legs intertwined, the TV screen showing snowy white when they awoke in the morning.

Once Alan got his weekend commute from Ottawa to Montreal properly organized, Saturday mornings turned out to be the best. The rhythm of their work week geared both of their bodies to wake up at nine o'clock at the latest, no matter how resolute their intention to sleep in.

After breakfast and a review of the Saturday papers, they usually took a trip to Jean-Talon Market. There they would be visually and gastronomically seduced by pungent cheeses, perfect fruits and vegetables, crisp salad greens and freshly baked breads and croissants. They might also pick out something fresh from the sea — mussels, scallops, salmon, tuna steaks or lobster.

Aside from sleeping together, going to the market Saturday morning was most akin to playing house for real. They got on famously. Arguing their position on food quality and culinary skills, they would try to outdo each other by relying on a mélange of curiosity, limited experience, expanding personal taste and bravado to make their points. Both of them came to realize before too long that they already had more sophisticated tastes for the finer things in life than either of their parents. For Alan this was comforting; for Susan, disquieting.

As Alan and Susan sipped their cappuccino together at La Bocca opposite Jean-Talon Market one Saturday in early December, they discussed their purchases. She'd won some of the arguments, he'd won others. Alan chuckled. The place was packed, but Alan was not distracted.

"I can't imagine Sam and Laura going to the market at Atwater or Jean-Talon together on the bus and actually enjoying it. He'd just as soon drive down in his latest Oldsmobile and wait for her to do the running around while he checked out fancy stereo equipment. Joint decisions? No way!" Alan had long ago concluded that his parents' relationship was less than egalitarian.

Susan smiled. In some ways, her family was similar. "Papa would never go near the market — that was Maman's job, and she'd do it only on weekdays so she could be home to wait on him Saturday afternoons and all day Sunday." She spooned off the milky froth and grated chocolate from her coffee. "God, this is good. Anyway, he'd work each Saturday morning, of course, closing off the books for the week at the trucking depot. But once he was home at one o'clock, he was king, and we all marched to his drum." Alan could hear the resentment creep into her voice. "Right up to his death a year ago, he kept up this routine. The regimentation would carry over to Sundays too. Mass at eleven each Sunday morning without fail. That was the rule. If you didn't want to participate, you didn't come home," she recalled angrily.

As Alan began to think about ordering more coffee, Susan went on to recount how each child in the Belair family had responded to her father's religious edict, a result of Roger Belair's strict upbringing in rural France before emigrating to Canada. Son Marc had complied; he'd even found solace in the church and pleased his father no end when he began studies to become a priest. "Too bad," she said, "Papa didn't live long enough to see Marc take his final vows next June." She made a mental note not to forget this event.

Alan caught the eye of their server, a thin brunette with bright red lipstick, and motioned for two more cappuccinos as Susan continued her story. "Antoinette was the opposite. She rebelled as a teenager. At sixteen, she'd stay at a friend's house overnight, even with a guy, just to avoid mass on Sunday. That was the start of a whole lot of trouble." Alan grew quietly uncomfortable at the mention of Antoinette, realizing that he would soon have to come clean with Susan.

"She and Papa had a very stormy relationship throughout her teen years. One moment, there'd be intense hatred and loathing, another moment there'd be demonstrations of affection and understanding that were deeper than anything that Marc or I experienced."

She stared off out the window at the sunlit street. The waitress brought their coffees. Susan smiled briefly, then resumed her story. "Funny thing, as Papa began to go rapidly downhill after his stroke, Antoinette appeared on the scene all prepared to rediscover the church and full of late-blooming repentance and compassion. In his final few months, she actually helped him go to mass each Sunday. The fact that he may have thought he'd redeemed the lost soul of his youngest daughter obviously made him very happy as he went to his grave." There was a hint of sarcasm in her voice.

"And what about you?" asked Alan, perhaps a shade too quickly, eager to get off the subject of Antoinette. Susan explained to Alan that her own approach had been more analytical, more rational. She'd gone along with her father's wishes all through law school, since she was still living at home. "But once I had a job and my own apartment, I stopped going to mass — absolutely, *fini*, no exceptions. I figured economic self-sufficiency meant I now had the right to live as I pleased." Susan smiled.

"How do you think he felt about that?" Alan looked intently at Susan as he stirred his coffee. She let out a small sigh.

"Right up until he died, Papa wondered whether his 'brightest, most successful' child would ever consent to being married in a church. I guess this must have hurt him."

"And I suppose that hurt you."

"Yes, it may have been why he and I seemed to grow apart in his last few years." Susan looked away and was silent for a few seconds. She turned back to Alan. "But I really couldn't do much to repair the damage, short of outright capitulation." Her voice was resolute but her eyes seemed to ask for approval.

"I guess not." Alan squeezed her hand.

La Bocca, crowded and noisy, provided wonderful cover for other interesting people that Saturday afternoon in mid-December. Bruno and Luigi Leonardo slowly finished their espressos just three tables away. It was rare that the sun should shine so brilliantly in December but this made their dark sunglasses seem almost appropriate.

"Gotta deliver him a message somehow. Let him know that he can't hang onto that fuckin' money forever. Somehow we'll track it down through that bitch livin' with the Frenchman," growled Luigi.

"Hey, stupid, we don' hafta deal with that dark-haired bitch. She thinks no one knows where she deposited the money. But we know." Bruno inclined his head in Alan's direction. "It's probably in his apartment on Peel Street. An' he's just sitting on it, hoping nobody'll notice while he goes up to Ottawa like some big shot. We gotta let him know *we* know, so he'll dig it out an' give it back to the bitch and Frenchie."

A germ of an idea was forming in Bruno's mind. He fingered the scar on his cheek. "Seems pretty keen on that blonde. Look at 'em over there, coo-cooing each other. What'cha say we give her a scare, like we used to in Salerno?" Bruno was grinning mischievously.

"Y'mean the curb treatment — with the Alfa Romeo?" Luigi was beginning to get the picture.

"Sure, just give her a little nudge. She walks home from work most nights — it's dark by then. We'll deliver the message in the next few days — a little Christmas present for lover boy. But no dents in the car, whatever you do. Just scare 'em a bit so maybe he'll turn over the money or deal with it somehow."

Regardless of the money, Bruno was beginning to enjoy the prospect of making the kind of mischief he'd enjoyed so much as a teenager in Sicily.

Yet another table at La Bocca was occupied by two straighter looking men with short haircuts. They were plainclothesmen from the Montreal regional office of the RCMP, following up on the lead given them by CSIS, which had been conducting Alan Chant's security assessment. From information provided by Hélène, CSIS had learned that Alan was dating Susan Belair. A CPIC cross-check of surnames had led CSIS to certain police information concerning one Antoinette Belair. This was passed on to the Mounties in Montreal, who quickly came to the conclusion that Antoinette and Susan were sisters, and that somehow Susan and perhaps Alan were part of Bertolini's project.

They would both have to be watched carefully. Moreover, they'd have to ask CSIS more about what Alan was doing in Ottawa.

The Mount Royal Tennis Club was closed from November to April, so that afternoon Susan kept to the familiar winter pattern she'd been following for over two years: a squash game at the Montreal Amateur Athletic Association, known to all simply as the MAAA. This historic old club was located on the west side of Peel Street, just below Sherbrooke — roughly half way, by taking a triangular route, between her office and her apartment. With a neoclassic exterior and an impressive foyer just inside the main entrance, it had the look and feel of an established men's club, accessible only to the privileged or affluent.

The MAAA had opened its membership to women in recent years, provided they were well sponsored and could contribute to the club athletically. After she had completed her first year of private practice, Susan had been proposed for membership by an admiring male classmate from McGill. The son of a wealthy investment dealer who'd been president of the Montreal Exchange, he'd been her squash partner at the McGill gym all through law school.

She'd enjoyed the MAAA even though it had been a financial sacrifice at the time. She was good enough to get a game with any number of members because she hit the ball like a man and was quick footed. Most of her squash partners, being male, were attracted by more than her athletic ability.

Susan had tried not to allow Alan's arrival on the scene interfere with her social and athletic life at the MAAA or the Mount Royal. This was not a problem during the election because he'd spent most of the days on the road with Savard, and it was lucky if she got to see him Saturday evening. After the election, when things returned to normal and Alan's commute to Ottawa became more routine, she'd occasionally include him in the activities at the club. Even when she didn't, she'd book her squash game earlier in the day to keep evenings free. Alan's pied-à-terre was only two blocks up the street.

However, when she did take him to the club as a guest, he wasn't always comfortable. It wasn't so much his squash game since he was a reasonably good player himself and could often beat her. But this club was her private preserve where she was in control — the guest tag, the signing of chits, the rules, the dress code, the whole bit. In a moment of weakness, he'd admitted to her that, in these circumstances, he felt insecure. She'd smiled, but with no real sympathy.

Chapter Fifteen

Outside La Bocca on that sunny day in mid-December, Alan kissed Susan and gave her a friendly nudge on the shoulder as he sent her off towards the MAAA for her squash game. He called Guy, whom he hadn't seen since before Christmas. They set up their own squash game at McGill's Currie Gymnasium for five that afternoon.

By then it was almost two, so he had several hours to kill. He dropped by the apartment on Peel Street to pick up the mail and a fur hat that he knew lay in the cupboard in one of those boxes. It would help ward off the icy blasts in the near-deserted Ottawa streets as he trundled midweek between government buildings.

The sight of all those boxes, most of which had not been touched since he put them there the previous June, reminded Alan of a hundred things he'd have to do — organize his personal papers, catch up on his investments, file his tax returns for the previous year and sort through all those miscellaneous files that he hadn't dealt with in the rush to close up his practice at Chant & Doucet.

What caught his attention were the two boxes of "wannabe" files. Like an unexpected rush of adrenaline, the dilemma of Antoinette Belair's attaché case containing her father's estate papers came clearly into focus.

He knew he'd been avoiding this matter. He toyed briefly with the idea of bringing it up with Susan, knowing full well that he wouldn't. It was ten months since Antoinette had trusted him to look after these papers. The fact that she hadn't contacted him recently really didn't change that.

In the closeness of that small room, Alan made a mental note to get in touch with Antoinette soon. The thought of what the attaché case might contain actually began to intrigue him. But the possible breach of an ethical commitment, combined with the unattractive prospect of sorting through the junk in those boxes, was too daunting, and he slowly closed the closet door. He'd come back to it again the next day or perhaps the next weekend, if other events didn't intervene.

🔺 🔻

"Hey, old buddy, how goes the practice?" Alan shouted out as he entered the locker room and saw Guy already dressed in regulation whites.

"Alan, my good friend, former partner and now my loyal public servant, it's been almost five months. A lot has happened," Guy grinned, putting his arm around Alan. "You'll be interested to hear about Russo. He's happy as a clam. I've been able to adjourn the security commission hearing on four occasions now. I'm pretty sure that if they try to start up next month, I can shut them down on an 'apprehension of bias' argument. One of the panel members used to be in the commodities business. If we can stall this one long enough, they might actually drop the charges," Guy boasted, with premature pride.

In his heart of hearts, Alan knew that Guy was better

suited to looking after scoundrels like Russo. Alan would have probably charged into a full-scale hearing before the Quebec Securities Commission, trusting his own advocacy skills to produce a victory for his client but with no guarantee of success. Yes, delay was probably the best strategy for Russo, given the facts, which slowly filtered back into his memory.

"There are a couple of other cases I want to discuss with you, but let's do it after," Guy said, sounding impatient. "Hurry up and get changed."

They played a hard game, bashing the little black ball off the four walls as though it were some ferocious animal that would attack them if they didn't strike first. Guy won, but barely.

They headed for the student lounge afterward, both still sweating profusely. Between gulps of ice-cold orange juice, Guy carried on with stories from the office. Hélène Lambert had left at the end of October. She'd received a much better offer from Richard et Langelier, where Alan had done his *stage*, and she was proving difficult to replace. But the practice was going well. Guy had had some notable successes, including a couple of new criminal cases promising huge fee premiums.

"Now, what about you? How're things going up there in Ottawa anyway?" Guy asked, inquisitively.

"It's very exciting. You wouldn't believe the volume of work," Alan responded enthusiastically. "But one false step, one unintentional leak to the media, one false call, and I could be back on your doorstep looking for work."

"And the new boss? Isn't he from Regina?" It was clear from Guy's voice that he, the cosmopolitan Montrealer, considered Regina to be little better than a frontier town.

"Baldwin's a great guy to work for, but he doesn't know

a hell of a lot about immigration. I don't want to sound immodest, but he delegates most of the tough cases to me for decision. Some days, I feel more like a judge than a political assistant."

They finished their cold drinks and headed off to the showers. Forty-five minutes later, saying their goodbyes on Aylmer Street, where they'd both parked, Guy mentioned casually, "Oh, I forgot to tell you — I had a call the other day from someone named Antoinette Belair. She was trying to reach you last week — wouldn't leave a number. I didn't want to give her your private number up in Ottawa or say you were living at Susan's on the weekends. Is she an old girlfriend, or just one of your 'wannabes'?" He had guessed that there was a family connection between Susan and Antoinette, confirmed when he saw that Alan was not amused by his question. He attempted a quick recovery. "I passed her over to my secretary who suggested she might reach you through Tom Baldwin's office in Ottawa. We gave her the main number. Hope you don't mind."

"No, that's fine." Alan smiled and was quietly relieved. He didn't want to have to explain about Antoinette and her father's estate papers to anyone if he could help it.

"Well, whoever she is, she must be something — I had another strange call a while back. It was a man with a deep voice, probably an American with a bit of a New York accent, and he asked if we had a client named Antoinette Belair." Guy watched his friend closely.

Alan looked mystified. He felt his shoulders tighten.

"I said no, not to my knowledge, but it might have something to do with my former partner. He's never called back," said Guy. "By the way, Alan, *is* she related to Susan?"

Alan's face said it all. "Well, I guess if Antoinette calls me in Ottawa, I can track down what this is all about. She first came to me last February. She was really nothing more than a 'wannabe' file. And yes, she's Susan's sister." Alan spoke the words very carefully, hoping his friend would understand not to explore any further.

Chapter Sixteen

When it finally became apparent to Antoinette by the end of the summer that Alan no longer worked at Chant & Doucet, she began to panic. At Hélène's suggestion, she called Alan at Savard's office in Ottawa. Unfortunately, by that time the election had been called and Alan was spending seven days a week crisscrossing the country as part of Savard's entourage, dubbed by the media as "The Second Coming." Her calls went unanswered and she assumed the worse.

Her only comfort was the knowledge that Alan was now a big shot up in Ottawa, which might make it easier to blow the whistle if he'd taken the money for himself. But if this were the case, *who* would blow the whistle? It couldn't be Marcel. He was an illegal. Antoinette herself could ask someone in Savard's office for help in tracking down Alan and the money. But how would she explain it — Alan holding her money as her trusted lawyer, or Alan as her occasional lover? And would they take her seriously?

Perhaps she could ask her sister Susan to help out. But she hadn't seen Susan since her father's funeral the previous January and even then, their relationship had been frosty. She was not prepared to take Susan into her confidence and tell her about Marcel and the money or how she had come to give it to Alan for safekeeping. For all she knew, Susan, forever the upright citizen, might feel it her public duty to call in the police.

So she procrastinated and did nothing. Late summer turned into fall as she and Marcel continued their fantasy life at 21 Terrace St-Denis. But Marcel was growing more edgy. They rarely made love anymore and he seemed irritable every time the subject of the money and Alan Chant's whereabouts came up. At the end of November, he gave her an ultimatum: "If you don't come up with the money within the next two weeks, I'll have Bertolini's guys go after it directly. Soon we'll get the call to move the white down to New York and I want that money immediately available. Anything that gives Bertolini the impression that we're hedging and might not deliver will put us both in serious danger. Now get it, and real soon," he said through clenched teeth.

After many attempts, Antoinette was finally able to penetrate the PMO's switchboard late one afternoon. The security officer on duty there connected her with the office of Tom Baldwin, the new minister of immigration where, he advised, Alan Chant had been installed as executive assistant. It was Monday, December 17th, and the nation's capital was beginning to shut down for the Christmas holidays. Holding her breath, Antoinette heard Alan's voice come on the line. "Alan, it's Antoinette Belair," she said. "At last, I've been able to reach you. We must talk as soon as possible."

"Antoinette, where have you been? I've been wondering when you'd call. Are you in Ottawa?"

"I'm at a pay phone in downtown Montreal. Have to be careful what phone I use these days," she replied, without for a moment suspecting that incoming calls to the PMO or to the immigration minister's office might be tapped for any number of reasons.

"Are you in some kind of trouble?"

"No, not really, but, well . . ." Her voice trailed off ominously.

"But what?"

"I do need your help, Alan."

Alan sighed. He suspected something shady, but it would also be a relief to deal directly with Antoinette and her papers once and for all. "Meet me at 3509 Peel Street next Saturday afternoon, December 22nd, at two. Don't tell anyone, and make sure you're not followed." Alan was nervous. He was more than a little sensitive to the prospect of attracting further CSIS scrutiny if their planned meeting became known.

Later that night, Antoinette told Marcel she'd contacted Alan in Ottawa and would be meeting him on Saturday afternoon of the following weekend in Montreal. She didn't tell him where. He didn't push. He had already set in motion his own surveillance.

Marcel had finally received instructions from Bertolini that it was time to move the heroin, hidden for eight months under the floorboards of the second bedroom at 21 Terrace St-Denis. He had rented a Volkswagen Jetta because it was fast and he didn't have much respect for North American cars. He would stow the cache behind the inside door panel for transit to Plattsburgh in upstate New York. Departure from Montreal was scheduled for late Saturday night, following Antoinette's planned meeting with Alan. With any luck, the drugs would be in

Bertolini's hands by Christmas and payment arrangements would quickly fall into place.

Not that Marcel was itching to grab the deposit money prematurely. He had long reconciled himself to the fact that the money came with dirty strings attached — in other words, they could never really touch it without incurring Bertolini's violent wrath until final delivery of the product was made and its quality established. Allowing Antoinette to make those flaky arrangements with Chant last winter and then not firming things up for the better part of a year was careless, in retrospect.

Marcel agreed to meet Bertolini's nephew Roberto in the men's washroom at the Texaco station two miles north of Plattsburgh. Already he was fantasizing about wrapping up this first major transaction. Perhaps then he'd find an excuse for a trip back to Marseilles during January and February to avoid the cruel Canadian winter that was descending on Montreal. The fact that he would have to cross two international borders carrying the passport of someone who had died almost a year ago seemed almost inconsequential.

"Yes, it'll be nice to have that money in our hot little hands, *ma chérie*," Marcel whispered to Antoinette as he pulled her close. "But first let's get our friend and partner Bertolini off our backs. He's been sounding nervous during our recent calls and I worry. Do what you can with Chant next Saturday afternoon. I'll call you that night from upstate New York, on the unlisted phone, using the earth station code. You can call me back from one of the pay phones down the street."

As Antoinette made her way up Peel Street that Saturday afternoon before Christmas, she felt very much alone. Unbeknown to her, she had lots of company. Jean Thibault and Eric Bourne were driving slowly northward in an unmarked car, trying to look very much the part of Saturday Christmas shoppers searching for a parking spot.

Across the street from Alan's pied-à-terre, Bruno and Luigi Leonardo sat in the Chrysler minivan that they had rented for surveillance purposes. Marcel had briefed them on the anticipated rendezvous.

In fact, the Leonardo brothers had inadvertently discovered Alan's apartment a month previously when they overheard Guy Doucet talking to some of his friends at Mamma Leonardo's shop at St-Denis and Rigaud. It seems that Guy, the opportunist, was mighty proud of his former partner Alan, who was now so close to the next prime minister in Ottawa. Guy was happy that Alan was able to get back to Montreal each weekend and looked forward to regular squash games with his old law partner at the McGill gym. Alan would have no excuse to miss a game, Guy had added, because he had taken a room on nearby Peel Street.

By going up and down both sides of Peel Street north of Sherbrooke, eliminating those buildings that obviously belonged to the university and carefully checking the names on the mailboxes or doorbells, Bruno and Luigi had figured out Alan's Montreal address. Now they were convinced they had pinpointed the location of the files moved from Chant & Doucet that hot afternoon in June. This had given them time to study the rear of the building to determine where and how best to enter when the time came.

Antoinette pushed the lower button on the porch outside the pied-à-terre as Alan had instructed her to do. Within seconds, he appeared at the door and let her in.

"Hope you don't mind all this secrecy. Your name came up during my security clearance interview. Seems like either CSIS or the RCMP may be keeping tabs on you for some reason. Any idea why?"

"Alan, I've no idea why they'd be interested in me," she said, shading the truth. She'd already decided to try to put him off the scent. Nervously, she lit a cigarette. "Incidentally, I know you're seeing my sister. Your former secretary Hélène mentioned it when I called last October to see if the attaché case containing my father's estate papers was still at the law office. Hope you don't think I was being too aggressive but I was beginning to worry — about the papers, that is."

Alan sensed a touch of desperation. "Sure, they're burning a hole in one of those file boxes behind that door," he replied, motioning towards the large closet. "You've been telling me for over ten months that you're going to choose one of the notaries I recommended. I'd still like you to do that so I could send the papers over to one of them. I told you then and I'm telling you now that I don't do successions work. Even if I did, I wouldn't have time now that I'm working in Ottawa. Hope you understand."

Antoinette exhaled as she stared hard at the attractive man in front of her. In the past ten months, she had tended to dismiss him as just another one-night stand who was providing an ongoing safety deposit service. But his boyish enthusiasm, his tall good looks and his nervous energy, which pervaded the small room, made for a provocative contrast with the mature, world-weary, almost fatherly persona of Marcel whose image flashed briefly before her. Maybe her sister wasn't so silly after all.

"Alan," she implored. "I've got to trust you. Those papers are more important to me than you'll ever believe. Hang on to them and give me a few more weeks. And don't tell anyone you have them, most of all Susan."

It had become clear to Antoinette, now that Bertolini's instructions had finally ordered them to move the white stateside, that she needed Alan more than ever for leverage for keeping some of the cash for herself.

"Antoinette, for chrissakes! It's been ten months." Alan tried to contain his mounting irritation. "I'd like to get rid of that attaché case, to be honest. What is it you've been up to anyway? CSIS and the Mounties know all about our little one-nighter at Tremblant. Asked me how long I'd known you, and whether I'd seen you since."

"What else? Did they ask you about—?" Antoinette stopped. She didn't want to give away her hand.

"The estate papers? No. That's really your private business with me, not theirs."

Antoinette let out an almost imperceptible sigh of relief. She put out her cigarette. "I appreciate that, Alan, more than you can believe." Relaxing at last, she tossed back her thick auburn hair and smiled flirtatiously.

Alan couldn't resist, the memory of that Mont-Tremblant night suddenly clear in his mind. He walked slowly over to her. He lifted her chin and kissed her moist lips, lingering longer than he should have. "Antoinette, you can trust me. But you're using me for something and I'm not quite sure what. Please don't leave it too long," he said, pleading gently with his eyes. "Now get out of here before the Mounties come busting in and ruin my career."

Bruno and Luigi watched intently as she walked down the outside stairs towards the street. She was carrying nothing, although Luigi wondered whether there was anything stuffed under her winter coat.

"Don't be so stupid, asshole, a million and a half bucks, even in thousands, would make her look fat as a pig. No big money on her, that's for sure," Bruno observed caustically, both to restrain his less experienced and impetuous brother and to vent his own frustration.

Thibault and Bourne were parked only two cars behind. They too watched Antoinette walk down the hill towards Sherbrooke. Taking note of the address on Peel Street, they glimpsed a male figure saying goodbye to Antoinette on the second-floor landing. Even if they had been able to see him clearly, it was far too early to blow the whistle.

That night, Alan and Susan planned to visit Huguette Belair on Carré St-Louis for a pre-Christmas dinner. This would be the family's first Christmas without Roger. Susan had not heard from Antoinette in over a month.

While Susan had gone for her usual squash game at the MAAA that afternoon, Alan had spent the few remaining hours after Antoinette's departure in utter agony. Eventually, curiosity and fear got the better of him and he opened the closet door. He lifted the lid from the box of "wannabe" files and pulled out the small brown leather attaché case. With a screwdriver and a penknife, he jimmied the lock of the case, careful not to cause any damage. He flipped it open. Inside was an unsealed large manila envelope. He emptied the contents onto his desk.

Alan had never seen so many American thousand-dollar notes before, all freshly printed, bundled and tied in packets of hundreds. The small white envelope with the handwritten instructions looked like yet another challenge he wasn't up to, so he left it unopened.

After scooping the money back into the envelope, Alan placed it in the attaché case, which he returned to the box of files. He shoved the box back into the closet. "This never happened," he muttered, trying unsuccessfully to convince himself.

When Susan left the MAAA at four-thirty, it was almost dark. A new moon appeared on the horizon and the cold air was crisp and clean. She felt good. She'd trounced her pudgy male opponent and enjoyed a cold Perrier in the lounge. After taking an invigorating shower and donning her bright yellow winter track suit with matching tuque, Susan rather fancied a brisk walk home to her apartment. The Christmas lights were spectacular and passersby seemed in a festive mood. Alan wasn't coming by until seven-thirty to pick her up for dinner at Huguette's so she had lots of time to savor the ambiance in the street.

As she passed the Musée des Beaux-Arts en route to Côte-des-Neiges, she didn't notice the small red Alfa Romeo slowly edging along behind her. Suddenly, with a loud screech of tires, the car catapulted forward towards her, careened up onto the sidewalk and came within centimeters of hitting her. Then it roared off.

Was this a fluke? After all, it was Christmas and there were a lot of intoxicated drivers this time of year. Stunned, Susan leaned against a lamppost to catch her breath. Pedestrians hurried by, heads lowered against the cold. No one seemed to have noticed the incident.

Crossing over to the west side of Côte-des-Neiges so she'd be able to see any oncoming traffic, she continued gamely up the hill. Just as she came to Cedar Avenue, the same red Alfa Romeo reappeared, headed straight for her. At the last minute, the car bounced off a snowbank and veered off. As the car sped by, the fat man on the passenger's side spat out the window: "Next time, bitch, it'll be your fuckin' lawyer boyfriend!"

Susan was terrified. She was sure they were trying to kill her — and possibly Alan — for no apparent reason. Arriving at her apartment, she double-locked the entrance door and collapsed into a frightened heap onto her bed. Only a telephone call from Alan at seven-fifteen to say that he was on his way to pick her up broke the eerie silence that pervaded.

Susan and Alan were a half hour late for dinner at Huguette's. He offered comfort and understanding, but could provide no explanation for what had happened.

At 21 Terrace St-Denis, as Antoinette was opening the door, she heard the listed phone ring several times, followed by her recorded message, "We can't come to the phone right now. Leave your name, number and the time

you called and we'll get back to you." After the beep, she recognized Marcel's voice. "This is earth station 081246581595. *Je t'aime*," he said, and then she heard a click.

For a moment, Antoinette was troubled. Marcel had said he would only use the earth station code on the unlisted phone. But this had come in on the other phone, the legitimate phone that was only to be answered by machine. Something was wrong.

Then she figured it out. No doubt Marcel had been unable to get through on the unlisted phone since she had not been home when he'd called. He was obviously in a hurry for her to call back, and, in fact, might be in real trouble.

Down the street, Swayze and one of Thibault's men, each with his headset on, looked at each other and smiled. Within fifteen minutes, they had figured out Marcel's code. With the assistance of Bell Canada and AT&T, they knew with certainty that the call had come from a pay phone at the Texaco station just north of Plattsburgh.

Chapter Seventeen

"*Â̂llo*, this is earth station 081246581595," Marcel whispered into the receiver, glancing furtively at the cars coming in and out of the Texaco station.

"*Oui*, come in earth station," Antoinette scribbled down the number, relieved to hear Marcel's voice. "Why'd you call the listed number with the answering machine?"

"*Écoute*, time's short. Had no choice. I tried the other line for over two hours. Don't use this line. Go down the street to the pay phone at the corner and call me right away. Hurry!"

It took Antoinette all of three minutes to get to the phone at the corner of St-Denis and Terrace St-Denis. She reversed the order of the number Marcel had given her and then dropped the first two digits. She dialed 518-564-2180.

"You must have spent a long time with that guy. Did you get the money?" Marcel asked impatiently.

"No, I didn't. You told me that the money had dirty strings attached until you could deliver the product."

"Christ, what do you think I've been trying to do?"

"Look, I can get it any time. Don't tell Bertolini and his guys exactly where it is in case they try to double-cross us."

"We've got a bigger problem." Marcel's voice sounded strained. "Met with Bertolini's nephew Roberto three hours ago, at the McDonald's restaurant down the road where we'd agreed. He was expecting four kilos. There was only one kilo of pure white in the package — the other three were shit! Luc must have switched the bags when he packed my valise in Marseilles. I should have checked it myself. *Le maudit!* Pocketed the $490,000 we gave him and took off."

"What are we going to do now, Marcel?" Antoinette, in a moment of panic, forgot Marcel's standing instructions and used his name.

"I told Roberto that we'd try to get him back half the money they paid us last winter. The way we figure it, that one-kilo package was worth one million, all in. If we'd delivered four kilos, that would be a total of four million, half up front just as we agreed and the other half on delivery."

A stocky, impatient man tapped on the pay phone door. Antoinette jumped. She made placating gestures through the window while trying to follow Marcel's story.

"—so, the way it works out," he was saying, "the Bertolinis overpaid us on the up-front, and they want a million dollars back *toute de suite*. That means half a million left for me — I mean, you and me. I told him I could get his million back in a couple of days but would have to speak to my partner in Montreal."

Antoinette noticed the slip. The bastard, she thought. She'd been right after all to look out for herself. "I guess I should have got the money this afternoon," she said, pretending to sound sheepish. At his end, Marcel shook his head. There wasn't enough time to get angry with her.

"*Ma petite*, listen carefully. Go back home and act as if

nothing's happened. I'm supposed to meet Roberto back here in half an hour but I'm going to try to take off across the border on the back roads before he gets here. I'll be back in Montreal sometime early tomorrow. We'll go over to Chant's place and grab the money. You do know where it is in his apartment, don't you?"

Antoinette played along. "Sure, I think I do. We should be able to find it easily."

"You'd better be right, *chérie*," Marcel said in a voice that was barely audible. Antoinette could feel his anger looping through the line.

As Marcel sped northward on Route 87 before hitting the back roads through Sciota and Mooers near the Quebec border, a white Cadillac pulled into the Texaco station. Roberto Bertolini had arrived ten minutes early for their rendezvous. He waited a full twenty minutes, then concluded that Marcel was a no show.

"Bruno, it's me — Roberto. I'm in Plattsburgh," he barked into the pay phone to the eldest of the Leonardo brothers. "That fucker the Frenchman tried to short-ship us. Owes us a million refund of the up-front. He was supposed to show up here with the money or an explanation but he's headed back to Montreal to pick up the girl or find the money, or both. Do whatever you have to do to get that money first, before he does," he ordered.

From their mobile communications unit parked opposite McDonald's, the DEA officers had seen the transfer of the heroin and their parabolic microphone had picked up snippets of the conversation about a rendezvous at some Texaco station. They had no idea which Texaco station — there were four of them in the region — and they were unable to hear when the meeting was to occur. But with quick action from AT&T, they were able to get central taps on all the pay telephones in each of the stations, even though they did not have enough men in the region to physically cover all four.

Careful monitoring and good luck led them to Marcel's call to Antoinette within minutes of its initiation. Four DEA officers arrived at the Texaco station eight minutes after Marcel's departure, but well ahead of Robert Bertolini's arrival.

As Roberto left the telephone booth, two DEA agents suddenly appeared out of the shadows, guns drawn, and barked at him to put his hands over his head. From the unmarked car that appeared to be filling up at the pump, two more DEA officers emerged.

"Okay Roberto, it's all over. Where's your pal the Frenchman? And who the hell is Bruno? You've got some singing to do, buddy," said the tallest of the DEA agents as he placed handcuffs on a distressed young Bertolini.

Using zoom-in photography, the DEA had managed to get a clear photograph of Marcel handing over his one kilo of heroin to Roberto. This would be key evidence in securing convictions and putting both of them away for a long time. More important, the DEA had known for many years that Roberto hated his uncle and continued to operate within the family only through fear. They reckoned that the chances of his squealing on Gus Bertolini, the head of the family, were very good indeed.

At RCMP regional headquarters in Montreal, Thibault, Bourne, Swayze and two other men listened carefully to the tape of Antoinette's call to Marcel, relayed by the DEA from Plattsburgh. Bell Canada and AT&T had done their job. Every word came through loud and clear. Within twenty minutes, one DEA vehicle was speeding northward from Plattsburgh and two RCMP vehicles southward towards the border point just west of the town of Champlain on the American side.

A third unmarked RCMP car turned the corner onto Terrace St-Denis and parked opposite number twenty-one to await the return of Antoinette from the pay phone. Inside, Thibault whispered to Bourne, "This is one hell of a way to spend the Saturday night before Christmas. With any luck, we should have this wrapped up by New Year's."

"I hope you're right. Our guys'll look after the prosecution of Bertolini and Gagnon stateside. Hope we're able to get the justice department legal beagles off their ass to move this one along quickly," Bourne said as he fixed his eyes on the entrance to Antoinette's building.

"Now if this little lady would just cooperate by coming straight home . . . It'll take a while in the courts but she's a goner," Thibault noted triumphantly. "They'll throw the book at her — aiding and abetting trafficking or maybe even importing. That is, unless she decides to sing."

They were both counting on Antoinette returning to the apartment from the pay phone. She had other ideas. Spotting the unfamiliar car with two men inside parked opposite her building, she'd immediately sensed danger. She retraced her steps partway down the block, then darted into the narrow alleyway leading to the rear of the building.

Seeing no one in the alley, she quietly climbed the fire escape to the rear entrance on the second floor. She entered the apartment without turning on any lights and, on her hands and knees, crawled into the bedroom to grab a suitcase, some clothes and cosmetics in frantic preparation for what might be an extended absence.

Just as quietly, she made her exit down the fire escape with suitcase in tow and set out for her mother's house on Carré St-Louis just three short blocks away. This required crossing Sherbrooke Street, a busy, well-lit thoroughfare that was still buzzing with traffic at eleven o'clock this particular Saturday night before Christmas. However, the sight of an attractive but nervous young woman pulling a suitcase across a busy intersection in the holiday season didn't strike anyone as particularly unusual. Thibault and Bourne were still staring intently at the front door of number twenty-one.

Huguette Belair had just gone to bed for the night, having spent a delightful evening with her eldest daughter Susan and her boyfriend Alan Chant.

"Maman, it's me — Antoinette. I'm in trouble. Please let me in." A long twenty seconds later, the lights illuminating the iron staircase leading up from the street clicked on, and Antoinette was safe inside. Huguette hugged her youngest child.

"What's wrong, *mon chou?* Let me call Suzanne. She and her boyfriend were here for dinner just half an hour ago. She can help you with whatever your trouble is, I'm sure."

"Please don't, Maman. Let me stay tonight and through Christmas. Perhaps for the rest of the holidays. Then I'll be on my way. I don't really want Susan involved. *Ça va?* And if anyone calls, don't let on that I'm here or that you've seen me recently."

"*Mais pourquoi?* I don't understand." Huguette looked anxious.

"*Écoute*, Maman, I've just broken up with my boyfriend, the guy I've been living with for over eight months. I don't want to see him right now, or anyone." She paused and looked away. "Besides, I may be in some danger."

"Antoinette, *mon Dieu!* What kind of danger?"

"Maman, please — don't ask me any questions."

Although deeply troubled, Huguette sensed that her silence could provide the greatest comfort, at least for the moment. "You're safe here, *chérie*. No need for worry."

Antoinette reckoned that she'd head for Alan's apartment on Peel Street when the time was right. First she had to figure out how to ditch Marcel. She'd come to that decision when it had become evident that Marcel was more obsessed with recovering the money than with her personal safety. Besides, thanks to Luc, their net share had been reduced by the Bertolinis to only $500,000. Soon they'd be arriving on the scene demanding the balance. She was sure this was why the unmarked car was parked opposite her apartment.

As she fell asleep in her childhood room with the white spool bed and the pink quilt that her mother had kept for her all these years, the RCMP were already solving part of her problem. Marcel Gagnon was arrested as he crossed into Canada and taken to St-Jean-sur-Richelieu to await the laying of formal charges.

Chapter Eighteen

"**C**an I get you a cup of coffee, *mon chou?*" Huguette's soft voice barely registered. Antoinette found it comforting. "It's almost noon. I didn't go to mass this morning because I was worried about you. Didn't want to leave you alone."

For Antoinette, the white spool bed and the pink quilt were beginning to put everything in perspective. On the run from the RCMP, her lover and the New York mafia, she was now the prodigal daughter returning to the protective warmth of her mother's home. Papa Belair would have been horrified. Any hint of this kind of trouble and she would have been out the door on her ear. But he was hardly a saint in his own right. She knew she could have called him on his hypocrisy.

Huguette was kinder and more warm-hearted, a stable and reliable pillar of love and understanding holding firm against the impending gale of intrigue, scandal and violence. There was real security in this home now that Papa was gone. For the moment, Antoinette found it to her liking.

"Antoinette, I want to talk to you about arrangements for Christmas. You know this will be the first year without Papa."

"*Oui*, Maman, I know. Christmas Eve was so difficult

for him last year. You and I took him to mass, remember? I think it was the last time." He had been in a wheelchair by then. With his speech gone, he couldn't even talk to all his friends, the families he had known for years. It had been so frustrating for him. "I was glad I could be there with him." Yes, she had been there towards the end, when it counted the most.

Huguette was hurt that Antoinette's focus was still on her father. "Well, Papa's gone, Antoinette," she said quietly. "We have this Christmas to contend with. Suzanne's coming over about noon tomorrow. She's going to help me prepare the tourtière and a fruit pie, and then we'll pick up a small turkey for Christmas day. I'm hoping both of you will go to midnight mass with me tomorrow evening. Then we'll have a small family dinner and open a few presents."

"I'm not sure I can stay, Maman. Give me a few minutes to get myself together," Antoinette said, sitting upright in bed, eyes fully open and heart beginning to pound.

As she began to put on her clothes, she was forced to confront reality. What was she going to do? Marcel would likely be back now and would be surprised not to find her at 21 Terrace St-Denis. She thought briefly about the two men in the car and wondered whether Marcel would be as observant as she had been.

If he went looking for her, one of the first places he might go would be the Belair residence, which he had visited the previous April to pick up the envelope he'd mailed from London.

The Bertolinis were another concern. She always suspected they had a Montreal connection. No doubt they would be making plans to get their money back and might have someone watching her.

She was also beginning to worry that the police had something on her. She remembered Huguette telling her last winter that the wallet she'd somehow lost at Tremblant had been returned by an RCMP officer. Glad to get the wallet back, Antoinette hadn't thought much about it at the time. Now she wondered whether her name was still linked in their records to the Belair residence on Carré St-Louis and whether they might come calling.

"Maman, does Susan know I'm here?" Antoinette inquired as she finished dressing and went downstairs into the warm, homey kitchen.

"Not yet, *ma p'tite*, I was about to call her to confirm arrangements for tomorrow. If you're going to stay, and I'd really like that, then I'll tell Suzanne. If you feel you have to go, then I won't mention it."

Antoinette noticed that Huguette kept calling her sister "Suzanne." It had been her father's idea to anglicize Susan's name, to ease his daughter's way in English society. (Roger, with his roots in Pont l'Évêque, had never felt very connected to the Quebec *nationaliste* movement.) Huguette had been silent at the time. Now it was clear that she'd disapproved. She'd been unable to stand up to Roger while he was alive, but now she'd reverted to using the name she'd given their first daughter at birth. Until now, Antoinette had been too self-centered and preoccupied with her own survival to notice.

Not that her survival was assured simply because she was under her mother's roof. Antoinette was confused. She wondered whether she could take Susan into her confidence, now that she'd decided to split with Marcel. Susan was a lawyer after all. She'd have some appreciation for how much trouble her younger sister was in for the misuse of Papa Belair's passport and her involvement in drug smuggling.

There was also the question of the money. She knew she wouldn't be able to tell Susan about this, particularly since it was still hidden with Susan's boyfriend. Besides, Antoinette wanted the money for herself. For her, it represented freedom — from Marcel, from the Belair family, from all those self-satisfied jerks who tried to hustle her into bed or get her hooked on drugs, from everything.

"Maman, I think I'd like to stay. You can tell — Suzanne. In fact, I might even stay for a few days until things get sorted out in my life." She could feel tears welling up now, brought on by genuine gratitude but also borne of fear that she was in real trouble and desperately needed help.

"*Bien sûr*, stay as long as you like," said Huguette, as she poured her daughter some more coffee.

"Maman, there may be some people looking for me. If they call or come to the door, tell them I'm not here and you haven't seen or heard from me for several months. I'm going to keep the blinds down in the bedroom all the time — I'm not going anywhere till I've figured out what to do. I can't go to mass with you tomorrow night. Perhaps Suzanne will. We can have a nice Christmas dinner when you get back."

"That would be a lovely treat for me, *mon chou*." Huguette turned to the sink so her daughter couldn't see her face. Nothing in her life had prepared her for something like this.

Antoinette knew Susan would find it difficult to break her vow never to go to mass again — the ultimate insult she had hurled at her father at the height of their disagreement. Antoinette would try to explain why it was important that someone go with her mother. This would lead into the more difficult explanation as to why she was on the run and had to stay out of sight.

♦ ♦

"Bonjour, Madame Belair, my name's Thibault from the RCMP. We were here last February — brought back your daughter Antoinette's wallet that had been lost up at Mont-Tremblant. We're trying to locate her now. Have you seen her recently?"

Thibault tried discreetly to look over Huguette's shoulder into the kitchen. It was four in the afternoon and darkness was falling, broken only by the Christmas lights starting to flicker on trees and balconies on Carré St-Louis.

Thibault and his partner had waited patiently outside 21 Terrace St-Denis until one in the morning before concluding that Antoinette had not come back from the pay phone. By that time, the streets were virtually empty. They'd realized that she'd sensed danger and fled.

Without being too obvious, they'd combed the neighborhood as best they could. At daybreak they had gone back to her old apartment on Avenue Laval, talked to the doorman at 21 Terrace St-Denis and even had a private chat with Mamma Leonardo, whose delicatessen the Sunday before Christmas was busier than ever.

It wasn't until mid-afternoon, while searching records back at regional headquarters on Sherbrooke, that they'd thought of checking at Antoinette's mother's — an obvious place of refuge only three blocks away.

"*Désolée*, I haven't seen Antoinette for several months. I don't know where she is. She's really not part of the family any more. She seems to have abandoned me since my husband died almost a year ago," Huguette said, quietly comforted by the fact that there was a grain of truth in her deliberate deception.

"If she comes back, madame, please give us a call," Thibault said, handing her a business card with the telephone number of the Montreal regional headquarters of the RCMP. "We want to have a chat about her knowledge of some rather serious events. She could be in some danger."

Huguette politely thanked Thibault for the information, closed the door and immediately headed for Antoinette's bedroom on the second floor to relay the conversation. Antoinette, wanting to stay close to the closet where she would hide if they decided to come in, had picked up only snippets.

"Antoinette, does this have anything to do with Marcel Gagnon, Papa's friend from the war who came around to see me last spring?" Antoinette was surprised that Huguette had made the connection. She should have remembered that Huguette shopped at Mamma Leonardo's from time to time for a special treat and may have seen them together there.

"*Oui et non.* Marcel and I were close friends at the time he came to see you, and for quite a bit after that. But not anymore. If he calls, give him the same answer you gave the police. And that goes for anyone else who calls too."

Huguette gave her youngest daughter a long, comforting hug. She had the good sense not to ask any more questions. Inwardly, she hoped that Suzanne would be able to help.

🔺 🔻

"Maman, your tourtière looks delicious." Susan had

arrived about three on Christmas Eve, having just left Alan after an intimate lunch at L'Express, a trendy Montreal bistro on St-Denis.

She was still jumpy after her frightening encounter with the Alfa Romeo two days previously. But she was sure now that the attempt to run her over was related to Alan. "Why else would the guy yell 'Next time, bitch, it'll be your fuckin' lawyer boyfriend'? Could it be someone you beat in court?" she had mused out loud to him that morning. "Or could it be one of those crazy cases in the minister's office that you're dealing with? Either way, you're a dangerous guy to be around. Good thing I like you," she had said with a tentative smile.

On this, their first Christmas together, Susan and Alan had exchanged modest gifts and enjoyed a savory lunch and a bottle of red wine together. Then they both went to their respective family homes for the rest of the three-day festive period — Alan to Sam and Laura's large house on Roslyn Avenue in Westmount, where Christmas had always been a glitzy event, and Susan to her mother's on Carré St-Louis, where Christmas had generally been an intimate family affair.

Alan had toyed with the idea of joining Susan to extend season's greetings to Huguette before leaving for Westmount, but their luncheon had gone on too long. Besides, because he and Susan had enjoyed Saturday night dinner with Huguette two days before they decided it wasn't necessary.

"Wish your mother a merry Christmas for me, Susan," Alan said as they left L'Express. "Is Marc going to be home from Brébeuf?"

"He should be coming in sometime later this evening although Maman was somewhat vague."

"What about your sister, Antoinette?" Alan dared to ask.

"Don't know about her — Maman was vague on that too. Unlikely she'll make it home this year, but what else is new?" Susan replied. She did not like lying to Alan, but her mother had telephoned the previous day to say that Antoinette was in trouble and that no one, absolutely no one, should know she was there.

"Well, *joyeux Nöel, mon amour*," Alan said, leaning over to give her one last kiss before hopping into his car. "Call me when you get back to your place on Boxing Day, and I'll be there in a flash. And stay out of the way of Alfa Romeos."

"Not funny, Alan. I'm still scared to death. Don't joke about it — maybe it's you they're after."

"Susan, I'll be all right. I'm going up to Ottawa for Thursday and part of Friday, to get rid of some paperwork and to get Baldwin's schedule organized for the new year. Be back late Friday for our usual weekend — if you can fit me in between squash games."

Susan grinned. "I'll try. Merry Christmas, Alan. See you Wednesday for sure. And I'm yours all weekend, except for Saturday afternoon."

Hurrying down St-Denis towards Carré St-Louis, her mind skittered between thoughts of her deepening relationship with Alan, images of careening red cars and wondering what sort of a mess her crazy sister was in.

Just as the tourtière was about to go into the oven, to be ready when they returned from midnight mass, the front door to the Belair home flew open and Marc appeared, dressed in his usual black with a clerical collar. *"Joyeux Nöel, tout le monde!"*

Huguette ran towards him, tears in her eyes, and embraced him as only a mother greeting a returning son can. Susan followed, politely affectionate. Privately, she was annoyed that Marc had caused Huguette such anxiety by arriving late without the courtesy of even a phone call.

"What a lovely surprise! Antoinette, my long-lost sister!" Marc hugged Antoinette briefly, more for Huguette's benefit than anyone else. Susan recognized the potential for discomfort, even embarrassment, and quickly began the ceremonial ritual of putting Maman's tourtière into the oven. Antoinette fetched Maman's fur coat from the front closet as a signal that they should be on their way to Basilique Notre-Dame, where the celebration of Christ's birth would begin in half an hour.

"How was midnight mass?" Antoinette asked, as Huguette, Susan and Marc returned to the kitchen, just after one in the morning.

Huguette was serene. "Fine. All our old friends were there, and virtually all of them came up to me after to say hello. *Franchement*, it was better than last year because there's no more uncertainty about Papa's health. It's a lot easier for people to deal with a widow and her grown children than a frail and dying old man whom they once remembered as strong, proud and vigorous."

It was two-thirty when they finished eating. Huguette, having violated her usual policy of abstinence by consuming two glasses of rich red wine, was the first to go up to bed. It had been a wonderful evening for her, perhaps the best since Roger's death. Marc soon followed. He'd been up since five in the morning for his daily prayers at the seminary.

"We're alone now," Susan said to her younger sister as they sat around the kitchen table, having cleaned up the dishes and put the food away. She poured herself another half glass of red wine. "Is there anything you want to share with me? Maman says you may be in a bit of trouble."

It was hard for Susan to offer an olive branch to her irresponsible and hedonistic sister. But families have to stick together, she thought, particularly at Christmas.

"Susan, I do need help." Antoinette also poured herself more wine and lit a cigarette. "I'm in a terrible jam. But you've got to promise me you won't tell anyone. I know you're a lawyer, but I'm asking you, sister to sister, can you please keep this to yourself?"

"You know you can trust me." Susan had put her invitation on a personal basis. She felt there wasn't much point in explaining again to someone like Antoinette an abstract concept like her lawyer's duty of confidentiality. Besides, she wasn't quite sure she wanted to be put in a position of professional rather than sisterly responsibility. "If two sisters can't trust each other, then who can they trust in this crazy world?" Susan added, trying to comfort Antoinette in a way she would understand. But she also realized that she was now on the hook psychologically, if not professionally, and that there was no longer any reasonable chance of backing away.

Antoinette swallowed hard. She took a drag on her cigarette. "Listen — remember Papa's friend from France during the war, Marcel Gagnon, who came to visit us during the Olympics?"

Susan didn't remember because she'd been away that

summer, working for a law firm in Toronto. But she'd recalled her father talking of his comrade in arms from the French underground and remembered hearing from Antoinette, or perhaps it was Marc, that Marcel Gagnon had made quite a splash when he visited during the Olympics. She took another sip of wine.

"You won't believe this, but Marcel Gagnon has been my full-time lover and partner for almost a year now." Antoinette then spilled out most of her story over the next hour to a wide-eyed and now silent Susan: the relationship with Marcel in the south of France, the reunion in London, the use of their father's passport, the cache of China white, the receipt of two million dollars, the apartment at 21 Terrace St-Denis and Marcel's delivery to Roberto Bertolini in upstate New York.

The only thing Antoinette was not prepared to disclose to her sister during her long monologue was the current location of the money and how it got there. Nor could she quite admit her feelings of guilt about her decision to abandon Marcel, her lover and father figure. There was also Roger Belair's deathbed confession. That would have to wait too.

After listening to Antoinette for over an hour, Susan was utterly stunned. The bottle of red wine had long been shoved aside. "Antoinette, you're in real trouble. You know they could put you away for a minimum of seven years for your involvement in bringing that stuff into Canada — not to mention the false passport for Marcel."

Antoinette gasped, but no words came out.

"The only leverage you've got is to offer to help the police round up Marcel and the Bertolinis — who are obviously much bigger fish — in return for their agreeing to go easy on you. I can't believe you'd get yourself into this kind of situation. What kind of relationship would you have anyway with a sixty-one-year-old drug dealer?"

They were both silent for a while. Susan could see that this offhand question hurt Antoinette deeply, so she backed off. Antoinette reached for another cigarette as Susan racked her brain for a solution to her sister's dilemma. Finally she spoke.

"I'll tell you what we're going to do. Does anyone else know everything you've just told me, other than Marcel?"

"No. It's all been kept between Marcel and me and the Bertolinis, although who knows where that connection could lead."

Susan immediately sensed danger. Although she wasn't a criminal lawyer, she knew from experience and from what Alan had told her that mafia involvement would almost certainly attract police surveillance. The prospect of Marcel and Antoinette's apartment having been bugged crossed her mind momentarily, but there was no time to worry about it now.

"Listen, the only way we're going to get you out of this mess is to offer cooperation to the RCMP. Boxing Day's a holiday. But Thursday and Friday are working days, and I plan to be in my office. It's not far from here — it's on Park. I'm going to call up the RCMP first thing Thursday morning and offer them a meeting with you — in my office. I'll try to get you the best deal I can. But you're going to have to cut loose totally from Marcel Gagnon. Hopefully, the Mounties will help you keep out of the way of the Bertolinis. Incidentally, you didn't tell me where the money's located."

"I can't. Trust me. The police won't be that interested in the money." She put out her cigarette. "It's the Bertolinis they'll be after, and their European source of supply."

"Don't be so sure, Antoinette," Susan replied sharply. Her sister's secretiveness irritated her. "The police are always interested in the proceeds of crime. It helps them establish their case when they go to court. Besides, they've been known to quietly use little 'finds' like that to finance their own operations." This was another tidbit that Susan had picked up from Alan.

"I can't tell you, that's all!" Antoinette's eyes flashed. "Don't push me on this." She rose quickly from the table and began to pace.

Susan watched her in exasperation. "Look, I'll do the best I can, but you're not making it easy." She got up and put their wineglasses in the sink. She wanted this bad dream to be over.

The deal negotiated at Susan's office on Friday morning took two hours of hard bargaining. At first, the police weren't interested in making a deal. Susan had to remind them that they were losing an opportunity of a lifetime and that it was irresponsible not to sacrifice one minor conviction for a chance to close down a major international drug ring. Eventually they relented under Susan's aggressive prodding.

Antoinette was to tell them everything she knew about Marcel Gagnon, the delivery of the heroin, the payment of the money, contacts with the Bertolini family and Marcel Gagnon's source of supply in France. If she lied or deliberately distorted information, the deal would be called off.

In return, she'd be charged only with aiding and abetting the use of a false or improperly obtained passport. Antoinette would agree to plead guilty and the Crown would ask that the sentence be suspended on appropriate terms and conditions involving a probationary period of two years.

Throughout the entire negotiation, there'd been no mention of the location of the two million dollars, although Antoinette had acknowledged its receipt from Bertolini's courier at Le Quatre Saisons the previous February. She also revealed that $490,000 had been paid to Luc Beaudoin in April during the handover in London, and another ten thousand had been used up in expenses.

"I've got to believe she wants that one and a half million for herself," Thibault said to Bourne as they left Susan's law office and got into their unmarked car. "The fact she won't say where it is tells me a whole lot." His dark eyes narrowed. "We'll keep twenty-four-hour-a-day surveillance on the Belair residence at Carré St-Louis. Sooner or later, she'll lead us to it if the Bertolinis and their guys don't get there first."

"If you're watching the Belair place and they come after him, don't hesitate to nab them right there and then. We'll give you all the help you need if these guys are from the U.S.," Bourne offered.

Thibault nodded. "I guess you and Swayze have got all the information you need to prosecute Roberto Bertolini and Gagnon. We should be able to deliver Gagnon to you before the end of January — mid-February at the latest, if our immigration guys keep their word. You've got to make sure that the legal wizards in Washington drag their feet for a few weeks and are slow off the mark in starting extradition proceedings."

"Don't worry, buddy. At ground level, we can get this done easily. This gal's information is just the icing on the cake."

Chapter Nineteen

"Tom, you said you would try and work at home in the evenings when I come to Ottawa." Carolyn was leaning back in bed looking peeved, her blond hair still neatly swept back, a copy of Chatelaine at her side and the end of the eleven o'clock news blaring from the TV.

"Honey, I tried but those guys from the department wouldn't let go. Morrison called the assistant deputy minister of immigration and all the directors and senior managers in for a special dinner meeting with me . . ."

"Uh-huh, tell me more," said a skeptical Carolyn.

"Seems some of them are feeling alienated because they perceive that I don't, or at least Alan and I don't, always follow their advice. It's just a matter of making them feel comfortable and showing them I don't have horns. Anyway, that was Morrison's observation."

Baldwin tried to change the subject. "Anything to eat left in the fridge?" he asked, as he headed towards the kitchenette in the cramped Park Lane apartment.

"Tom, it's almost eleven-thirty — what's going on? You said it was a dinner meeting. Most people in Ottawa finish dinner by eight and are sound asleep by ten."

"Well, we didn't get started until seven and the service was slow in the Blue Room. Didn't finish until after eight and I had to do a lot of the talking so I barely had time to eat. Then I had to go back to the department to meet with Forrester," Tom explained, poking about in the refrigerator.

"I see, just the two of you. What was she wearing?" Carolyn asked tartly, enjoying Tom's discomfort and now somewhat miffed at playing second fiddle to another woman.

"I don't remember what she was wearing. Always dresses like a lawyer ready for court. Seems there's been trouble brewing between my department and hers. I can't go into it really but it could develop into a major policy split over immigration adjudications. I think I understand what the problem is now, even though it's all legal stuff — going to speak to Alan in the morning to see if we can resolve it." Tom arrived back with a piece of cold chicken on a plate.

Carolyn was still looking at him, amazed that he didn't yet notice she was really annoyed. Tom took a bite of chicken. "You know, Carolyn, one of the few remaining benefits of supporting Forrester for the leadership is that we can get together like this in situations of interdepartmental warfare and work things out. I'm not sure the situation would be the same with some of the other ministers — especially the right-wingers who supported Savard."

Carolyn wasn't fooled by any of this. She knew that Tom had been attracted to Forrester the first night he had laid eyes on her at the Ramada Inn in Regina almost nine months ago. He had talked about her incessantly during the leadership campaign. She knew he was only telling half the truth when he attributed his abundant enthusiasm to nothing more than his zeal in whipping up support from Saskatchewan delegates.

Once Savard was installed as leader, Joan and Tom had become ordinary mortals seeking election in individual constituencies. While they had less contact than during the leadership campaign, they had made a point of talking weekly on the phone over the summer and into the fall. But now that she was a senior minister and he a junior minister, they barely had time even for telephone calls, although they did share small talk during the coffee breaks at cabinet committee meetings.

In the four weeks since the swearing-in, she and Tom had had lunch twice. At the Grill Room in the Chateau Laurier they discussed the loose ends remaining from Joan's leadership campaign, for which there was still a large debt. The other lunch was at the Four Seasons, where they shared mutual concerns about Savard and his henchmen in the PMO. They both feared that the throne speech for the opening of Parliament in January would swing too far to the right, away from the "caring" agenda upon which they'd all been elected.

Carolyn thought back to the previous Thursday, when she and Tom had spied Joan at the government caucus Christmas party in the West Block on the Hill. She was with a tall, white-haired retired Toronto broadcaster, now a senator. Tom knew that this was only a relationship of convenience although he and Carolyn had agreed that Joan and the senator made a striking couple.

"Tom Baldwin, let's get one thing straight. If you want me here in Ottawa, you'll have to pay some attention to me," Carolyn declared, now sitting upright in bed. "I don't care if it's Savard or the Lord almighty demanding your time and attention. When I'm here, you're here, do you understand? Otherwise, it's back home for me and I'll see you on weekends, if you're lucky. I've got lots to do in

169

Regina. The IODE wants me to take on responsibilities for all the province, and there's still lots of work to be done at the hospital. Anything's better than being stuck in this antiseptic apartment here in sterile Ottawa." With that, she turned off the bedside lamp, lay down and motioned for Tom to come to bed.

Tom complied without argument. But as he lay there, the adrenaline still flowing, he felt squeezed, pushed and pulled in every direction. So many decisions and so little time: the deputy, the department, the PMO, cabinet committees, caucus, the media, the constituency office, the party, the local riding association, Forrester and now Carolyn. In January, it would be worse with the convening of the House and the daily preparation required for question period.

It seemed everyone wanted a piece of him. There just wasn't enough to go around. Nothing in his background had prepared him for this, not even the hectic first few months as chief of the medical staff. Thank God for Alan Chant. Without him, he'd be lost. And he knew he could rely on Forrester if he got in a jam, although Carolyn would never understand.

Fortunately, sleep came easy to Tom. Within minutes of his head hitting the pillow, he was fast asleep and snoring loudly, much to the consternation of an angry Carolyn, lying wide awake with her back to him.

The Christmas break was good for both Tom and Carolyn. After fighting a whirlwind election campaign, being sworn in at Rideau Hall, taking on a new department, getting to know key staffers like Alan Chant and dealing with the first wave of sensitive cases left over from the previous minister, Tom's return to Regina a week before Christmas came as welcome relief.

He was a celebrity in his home town. Everywhere he went, people recognized him. The Baldwins' social agenda was full to the point of overflowing. The medical staff at the hospital invited them to be guests of honor to their Christmas party. And, happily, the constituency office seemed to be less busy as people with problems looked more to family and friends during the holidays than to the government for solutions.

Tom and Carolyn spent Christmas Eve with his parents, first going to church and then sitting down to a sumptuous late supper of oyster stew and glazed ham — a Baldwin tradition going back several generations. Coming home at one in the morning, they fell asleep in each other's arms, after expressing the faint hope that no one would dare wake them before noon the next day.

This worked for Carolyn, but Tom awoke sharp at seven in the morning. There was no call from Denis Forget, no briefing books to read on the way to the office, no emergency calls from Alan or the deputy, but he couldn't shake the rhythms of his Ottawa schedule.

Not wanting to wake his wife, he slipped out of bed and went into the den where he turned on the TV. A wasteland, it seemed to him — mostly American church services with evangelical preachers exalting the glory of God. "Guess the Yanks try to be first with everything, including praising the Lord," he joked to himself.

At eight o'clock, Queen Elizabeth began to deliver her Christmas message. Tom remembered as a small child getting up on Christmas Day and listening to a very young Queen Elizabeth II deliver her radio Christmas message to her subjects throughout the world. Her speech had then seemed inspirational, yet remote. Today, the Queen's televised message struck him as more relevant, touching on starvation in Africa, continued fighting in Central America, the uneasy peace in the Middle East and the utter senselessness of terrorist acts throughout the world but especially in the United Kingdom.

Watching the Queen deliver this message, he concluded that there was a place for moral leadership in the world but he wasn't quite sure it came from those holding elected office. He was glad she was there to do a job that had to be done.

That Christmas morning Tom took a long walk in the empty streets of his home town. Christmas lights were glowing bright even though it was daytime. He could spy happy families in warm living rooms with small children opening gifts. Occasionally, excited youngsters appeared on the street trying out a new toboggan or a toy and the occasional family carried gifts over to a neighbor's house. Tom was delighted to tip his hat and wish them all a merry Christmas. Somehow, Ottawa seemed a long way away and rather unimportant.

As he watched the children playing, he couldn't avoid thinking about an emptiness in his own life. God knows, he and Carolyn had tried to have kids. After three miscarriages, they had come to realize that she couldn't carry a child to term. She'd been willing to try a fourth time but Tom knew from consultations with his medical colleagues in Regina and Toronto that it was futile.

They had talked about adopting and gone as far as an initial visit to the agency. But it seemed so complicated. They would have to wait at least two years, and even then there were no guarantees that a child would be placed with them. Then politics intervened. He turned up his front path.

"Merry Christmas," Tom whispered in Carolyn's ear. It was close to noon on Christmas day and she'd slept right through. She reached up and pulled him down on the bed beside her.

"Well, Honorable Tom, how'd the minister like to give his wife a real Christmas present?"

Still cold from his walk, Tom had his clothes off in a few seconds. Her warmth struck him, just as his chill excited her. They spent the most pleasant hour together they could remember since the election — no phone calls, interruptions or distractions. At least almost none.

At one o'clock, the head of emergency called from the Regina General Hospital: "Tom, I hate to do this, especially on Christmas day, but everyone's away and we've got a woman here in great difficulty about to pop. I haven't done a C-section in a long while and we're afraid we may lose the child unless somebody qualified gets here real soon."

"Sure, be there in fifteen minutes," he said instinctively. Somehow this use of his skills seemed more important to Tom than anything he would do as a cabinet minister.

Carolyn winced, but understood. "Call me when you can," she said, kissing him on the cheek as he rushed to get dressed.

"Well, the turkey's carved — will Tom make it?" Erik Thorvaldsen asked his daughter Carolyn as the family gathered to say grace around the Christmas table. A moment later, the doorbell rang and Tom appeared, looking exhausted but happy.

"Well, we saved the baby. The mother's in bad shape but she should pull through. Three hours in the O.R. Haven't had one like that for a while. Looks like I'm just in time for dinner."

A tear of pride came to Carolyn's eye as they all hugged Tom and rushed him to the table. Pre-dinner grace and expressions of thanks to their maker for the gift of life took on special meaning that Christmas day.

Tom and Carolyn managed three days of skiing at Banff between Christmas and New Year's and spent a quiet New Year's Eve with some doctors from the hospital. Though their friends were glad to see them, they were clearly uncomfortable at having a star, this political curiosity, in their midst.

Tom tried to divert any questions about Ottawa by provoking a discussion about the general situation at the hospital, in particular the yet-to-be-completed process of selecting his successor as chief of medical staff. This started most of them talking although there were obvious sensitivities. Two of the candidates were at the party.

"Come to think of it, politics dominates everything, no matter what the institution, profession or social setting. It's the same process — just different venues," he observed philosophically to Carolyn on the drive home.

Chapter Twenty

"*Pour vous, Monsieur Doucet.*" It was only the second day on the job for Madame Landry, the new receptionist/secretary at the Doucet law office. She was the temporary replacement for the much-missed Hélène Lambert, who had left at Christmas. Guy had turned to an agency, and they had produced this so-called "experienced" woman who acted as if she'd never worked in a law office.

"He says he's calling from the legal aid office at St-Jean-sur-Richelieu. The director there says he remembers you from the many cases you had as special prosecutor for the attorney general of Quebec."

"Put him through. Not so sure I'm looking for legal aid cases these days, but what the hell," said Guy as he closed the door to his office.

"*Bonjour*, my name's Laforêt, first name Jean-Claude. Director of legal aid down here in St-Jean. There's a somewhat unusual application for legal aid on my desk for a guy allegedly involved in a big drug deal in upstate New York. Picked up by the Mounties when he came across the border into Quebec."

"How did you get my name?" asked Guy.

"Says he wants an experienced criminal lawyer who knows his way around the government, and asked for some suggestions. I immediately thought of you because I once watched you in court when the government was your client, prosecuting some businessman for fraud." There was a pause as Laforêt waited for his flattery to sink in.

"Don't do much of that anymore. It's hard to work for the government and still build a practice." Guy was gearing up for the inevitable discussion as to whether he would do legal aid work at the customary reduced rates. But he wanted to hear more first. "Who brought him in and when?" he asked.

"Two Mounties brought him into the detention facility here in St-Jean just before Christmas. They kept him for a full day of questioning. Seems they can't decide what to do with him."

"How long's he been in jail?"

"Poor bugger's been in for close to ten days. Anyway, he's applied for legal aid. The application came in here two days after Christmas but unfortunately there was no one here to process it till yesterday. Obviously he needs somebody solid to represent him."

"Any charges been laid?"

"Nothing under the criminal code, but he produced a dubious passport — said he's a Canadian citizen but there's some real doubt about that. We're not even sure what his real name is." Laforêt chuckled. "From what I can tell from the court records, they've booked him under the Immigration Act for entering Canada with a false passport. But I somehow gotta believe there are drugs involved, maybe stateside."

"What makes you think that? Was he bringing drugs into Canada?" Guy asked. Against his better judgment, he was intrigued.

"Well, I heard the Mounties talking about working

with the DEA on this one. That's gotta make it big. Also, they want to move him up to the main holding cells in Montreal, but they aren't saying when."

"Why me? You don't even know whether this is a serious drug case or just a simple immigration offense," Guy observed dryly.

"Just a feeling in my bones that this one's pretty big. I figure by recommending you take the legal aid certificate for this guy, it'll scare the living bejesus out of the police and get them off their duffs to do something." Jean-Claude Laforêt took his job seriously. In his world, every criminal was entitled to legal representation, particularly if the police were deliberately dragging their feet.

"About the question of fees, Mr. Laforêt. You guys pay only sixty-five dollars an hour, and that hardly covers the lights and telephone in my office."

"Well, Mr. Doucet, everyone in our profession has a duty to give something back to the system — which, by the way, enables you guys to make a pretty good living. I understand you used to have a young partner called Chant who did a lot of legal aid cases in Montreal when he first got out of law school. Gone up to Ottawa now to work for the prime minister, somebody told me."

Now Guy knew the real reason why Laforêt had called him. The case might be political, and this fellow obviously needed some high-powered help. Guy had never worked on a case where the DEA was involved. It might be interesting and lead to other, more lucrative work. As to whether Alan could help, that would have to wait.

"*D'accord*, I'll help you out, Mr. Laforêt. Any idea when they're thinking of moving him up to Montreal? If it's not soon, I'd better get down to St-Jean and interview him there."

"I think that's the best thing. I doubt the Mounties will do anything before the weekend. Can you get down tomorrow?"

"Guess I'll have to make time, won't I?" Guy said. He knew that keeping anyone in custody for over ten days without explaining the charges was indeed a travesty of justice — even if it was during the Christmas holidays and even if the guy was a big-time drug dealer.

The interview in St-Jean the next day went well and finished up in mid-afternoon. Driving home towards Montreal along the Richelieu, Guy began to consider all the possible proceedings that could be taken against his new client, Marcel Gagnon.

He had heard from a nervous Marcel what he believed was a bizarre but complete tale of plans to run heroin from Europe via Montreal to the Bertolini family in New York. Only the first delivery had been made, and had taken much longer than anticipated because of Bertolini's foot-dragging over giving delivery instructions. According to Marcel, Gus Bertolini was the mastermind, the driver behind the scheme. Marcel was just the mule.

Some things were clear from the outset as a result of the Mounties' questions to Marcel, which he'd described in some detail to Guy. The DEA wanted to prosecute Marcel, together with Roberto Bertolini if possible, in the United States. That was where the delivery had taken place. Obviously both the RCMP and the DEA knew about it and had pretty good evidence.

Guy made a mental note to check with DEA or justice officials in upstate New York to determine whether

Bertolini had been picked up yet and charged. Regardless, Guy reckoned that the Americans would soon begin extradition proceedings to get Marcel handed over as quickly as possible.

It was not clear what the RCMP would do. Marcel had admitted to Guy that he had come into Canada with a phony passport. But Guy found it hard to believe that they would be satisfied with a simple prosecution under the Immigration Act. Even if the Mounties obtained a conviction, Marcel could only be put away for a maximum of two years.

There was also the far more serious offense of importing under the Narcotic Control Act, which called for a minimum sentence of seven years. However, Guy wasn't sure that the RCMP had gathered enough evidence to sustain such a charge. Besides, the Mounties were tending to shy away from importing as an offense, especially since the seven-year minimum was under attack by criminal lawyers across the country as a violation of the Canadian Charter of Rights and Freedoms.

A more likely charge was possession for purposes of trafficking under the Narcotic Control Act. Marcel, however, could not enlighten Guy as to whether the police knew he'd hidden the heroin in his Montreal apartment for over eight months before delivering it to Roberto Bertolini.

The only other thing a mystery for Guy was whether Marcel was acting on his own in Canada or whether he had a partner. He would pursue that line more vigorously at their next interview, perhaps after Marcel had been moved from St-Jean to the holding cells near the court house in Old Montreal.

Rounding the corner off Rue de la Commune onto St-

Pierre, Guy glanced at his watch. It was a quarter to five on a dark Friday afternoon. He knew Madame Landry would be out the door at five on the dot so he double-parked his car. He found her cleaning up her desk for a quick exit.

"*Encore une petite chose*, Madame Landry. Before you go I want you to pull out a research file for me so I can do a little work over the weekend. The general title is 'Extradition Act.' It seems that our new client down in St-Jean is very popular with our American friends. We may well see a formal visit from the U.S. consul general in Montreal early next week. I want to be prepared."

The tension in the boardroom on the fourteenth floor at Place du Portage Phase IV in Hull was palpable. Douglas Morrison, deputy minister of immigration, had called the meeting late that Friday. Neither the minister nor Chant were there. Baldwin had gone back to his constituency in Regina and Chant had left for his usual weekend in Montreal.

Bill Kirke and Frank Legault had wanted to move expeditiously when the RCMP asked for an inquiry under the Immigration Act in order to quickly deport Marcel Gagnon. The case was really quite simple. Gagnon had come into Canada with an improperly obtained passport. The requisite written report describing this case had been sent to Morrison, and all he had to do was to agree that an inquiry was warranted.

An adjudicator could be in place Monday morning, with a deportation order likely to follow immediately after the hearing. This procedure would make things easy for the DEA, who would immediately pick Gagnon up as soon as he crossed the border and prosecute him together with Roberto Bertolini. Apparently the nephew of the New York drug kingpin was prepared to squeal on his notorious uncle in return for a plea bargain.

Bev Callen, elegant in a gray flannel suit, was clearly disturbed. "John, the shit will hit the fan over in justice if we're seen shipping this guy out with unseemly haste. Christ, he didn't even have a lawyer until this afternoon, and now we're supposed to hand him over to the Americans lock, stock and barrel on Monday without even the pretense of due process. I don't like it." Callen allowed his displeasure to sink in for a moment, then continued. "The Americans should go through the normal extradition process. They'll get him in the fullness of time. In the interim, we can fulfill our responsibilities by proceeding under the Immigration Act if the evidence isn't good enough to charge him under the Narcotics Control Act."

Morrison was distressed. Normally unflappable in situations like this, he would usually opt for expedited removal without blinking an eye. But a couple of things were gnawing at him. First, he wasn't sure his naive young minister, Tom Baldwin, would back him up if the whole thing came out in public, especially with that civil rights lawyer Alan Chant whispering in his ear. Second, he'd had his fill of those bastards over in the justice department. Since the arrival of their new minister, that hard-nosed, high-and-mighty female from Toronto, they seemed more obnoxious than ever.

"Does CSIS have anything to say on this one?" Morrison asked.

"Nope. We called Francine Côté just before lunch. She said that CSIS isn't into drugs yet and that neither Gagnon nor the Bertolini family are threats to the security of

Canada. But she suggested that the RCMP should be able to do what they want — the DEA will return the favor for sure." Callen closed his file and looked straight at Morrison. "Your call, Mr. Deputy. The Immigration Act gives you and not the minister the authority to direct that an inquiry be held."

"Refresh my memory, Bev. What kinds of issues will Gagnon's defense counsel raise in extradition proceedings, if that's the way we go?" Morrison wanted to weigh his options carefully. He shifted his gaze to the window. A light snow was falling.

"Their main argument is that the fugitive's alleged crime is an 'offense of a political character.' That's not a defined term. It can mean anything they want it to mean. They'll no doubt argue that Gagnon's being used by the DEA as cannon fodder to crack the Bertolini family."

"Is that going to fly?" asked Bill Kirke.

"I'm not sure it will hold up here, particularly since there seems to be pretty good wiretap evidence that Gagnon was carrying the heroin when he left Canada and was actually responsible for bringing it here in the first place."

"Anything else?" Morrison asked.

Callen removed his glasses and, extracting a monogrammed handkerchief from his breast pocket, set about meticulously polishing the lenses as he spoke. "The other factor to keep in mind is that even if the judge is persuaded to surrender Gagnon to the Americans, he can still appeal to the minister of justice on virtually any ground. Then it'll be Forrester who makes the ultimate decision regarding surrender."

"That'll be just lovely," said Kirke sarcastically, who'd been fiddling with his coffee cup while Callen spoke.

"He can also appeal to the Court of Appeal, but most defense counsel go the political route. Certainly that'll be the case as long as Forrester holds office." Callen put his glasses back on and looked expectantly at Morrison.

"And if I direct an inquiry and the adjudicator orders deportation and we get him out that way, what happens to the extradition proceedings?" Morrison asked, turning his pale eyes on Callen.

"Well, that'd be the end of it." Callen neatly folded his handkerchief and replaced it in his pocket. "The Americans usually take a month or so to get extradition proceedings started. I wouldn't expect they'll have even begun to prepare their depositions let alone navigate all the paperwork through the State Department. In my view, we've got clear sailing before extradition proceedings will kick in."

That was good enough for Morrison. "Let's go for it. What have we got to lose? We're far more comfortable taking our chances with the inquiry before an adjudicator. Can't see taking any political heat for deporting a drug dealer who entered Canada on a false passport." He looked at Legault, who'd been sitting silent and ramrod straight until then.

"No disagreement with that conclusion, Douglas."

The meeting concluded quickly. They all headed for their cars in the parking lot except Legault, who couldn't wait to call Thibault in Montreal. "*Victoire*, Jean! Tell your friends at the DEA that they'll have the Frenchman before Valentine's Day."

As he left the building, Legault made a mental note to brief Alan Chant on this one in case it ever came up between Baldwin and Forrester. But he was in no hurry.

Chapter Twenty-One

E ven though Parliament wouldn't open till January 15th, Tom was back at his desk in Ottawa the day after New Year's to get ready. He was facing a full round of departmental briefings, a new group of sensitive cases requiring decisions, meetings with visiting dignitaries, a full slate of cabinet committee meetings, and policy proposals from the department and non-governmental advisory groups. He was also scheduled to go back to Regina each weekend in January and Alan had managed to line up some government business that would keep him there for a couple of weekdays as well.

Carolyn had originally planned to come for the opening of Parliament and the social events that followed. But then she decided to stay in Regina for two or three weeks to help reorganize the women's auxiliary office at the hospital and visit with friends whom she hadn't seen since before the election. She didn't really want to go to Ottawa any earlier than was necessary. January was a good time to avoid the nation's capital.

"Minister, this week is the calm before the storm," Alan said, beginning his daily briefing that second Monday following New Year's. "There's the throne speech tomorrow, followed by speeches by the two opposition leaders on Wednesday and the reply by the PM on Thursday. Other than being in your seat those days, there's not much for you to do and it's unlikely anything affecting your department will be raised."

Tom nodded. "Good. I'd rather ease back in than plunge back in."

Alan smiled. "By Thursday, we should have been able to get most of the departmental briefings and paper work behind us, if we keep our noses to the grindstone." Alan continued, trying to sound casual. "I was going to suggest dinner Thursday night, perhaps at Café Henry Burger over in Hull. You might have heard some people refer to it — mistakenly — as 'Café Henri Burgé' because it's a classy French restaurant. Anyway, there are some special people I'd like you to meet who just happen to be in town that day. It'll be an interesting group."

Tom looked uncertain. "Who'll be there?" he asked.

"First, there's my father, Sam, who'll be here for the day seeing Revenue Canada with his lawyer. I don't think you know her — Felicia Fortin from the Stewart Beauchamp firm in Montreal? She's quite a lady. My father relies heavily on her to keep his tax bill down." It was not clear to Tom whether Alan was proud of Sam or apologizing for him.

"Who else, Alan?" Tom was becoming interested.

"Well, my girlfriend Susan Belair is in town from Montreal seeing some folks in the department on problem cases. I told you Susan's an immigration lawyer with her own small office on Park Avenue, didn't I?"

Tom now understood how Alan always seemed to have his ear to the ground when it came to complex immigration cases. He wondered how he found time for a girlfriend since he seemed to be working all the time.

"So there would be five of us at Henry Burger. Does

that work for you?" Alan inquired, genuinely hoping that he could introduce his boss to the two most important people in his life. Besides, if Tom came, Alan would have no qualms about putting the bill on the ministerial expense account.

"Well, maybe I'll try to get a 'date' since Carolyn's not coming down until the end of the month," Tom added. Now it was his turn to try to sound casual. "I'll let you know."

A moment later, Tom was on the line to the PMO, asking to be connected to the minister of justice. It took all of three minutes to track her down.

"What a pleasant surprise, Tom. Where are you? In Ottawa?" Joan's voice came through loud and clear.

"Yes, I came in last night from Regina. You wouldn't believe what these guys in the department have lined up for me this week — but I guess they want the decks cleared before House sittings start for real," Tom added. "Where are you?"

"Well, I'm down here in Toronto trying to close out some files at my old law office, some things I should have gone through before the election but never got around to. My department in Ottawa is screaming, but that's tough. I'll be down for the opening tomorrow. Told them I wouldn't see any officials until Thursday and then only in the late afternoon and early evening. Guess you and I have to be in our seats to hear Savard that day." Forrester sounded defiant.

"Well, Thursday is what I was calling about, to see if you were free for dinner that night in Ottawa. It's been too long — haven't seen you since the caucus Christmas party and that was a zoo."

"Sure was. Did you see who I had to squire around that

night? Senator Smoothie."

Tom remembered all too vividly his brief rush of jealousy on seeing Forrester in the company of the dashing senator. But he wasn't going to admit that to her. "You both looked like you were having fun," Tom chuckled wryly.

"Ah, go on. He's a harmless old bird. Fancies himself as a ladies' man, but it'll never happen, at least not with me. Not my type." There was a pause and then she said: "Sure, I'll have dinner with you Thursday, provided I can catch the ten o'clock plane home to Toronto. My departmental guys can go screw themselves. If we don't finish, they can catch up with me next week. What'd you have in mind?"

"Well I'm putting together a small group with my executive assistant Alan Chant. Three of them are lawyers and you'd make the fourth. I'm sure they'd be delighted to have the minister of justice join them. Chant is the young hotshot lawyer sent over from Savard's office. You'll like him."

"Well, if that's where he came from, I'm sure he didn't vote for me last June," Forrester observed acidly.

"Don't worry — he wasn't even at the convention. His old man was one of Savard's Montreal bagmen. He'll be at the dinner, too, with his tax lawyer Felicia Fortin. It wouldn't hurt you to get to know people like Sam Chant, given the financial situation we still have to deal with. Just remember, it's guys like Chant senior who really drive political financing." Tom had begun to pick up steam, sounding more like a seasoned organizer than a political neophyte and the youngest minister in the Savard government. And Forrester's one weakness in the leadership campaign had been financing. Tom was getting the benefit of Alan's five-month crash course in politics in the

Savard office. "You know, Joan, all those lawyers who toadied up to you before Christmas in order to make your QC list at New Year's are notorious cheapskates when it comes down to actually writing a check."

After his call to Forrester, Tom buzzed Alan on the intercom. "Alan, there'll be six of us on Thursday," he said, with just a hint of smugness. "You can tell your dad, but don't tell your other lawyer friends — we'll be joined by the minister of justice. I hope they recognize her when she walks in."

The conversation at Henry Burger turned out better than Alan had expected. Sam had been charming and humble. He used the "f" word only once, in a weak moment when describing the separatists running the provincial government in Quebec City. "We'll get those SOBs out before too long, just you watch!" Sam had added. Despite the colorful language, Alan had to admit that he had gained new respect for his father, whom he had previously dismissed as a political sycophant.

Susan, quiet yet radiant, got on well with Baldwin. They discussed refugee policy and the need for increased financial assistance to immigrant women. She told him about her immigration practice in Montreal but shrewdly avoided discussing specific cases, although she knew Baldwin wouldn't have known the details anyway.

Susan hadn't even told Alan what particular cases had brought her to the department that day. He hadn't asked, preferring to keep up the fiction of an arm's-length professional relationship between them.

Felicia Fortin and Joan Forrester hit it off famously.

They were about the same age but from different legal disciplines. Trading war stories, they talked primarily about the politics of large law firms and the pressures on women partners who wanted to get ahead.

Tom picked up on this part of the conversation. "Just like I was reminded in the hospital back in Regina at Christmas time," he observed. "Every institution, every profession, every firm has a political process underlying its power structure. It's no different than what goes on here in Ottawa, except we do it in a fishbowl, not behind people's backs."

Felicia couldn't resist. "But even here in Ottawa, I'm not sure everything is done in the open either, Minister," she said with a smile, winking at Forrester at the same time. "I'm sure there are still old scores from the leadership convention last June that have yet to be settled."

Joan Forrester's smile turned to a frown. "There's no looking back, we're the government now. Tom's right, we're in a fishbowl. We can't be seen to disagree publicly — cabinet solidarity and all that. We do have disagreements from time to time, or at least our departments do. But we usually settle things and emerge united. Right?" She was smiling again as she glanced pointedly at Tom.

Tom nodded. "Of course."

Felicia looked openly curious. Her eyes darted back and forth between Forrester and Baldwin.

"Matter of fact, Tom and I have got a doozer brewing right now that I'm going to be chasing him on. But we'll deal with it, personally if we have to." Joan finished her little speech staring directly at Tom, who looked mildly uncomfortable. "Now I've got to catch my plane for Toronto. Nice to meet all of you. Alan, look after Tom. He needs all the help he can get. Susan, you look after Alan

— make sure he stays healthy and doesn't leave the law for good." .

"Sorry you have to leave, Minister," Alan said. "We've enjoyed your company."

"Sam, hope you guys sock it to the Péquistes when the Quebec election comes. If a justice minister from Toronto can help, call me — my French is improving," Joan smiled, her hand resting on Sam's shoulder.

"Don't be surprised if we do call you down to Montreal. That'd be great," Sam offered, beaming.

"And Felicia, we must do this again — but next time on my turf when you're down in Toronto. We still have a lot of ground to cover."

"You bet, Joan." Felicia gave Joan another conspiratorial wink. "Safe trip."

Tom walked Forrester to the waiting limousine in the parking lot. "You know, Joan, I wonder what would have happened if you'd won the convention. We might be doing a better job today, particularly on social policy. And I worry about the ethics of some of the guys around Savard, although Sam seems like one of the better ones." Tom tried to sound positive.

"Don't be so goddamned naive, Tom. If I'd won, I'd be sitting as leader of the Opposition and you'd be a backbench critic on health care or whatever, if you'd been lucky enough to buck the tide and get elected in the first place. With Savard, we've got power. Without power, we're nothing."

"I suppose you're right." Tom looked away pensively, but she drew him back with her steady gaze.

"But we do have one little problem developing, Tom. I wasn't just kidding a few moments ago inside. It seems your department, with the blessing of the RCMP, is thinking about using your Immigration Act to get around my Extradition Act and screw up the normal course of justice. You'd better well fucking understand, I won't allow it. Get briefed, Tom, because I'll be over to see you if it's not resolved soon."

Tom was taken aback. He'd never heard Forrester speak that way before. "I'm not aware of the case, Joan. The officials obviously have been keeping it to themselves. I'll have Alan look into it," he said, earnestly. "And you can come over any time you want. I'm always glad to see you."

Forrester looked briefly into his eyes, then kissed him squarely on the lips. She allowed the kiss to go on a second too long. Tom was even more taken aback. He glanced around. The limo drivers were acting as if they'd seen nothing unusual.

"Thanks for dinner, Tom." She squeezed his arm. "Now get back in there with your able assistant and his interesting friends. You're lucky to have him, more than you know." Joan jumped into the back seat of her waiting limo, and with a wave sped off to the airport, leaving an astonished Tom Baldwin staring after her.

Chapter Twenty-Two

"Hi, boss, what's up?" Alan called across the room to the humorless Martha Kulyk, fresh from his ride from the Ottawa train station with Denis Forget. It was the third Monday in January.

"You lawyers are all the same," she shot back, dryly. "You never ask a question without knowing the answer. Everything I have to tell you was in those damn briefing books that I came in at six-thirty this morning to prepare. You'd better read 'em — there's no way I'll summarize it for you now."

"Just kidding. Wanted you to know that you're still in charge," he laughed. Alan didn't mind her little put-down. Several weeks earlier he'd come to the conclusion that it would serve everyone's interest if she still thought she was running the office, screening what both he and the minister were given to read. That way, she'd work harder on the superficial stuff and keep her nose out of the tougher issues coming out of immigration enforcement.

Alan had already established a separate channel of communication through Joe Bédard and Dominique Rodriguez. Bédard or his assistant would send the briefing books for the sensitive cases that needed the minister's attention to Dominique, who would place them in the small safe in Baldwin's inner office.

Alan had made arrangements for this safe through Frank Legault. He believed a more direct channel of communication would encourage candor. This in turn would enable Tom and Alan to make quick and fair decisions that would stand up under public scrutiny.

"When's the minister getting into town?" Tom called over his shoulder.

"Late tonight on the Air Canada flight via Winnipeg," Martha replied, without looking up. "Callen and his team want another go at the minister on sensitive cases that have been piling up. Can he make an eight o'clock meeting tomorrow morning? He's got the Economic Development Committee at ten, and a courtesy call from the Jamaican ambassador at eleven-forty-five," she said, checking her daytimer.

"Sure! That's what he's here for — to deal with the tough cases. I'll meet him at the airport tonight and put him to bed with a few notes." Alan's voice trailed off as he walked into the minister's inner office and locked the door.

True to form, Dominique had put the briefing books in the safe. Alan took them out and resolved to get through each case before supper so he could properly brief the minister, whose plane arrived at nine-thirty that evening.

The first day on the job for McGill Legal Aid started with a visit to the holding cells, and it had been a terrible experience. At seven-thirty in the morning, Alan was not ready for the smells, the cries, the disruptions, the jostling. He wondered how he would ever assemble a complete dossier on the prisoners in cells ten through sixteen before Court started at ten o'clock.

His first instinct had been to try to interview each person.

That turned out to be a hopeless task. Few of them were sober enough to talk. Even if they were, what came out was gibberish, half truths and wild exaggerations — in between the vomiting, retching or just plain passing out.

A friendly young police officer noticed his dilemma and suggested he come with him to the adjacent interviewing room where cleanly typed "dope" sheets were produced for each of the seven prisoners. This was the information Alan was looking for — clear, concise and chronological.

But something gnawed incessantly at the back of his mind, particularly after the first couple of days when his selected "clients" had not fared too well on their bail hearings. Suddenly it had dawned on Alan that he'd been had. He'd forgotten the first rule of criminal defense counsel — never accept police evidence without independent corroboration.

Alan contrived a procedure to get better evidence. Instead of arriving at seven-thirty, he'd be there at six each morning to join the Salvation Army workers who were allowed into the holding cells to attend to the prisoners' spiritual and physical needs.

That Alan was a duty counsel and not a member of the "Sally Ann" didn't seem to bother the jail guards at that time of day. It was awfully early in the morning. But the background information he got from careful questioning and encouragement, with the support of the Sally Ann staff, often produced the hard evidence he needed. In the ensuing weeks, his success rate on bail applications shot up.

"Minister, we've got an action-packed week ahead of us. Hope you got a good rest on the weekend. We're in for a few long days," Alan warned Tom at the airport as they climbed into the black Chevrolet Impala for the drive to the Park Lane.

This was not what Baldwin wanted to hear. He'd had a

hectic time in Regina. He'd been guest speaker at a special award ceremony at Campbell Collegiate on Friday night, and on Saturday he'd worked in his constituency office from nine in the morning until three in the afternoon, after which he'd spent two hours taping a local community TV program. He and Carolyn had ended their Saturday by attending a dinner at the Polish Hall. As guests of honor, they'd filled up on cabbage rolls, sausages and long-winded speeches, few of which were in English.

Sunday morning Carolyn and Tom went to church. That afternoon his local constituency association had scheduled him for a guest appearance at the skating rink, where he had been suitably introduced. His only real "down time" with Carolyn had been on Sunday evening when she had cooked him some veal parmigiana (his favorite) and opened a half bottle of Barolo (another favorite). Over dinner, she filled him in on all the gossip from the hospital. The new chief of medical staff had not yet been chosen but the race was down to two candidates.

Even then, as they'd stretched out after dinner on the couch in the TV room to watch the local news, he couldn't get away from work. There was the president of the Sikh association in Regina condemning the minister of immigration for threatening to deport a poor epileptic Punjabi girl without so much as a hearing. Tom didn't have the faintest idea what the case was about. But he was sure he'd be briefed when he got back to the office in Ottawa on Tuesday morning.

On Monday, as the acting regional minister for the prairie provinces, Tom had a full schedule of appointments at the downtown government office in Regina. His more senior cabinet colleague and president of the Canadian Wheat Board, the Honorable Ian McKellar from

Manitoba, was out of the country on official business. So Tom had to stand in.

By two in the afternoon, he had spent six hours listening to a variety of complaints. The vice-president of the National Farmers' Union was concerned about the Savard government's proposal to disband certain marketing boards, the proponent of an oil upgrader facility in eastern Saskatchewan asked for a commitment of federal subsidies, and the president of one of Saskatchewan's largest wheat pools was angry about bureaucratic inefficiency at the wheat board.

Their complaints had nothing remotely to do with Tom's department, but as a team player, Tom was the eyes, ears and voice of the Savard government at that particular time and place in western Canada. Tom had found that with his medical training he was a better listener than most politicians he'd encountered. Still, his inability to provide instant prescriptions, cures or relief was acutely frustrating.

The last appointment that day had been the Saskatchewan vice-president of the ruling party. He had a litany of complaints all centered on his perception that the Savard government was ignoring the party faithful in the appointments process. "Not only have you guys been slow off the mark in removing the supporters of the previous government from the federal agencies and boards that matter out here, but the few appointments you've made involve very few of *our* party people. What the hell is going on up there in Ottawa? You're forgetting the very people who worked so hard to make sure you got there in the first place."

Tom was genuinely confused. Because he'd had so little experience in party politics before attending the leadership convention and seeking the nomination in Regina East, he was still viewed as an outsider by suspicious party regulars. He'd had no idea whether the government had been unusually slow in making appointments — it was only two and a half months since they'd been sworn in — or whether they had been politically unwise in seeking out the brightest and the best, regardless of political affiliation. All he knew was that the appointments were handled exclusively by Savard's office. Only at the last moment was he even consulted about the Saskatchewan candidates, usually with a cursory phone call from the PMO asking if he had any objections to the appointment of so-and-so to such-and-such agency or board.

"Listen, my friend, I'll take up your concerns with the prime minister this week." Tom spoke soothingly to the party vice-president. "You have every right to be annoyed. We're aware of the important role you and all the others played in the election and we won't forget."

Baldwin knew the man didn't like him and that his attempt to pacify wouldn't cut much ice. After all, the vice-president had been a Savard supporter from the beginning and now felt he was being frozen out. It galled him that this young Dr. Baldwin, who'd supported Forrester and was a relative newcomer to politics, was sitting here in a minister's chair with all the perks of office while he, the experienced and faithful political warhorse, had received nothing. Tom vowed to speak to Alan about doing something for this fellow, if only to quiet him down.

🔺 🔻

"Alan, you wouldn't believe the crap they put me through

yesterday in downtown Regina," Baldwin sighed in the back seat of the Impala. "Can you do anything with your buddies at the PMO to spare me the agony of having to go through that hell when McKellar's away?"

Alan smiled sympathetically. He wasn't about to admit that he'd been responsible for putting Tom through the wheat board hell. The previous Thursday, when Savard's ministerial coordinator called, Alan had volunteered Tom's services more as a personal favor to be paid back later than anything else. He changed the subject.

"We're being visited tomorrow morning at eight o'clock sharp by the fabulous five with the latest sensitive cases that need your immediate attention," Alan said to the somewhat subdued Baldwin. "No doubt you remember our last go-round before Christmas. I'll bet those five are indelibly imprinted on your mind by now — Callen, Kirke, Bédard, Legault and Côté," Alan recited. "Now if you tell me you remember their titles, I'll dispense with the reintroductions tomorrow morning."

Tom dutifully rhymed off the titles, hesitating on Francine Côté's. Alan chuckled as he helped him out. "Director General of Counterintelligence."

Tom finished off. "—with the Canadian Security Intelligence Service."

"Right. Now, Dominique has produced some terrific background stuff from the department, which I spent the last three hours reviewing." Alan handed Tom the thick green briefing book. "I've read it all and highlighted the important passages in the usual way. Hope you agree with my recommendations. Based on our last session, you're on a bit of a roll."

"Why do you say that?" asked a bemused Baldwin. "I thought we were in trouble when that Concordia professor had a heart attack and died, and the university blamed it on me for not renewing his work permit."

"Well, we lucked in on this one, in the end. Seems there was a big exposé at the Cuban consulate in Montreal last week. Apparently CSIS was able to turn one of their liaison officers who spilled the beans on the Cuban's entire spy network in Montreal and Ottawa, including the involvement of one Professor Firestone."

"No kidding!" Tom shook his head in amazement. "But will the public know?"

"External Affairs plans to PNG three Cuban officials next week and it'll be all over the media. I've persuaded the press officer at external to include a reference to Firestone in the backgrounder that goes out. I also leaked this information to a couple of friends in the press gallery. You'll be totally vindicated."

"A pleasant surprise! I just hope your little leak doesn't come back to haunt. I almost wish you hadn't told me. All right, what about those other two cases we dealt with before Christmas?" Tom looked out the car window. They were driving along the canal. Despite the late hour, a few brave skaters glided by on the shimmering ice. Tom reluctantly tore his eyes from the scene and turned back to Alan.

"Juan Barcelona, Chilean ship jumper. With the support of the two Vancouver area MPs, he's been allowed to stay on a minister's permit, gainfully employed as a stevedore on the Vancouver waterfront. Hoping to save enough money, along with his roommate who looked after him when he first jumped ship, to buy a small house in Vancouver's east end. Should qualify soon for permanent resident status. Dr. Baldwin gets high marks as a case-sensitive minister who listens. And the gay community in Vancouver is not displeased."

"Okay. Can't quarrel with that outcome. What about the other one — that convicted commodities broker with a new identity?"

"Fred Milanowski — right. You'll remember the RCMP actually wanted him out in the end because he didn't provide the kind of undercover help they thought was useful."

"And I said he should stay, on the basis that a deal is a deal."

"Correct. Well, this gave Milanowski renewed incentive to go public in the investigation into the Winnipeg airport concession. He's doing an interview next week with W5 on CTV and the senator alleged to be involved, the good friend of the PM, is going to be front and center. Senator Semeniuk and his people are already preparing to fight back. Their main point of attack will be the fact that their accuser, Milanowski, is a convicted criminal in the United States who shouldn't have been allowed into Canada by the RCMP in the first place — he was allowed to stay on at your insistence even though the Mounties now want to remove him. It'll come down to credibility — the senator or Milanowski."

"How do you think that will go?" Tom looked nervous.

"I have a feeling that the public will side with Milanowski if he's treated fairly on W5. And that will support your decision, Minister. But I have to warn you — the PM'll be privately pissed off at you if his good buddy the senator goes down."

As the Park Lane came into sight, Alan could see that Baldwin was getting tired, and that he'd reached the end of the road with this impromptu briefing. It was a long shot whether Baldwin would even open the thick briefing books before falling asleep that night.

"Sometimes I think the sun will never rise," Alan had said, yawning, to his Salvation Army colleague as they entered the holding cells underneath the old court house that cold November day in 1977.

"You know, God looks with kindness on those who sleep very little," replied Major Dunphy, a lifer with the Salvation Army who still enjoyed performing the Lord's work in the middle of the night. "My sleeping is not going to improve the situation of these unfortunate people, so I simply do without," Major Dunphy had noted modestly.

Alan felt chastened. By the end of his first year of McGill Legal Aid, Alan too had learned to do without sleep. Hit the books from six to eleven with forty minutes off for supper in the evening, then home by midnight to sleep for a few hours and up at five in the morning to be downtown by six to start the day — that had been his routine.

After all, he reasoned, if an old fellow like Dunphy could learn to do without much sleep, then a fit young man like himself had no excuse.

Chapter Twenty-Three

"Good morning, Minister, we're back with another group of sensitive cases requiring your personal attention. Hope you and your family enjoyed the Christmas break," said Bev Callen, starting the early morning meeting without even looking up. He didn't bother to acknowledge Alan Chant. Tom Baldwin reached for his glass of orange juice. He was trying to cut down on coffee.

"Unlike the other cases we disposed of several weeks ago," Callen was saying, "these have all come to the surface since the new government was sworn in. So the political problems they're creating will be seen as resting squarely on your shoulders and it will be harder to lay the blame on the previous government." Callen straightened his glasses. "Minister, I hope you don't think I'm being overly candid," he added, hinting at the list of immigration horrors that he and his officials were about to unveil.

"No, I appreciate your forthrightness," replied Tom, sounding less than eager. He wasn't sure he was ready to play King Solomon yet again.

"Bill, why don't you take the first one?" asked Callen, carefully moving his coffee cup away from his papers. Bill Kirke stood up, a wiry bundle of nervous energy, no taller than five foot four. Clutching two yellow pages of handwritten notes obviously prepared late the previous evening, he began to describe in hushed tones the troublesome case of Millicent Wright.

"This lady has created a real hornet's nest for us down in Toronto, Minister. She's a Jamaican mother of three, no husband, currently working illegally as a domestic with a prominent Rosedale family for far less than the minimum wage. It seems she got into the country as the fiancée of a young Canadian, originally from Jamaica. He's purportedly the father of two of her children and he originally sponsored her immigration application as a member of the fiancé/family class." Kirke paused and gulped down some coffee. "Like so many cases of this sort, she was deserted shortly after she arrived. The gentleman is nowhere to be found so his sponsorship commitments are worthless. Millicent Wright, in desperation, turned to prostitution for financial survival." Kirke looked up to ensure the minister was still with him.

Without glancing up from his briefing book, Baldwin asked Kirke to continue. He had already reviewed the highlights of this case and noted Alan's recommendations. But he wanted to hear Kirke tell the whole story.

"Millicent Wright soon found herself pregnant again and took refuge in the local Roman Catholic church, which counseled against an abortion and helped her through the pregnancy and the intricacies of obtaining welfare," Kirke said, fidgeting with a pencil.

Looking slightly bored, Francine Côté, who had been sitting quietly in the far corner of the boardroom, got up and poured herself more coffee. Tom glanced up at her. She was even better dressed this time — a smart Chanel-style suit in burgundy wool with gold buttons. Conservative in cut, it still displayed enough shapely leg to make her more than a little interesting. She still gave the impression that she had more important things to do than attend this meeting with a bunch of immigration types.

Kirke also stole a furtive glance at her, then continued with his briefing. "But she wanted greater security and financial independence, so she took an illegal job as a domestic with a prominent Rosedale family." Kirke swallowed tensely before launching into the next revelation. "We're told by our officials in Toronto that the employer, Henry Street, is a partner with a major law firm and a well-known political supporter of the prime minister. In fact, he was one of his key Toronto organizers in the leadership convention held last June."

Christ, thought Alan, he must have missed that. Or maybe it wasn't in the briefing note.

Nervously, Kirke continued. "Apparently, one of the Rosedale neighbors found out about the illegal nanny and called our enforcement people — not so much because they wanted to cause difficulties for this poor woman, who was just trying to support her kids, but to embarrass Henry Street who is not well regarded by some in the neighborhood."

Baldwin was amazed at the gossipy nature of this information. Clearly, it hadn't been fully set out in the written material. Immigration officials seemed to have their own sources of local political intelligence.

"Now, Minister, there are two sides to this case. On one hand, the focus is on humanitarian and compassionate grounds — three innocent kids, a single mother trying to make ends meet, and her exploitation by a prominent citizen who, uh, should know better," Kirke added cautiously. "This is the side *The Toronto Star* will pick up if they get hold of it. On the other hand, if you appear too lenient on on this, you'll simply encourage people to use the fiancé category to beat the system. Instead of two thousand cases annually, we'll have ten thousand, the bulk of them from Third World countries." Kirke tried to smooth out his notes, which looked almost as rumpled as his gray suit.

"Any political angle on this?" asked Bédard.

"You bet." Kirke turned the second sheet of paper over. "First, the woman sought help from the Jamaican-Canadian Association. They've got a direct pipeline to the immigration reporters at the Toronto Star. I know the Jamaican ambassador is coming to see you later — he'll also ask you to be lenient. However, the Rosedale–Moore Park Association has indicated to our officials that they hope you throw her out — seems some of their members don't like having black nannies with kids in the neighborhood, especially if they're illegal. Unfortunately, most of these members don't seem to like Henry Street."

Baldwin looked again at the briefing note. In the margin Alan had scribbled: "Allow her in through a minister's permit, but impose strict conditions."

Baldwin asked Kirke and Joe Bédard what conditions they would suggest imposing if he decided to allow Millicent Wright to stay. They had a list. It contained no specific conditions to be applied to Millicent Wright personally, but rather suggestions for preventing future abuses of the system.

First, they wanted tougher fiancé rules restricting the spousal dependency category to persons who were actually married, at least for those countries where most of the abuse originated.

Second, enforcement wanted to send a strong message to Air Canada, Air Jamaica, Air India and other carriers serving Third World countries, outlining their obligations to pay for return air flights for those people who arrive without proper immigration authority. This would force the airlines to be more careful in determining who was permitted entry into Canada before they boarded the plane.

Third, they requested that advance information about the first two proposals be sent to the minister's provincial counterparts responsible for general welfare assistance. These changes would greatly help provincial politicians and their officials, who would no doubt then provide political support.

"If you adopt these three simple proposals, the department will recommend a minister's permit for Millicent Wright," Kirke concluded. Tom looked briefly at Alan who pretended not to notice. Taking this as a positive sign, Baldwin said, "Sure, go ahead."

Once he'd heard the conditions, which seemed eminently reasonable and politically smart, Alan let Baldwin appear to decide this one on his own. However, he wondered what Baldwin would tell the Jamaican ambassador when they met later that morning. More important, he wondered what Baldwin would say to Savard when this case hit the press and the PMO got the inevitable call from Henry Street complaining that his reputation had been tarnished by this upstart young minister and his over-zealous officials. He made a mental note to call the PMO with a "heads-up" warning.

He would also call the reporter covering the immigration beat for the *Star* in Toronto to give her the appropriate spin on the case before it actually broke. She'd been part of the *Star*'s Ottawa bureau when the new government came in. Alan had met her briefly at the press gallery dinner in late November before she'd been re-assigned back to Toronto. New to immigration, she would appreciate the advance notice and hopefully return the favor with a story sympathetic to Baldwin.

In a condescending voice, Callen jumped in. "Minister, you're on the right track this morning. But the next case isn't quite as easy." He nodded to Bédard, who pulled up a file labeled "Stanislaw Zawacki."

"This is a strange one, no question about it," began Bédard. "If it hadn't achieved such prominence within the Polish community, we could have dealt with this as a normal 'ship jumper' case and returned this fellow immediately to his ship. That would have been the end of it."

The reference to the Polish community caught Baldwin's attention. He wondered if the adulation lavished on him Saturday night at the Polish Hall in Regina had any connection. He vaguely remembered a telephone call the previous week from the member of Parliament from Toronto Parkdale–High Park, Jan Kepal. Of Polish extraction himself, Kepal had recounted the tale of some beleaguered Polish sailor in St. John's, Newfoundland.

Stanislaw Zawacki was a twenty-two-year-old seaman from a Polish vessel that was fishing off the banks of Newfoundland. On leave for a day in St. John's, he met and fell in love with a local beauty named Bernadette Kelly. He jumped ship and within three days the couple had persuaded a priest, Father Sean O'Flaherty, to marry them.

"They were still celebrating their honeymoon when immigration officials, acting on complaints from the ship's captain and Bernadette's parents, entered her apartment and took him off to immigration detention to await a hearing. The trouble was," sighed Bédard, running a hand over his balding pate, "we couldn't move fast enough to get an adjudicator in place. Within hours, the Canadian Polish Congress got wind of things and arranged for local counsel for Zawacki."

Bédard then recounted how the *S.S. Polgar* hurriedly left port to return to Gdansk — apparently there were undersized cod stocks in the hold — leaving behind one hell of a problem. The adjudicator ruled that Zawacki had entered Canada illegally and was therefore subject to removal or deportation. But he noted that Zawacki now appeared to be legally married to a Canadian, which meant the minister could issue a permit. Bédard closed the file and awaited the minister's response.

Tom cleared his throat. "Well, ladies and gentlemen, Mr. Chant and I have had Dominique try to get a little more background on this one since we know how aggressive the Canadian Polish Congress can be in defending their people." Tom, looking down at Alan's handwritten notes, didn't really have to spell this out. The immigration officials in the room knew full well of the interest in the case. What they didn't know was that Kepal, the Parkdale–High Park MP, had been part of Forrester's team at the leadership convention seven months previously and had worked closely with Baldwin.

Working from Alan's notes, Baldwin explained that Zawacki was not a political refugee. He'd simply been looking for a better way of life and chose this particular shortcut. Furthermore, there was evidence that his relationship with Bernadette Kelly had soured. Bernadette appeared to be having second thoughts and church authorities, when consulted, felt there would be no problem having the marriage annulled if that was what the young woman wanted.

"And so," Baldwin concluded, "no minister's permit for this one. Look after him in detention until the next Polish ship comes into port and then arrange with the captain to have him taken on as crew." Bédard nodded and scribbled on his briefing notes. Tom took a sip of juice. "Dominique, when we finish please set up a call with Jan Kepal so I can explain why we're doing what we're doing. I hope he'll be able to quiet down the Congress but, even if he can't, I think we're on pretty solid ground here. I should call my host at last Saturday's banquet in Regina as well."

Alan couldn't avoid a self-satisfied look. Baldwin had followed his advice right down the line. Dominique's spadework had been superb. The department would regard this as a win. But the minister had let Bédard and his enforcement staff know, without beating them over the head, that their work had been somewhat superficial. Alan looked over at Dominique. He remembered Susan telling him she was a "keeper."

It was Callen's turn to move on to the next case. "This one, Minister, is somewhat more complex. It involves Victor Chen, a young landed immigrant operating out of both Toronto and Vancouver, as well as Hong Kong. Unfortunately, we don't have a clear consensus on this case. We need a decision, one way or the other."

Callen suggested that Frank Legault, the director of control and intelligence, explain why he thought Chen should be invited to leave Canada through deportation or voluntary departure. Then Francine Côté from CSIS would explain why she and her colleagues believed Chen should stay.

Legault began. "On the surface, Victor Chen appears to be just another one of the several hundred thousand highly motivated Chinese immigrant entrepreneurs who've emigrated to Canada from Hong Kong in the past few years. He's in his mid-thirties, single and holds his Ontario real estate broker's license. He operates out of a storefront location on Dundas Street West in Toronto."

Apparently, however, Chen didn't spend much time there. Through the RCMP and the Metropolitan Toronto Police, Legault had learned that Chen was a member of the Kung Lok. A secret Chinese organization dating back eight centuries, its methods involved extortion, violence, bribery and intimidation. With principal cells in Hong Kong and Guangzhou, the organization had spread its net to new frontiers — San Francisco, Vancouver and Toronto. Legault paused to let this information sink in.

Baldwin looked around the room but everyone was watching Legault, except Francine Côté who was looking down at her notes. Legault continued.

"As a landed immigrant with a real estate broker's license, Chen began to travel more and more throughout southeast Asia in search of investors anxious to tap into the Ontario residential market, which was believed to be underpriced by world standards. But the RCMP drug squad has advised us that Chen, under Kung Lok influence, would also act as a drug courier, supplying heroin at wholesale to mainstream distributors in Vancouver, Toronto and occasionally New York."

Kirke began to shuffle his papers. Legault frowned at him and continued his briefing. "It appears that Chen was tied in with one of the drug kingpins in New York, a person identified by the DEA as Gus Bertolini, whose tentacles reach into Europe and South America, as well as northward to Montreal, Toronto and Vancouver." He turned to face Baldwin.

"During Chen's last extended trip to Hong Kong, the RCMP and enforcement people cooked up a little scheme.

As you know, Minister, if a landed immigrant is outside Canada for longer than six months without a returning resident permit, immigration status is lost unless he can prove he didn't intend to abandon Canada as his place of permanent residence."

"Yes, I'm quite aware of that rule, Mr. Legault." Baldwin remarked, with a hint of sarcasm.

Legault went on, unperturbed. "Chen was returning to Canada after an absence of over eight months, so he was detained at Pearson International Airport on a flight from Hong Kong via Los Angeles. He's now in immigration detention out at the Celebrity Inn on Airport Road and he's retained Manny Brown, the well-known immigration lawyer, in anticipation of an inquiry, which would likely start next week. Our choice, Minister — really your choice — is whether to proceed to inquiry, which could take several weeks of hearings with no guarantee of success, or simply fold our operation and let Chen back into the community to be dealt with by more traditional law enforcement means. The Mounties aren't sure they have enough hard evidence just yet to convict him of importing, trafficking or extortion — or anything for that matter."

"Well, that's a shame. Sounds like this criminal shouldn't be running loose," Tom said, as he shifted in his chair.

"We'd like to continue the inquiry and get him out. I am sure you're sympathetic to that, Minister, since I know both you and other members of the government have spoken out against the growing international drug trade and would want to shut down an operator like Chen — even though you couldn't take political credit for it in exactly those terms."

Legault then nodded towards Francine Côté in the corner who had finally raised her eyes from her notes. "Ms. Côté, I know, will have another view on this case," Legault added in a slightly patronizing tone.

Côté got up and joined the others at the table. "Well, gentlemen and Ms. Rodriguez, there *is* another perspective here, which relates to the security of Canada. The fact is that Chen, scoundrel that he is, provides undercover information on the Kung Lok. We've been able, through local police forces, to protect a number of lives and save millions of dollars thanks to advance warning. In short, Chen has been a valuable tool for neutralizing Kung Lok operations in Toronto and Vancouver. It would be a shame if he were lost," she said matter-of-factly, with the entire room hanging on her every word.

"However, as director general of counter intelligence at CSIS, I want to share something with you on a highly confidential basis. I trust everyone here has a top-secret security clearance," she said, looking around the room. Alan breathed a quiet sigh of relief. His clearance had come through from the PMO only a couple of weeks before Christmas.

Francine Côté lowered her voice. "In addition to his other activities, Victor Chen is a middle-level agent of the Chinese government, tasked to report on the political activities of Chinese students in Toronto and Vancouver. We discovered this about a year ago after one of his infrequent visits to the Chinese consulate on St. George Street in Toronto. One of our intelligence officers, a young Chinese, confronted him on this and, using background information from the RCMP and the Toronto police, was able to turn him to our benefit about six months ago."

Callen cleared his throat. "Yes, but how good is the information he's providing?"

"I can't say more, except that Chen is highly valuable as a double agent. We don't want him removed from the scene, at least not just yet," Côté concluded. She stared coldly at Baldwin. Kirke stopped fidgeting with his pencil. Then she continued in an unexpected direction.

"Far be it from me or anyone in my organization to give political advice, Minister. But consider the options: if you proceed against Chen, you risk losing after a very long and expensive hearing, which won't deal with his activities as a drug dealer. Instead, the inquiry will focus on the fact that he's stayed outside Canada more than six months — hardly a hot issue."

Baldwin reluctantly nodded.

"Even if you win, Canada loses because we'd no longer have Chen available to neutralize the Kung Lok or advise on Chinese intelligence activities. This is not a case in which you'll get a lot of political credit either way, Minister. So I hope you'll do what's right for the country." Côté sat down.

Legault was barely able to contain his anger. "Well, Minister, if we're talking about giving political advice, I don't need to remind you the public will be pretty upset if they perceive you've gone soft on a known drug dealer."

"That's enough, Frank," cautioned Callen, hoping to find some form of middle ground between Côté and Legault that would be a comfortable resting spot for the minister.

Alan had worried about this case when he read the briefing note: here were two powerful departments with opposing recommendations, both meritorious on the surface but in direct conflict with one another. His instinct was to recommend that Baldwin back up his departmental officials. Legault's argument of "no truck nor trade with drug dealers" struck him as sensible and cautious.

The CSIS position seemed a little too clandestine and conspiratorial to be real.

But Baldwin was obviously impressed by Côté's presentation. "What I see here is a no-win situation. If we proceed to inquiry and win, it may hurt Canada. If we don't proceed to inquiry and let Chen back into the community, I may help Canada but hurt myself politically and perhaps hurt some innocent people who use his horrible product. If it's a no-win situation, then I opt for the pro-Canada choice. CSIS is doing good work here and I think we've got to back them up," the minister concluded.

Baldwin was also thinking of those thousands of Chinese students in Toronto and Vancouver being spied on by a foreign government. This struck him as a severe restriction of the sorts of freedoms that Canadians prized. Chen the double agent could provide a valuable counterbalance.

Alan looked glum. He feared that with Chen's New York connection, he was running drugs big time. This case could come back to haunt Baldwin but there appeared to be no turning back now.

Côté was already packing her briefcase to head back to CSIS headquarters with the good news. The last sensitive case for the day had no security concerns so both Côté and Legault were able to leave. Baldwin leaned over to Alan and whispered, "Can you imagine the conversation those two will have in the elevator on the way down?" Alan nodded with a faint smile. He was wondering if the minister's decision would have been the same had the CSIS presentation not been made by an attractive and intelligent female.

"The last case today, Minister, is in your political backyard, both politically and professionally," Callen began. "I'll let Bill Kirke run you through it."

Kirke stood up, adjusted his tie, which had gone askew, and began to reel off the facts of yet another insoluble case that he knew would make the department look bad and the minister even worse.

"Rauinda Singh came to your home town, Regina, from New Delhi with her family as an assisted relative. She's only seventeen. Apparently, she's epileptic but this was never disclosed to our interviewing officer in New Delhi or discovered on her medical examination there. The sponsoring relative was her older brother, Shamsar Singh, who had emigrated to Canada from the Punjab. In 1983, he decided to bring his father and mother and teenage sister to Canada."

Baldwin began to recall the story he had seen on TV and read in the *Leader Post*. The leader of the Sikh community in Regina had labeled him as hardhearted for seeking to deport this young Sikh woman.

Bill Kirke explained that Rauinda Singh apparently suffered a seizure inside the arrivals area at the airport in Toronto after the family had passed through customs and immigration. Airport officials took the girl to the immigration waiting area where the airport duty doctor diagnosed the problem. After taking a brief history and learning of the epileptic condition, he administered a mild dose of phenobarb. Immigration officials immediately revoked her visa on the grounds of medical inadmissibility, but, on a compassionate basis, allowed her entry as a visitor for up to three months.

Three unique factors complicated the case. First, the family now claimed that Rauinda was not an epileptic and that the seizure at Pearson Airport did not take place. Second, the Singhs claimed that even if the young woman were medically inadmissible, she had no relatives back in

India and her only means of support was to stay with her family in Regina. According to Canadian officials in New Delhi, however, she had a close uncle who was a business-man there, with whom she had lived for two years. Third, she was now apparently engaged to her brother's business partner in Regina and he was quite prepared to marry her if that's what it took to keep her in Canada.

"Unfortunately," added Kirke, pulling at his tie again, "this case has caught the attention of a young reporter at *The Regina Leader Post*. There've already been two stories with photos showing a relatively healthy Rauinda Singh at the bedside of her elderly mother and father." Kirke closed his file and sat down, looking first to the minister and then to Alan.

Baldwin was in a quandary. "Are you suggesting that she and her family lied to immigration officials in New Delhi by suppressing her medical condition?" questioned Baldwin.

"Yes sir, that appears to be the case," answered Kirke. Callen nodded his confirmation.

"And are you satisfied with the authenticity of the med-ical report by the duty doctor?" questioned Baldwin fur-ther, sounding much more like a doctor than minister of immigration.

"Yes sir, our enforcement people met with the duty doctor and he's prepared an affidavit, with his report attached," Kirke replied dryly.

"And have our officers in New Delhi reaffirmed that there is in fact a close uncle able to receive her if she is returned there?"

"Yes sir. We have a complete dossier on him, including a statement that he and his wife would welcome Rauinda back."

Baldwin looked thoughtful. Alan's notes suggested that it would be politically dangerous to kick her out and that he should consider some basis for allowing her to stay, if for nothing else than to get the media off his back. Baldwin was uncomfortable with this recommendation. He had no tolerance for people who tried to cover up medical evidence or deny a legitimate diagnosis. Moreover, the contrived marriage was too much for him to stomach. Most folks in Regina would feel the same way.

Alan intervened, hoping for leniency. "Minister, like so many of these cases, you can't win here. But you can lose big time if you get on your high horse of righteous indignation and kick her out. Not only will the *Leader Post* fry you for lunch but they'll call in *Canadian Press* and the CBC. The media will love this one and you'll be denounced by every Sikh leader from St. John's to Victoria. May I suggest that you let Bill Kirke quietly advise the family that a minister's permit will be issued on humanitarian and compassionate grounds?"

Kirke supported this approach. He felt that if Rauinda managed to avoid the provincial healthcare system she'd get landed status in five years.

Baldwin nodded his assent. Alan had laid out his arguments in the briefing memorandum, and Kirke had fallen right into line.

Baldwin's power to decide had been effectively usurped. The transition was virtually complete. Alan Chant was now more or less running the department, and his primary task was to protect the government. Medical authenticity, deceit, contrived circumstances — none of these would be permitted to get in the way of making the politically appropriate decision. That's the way Savard had wanted it when he asked Alan to work for Baldwin.

Except for the Chen case, it had been a good day for Alan. And it was only ten in the morning. He had less than an hour to catch his train to Montreal.

Chapter Twenty-Four

Marcel Gagnon's file did not arrive at the State Department in Washington until Monday, January 14. Even then, it was incomplete. Although the DEA knew about Gagnon's source of supply in the south of France and the accomplice who helped transport the heroin from France to England, the United States justice department had somehow left out these important details.

However, the dossier was fairly complete in other ways. It described how Gagnon's girlfriend, one Antoinette Belair, had received a sizable downpayment in early February 1984, at Le Quatre Saisons in Montreal, how Gagnon had entered Canada with the China white, where he had lived and what he'd done for the rest of 1984. This file represented a major investment of time and resources — a full year's work by criminal intelligence experts from the United States, Canada, Great Britain and France using some of the most sophisticated surveillance equipment and techniques available anywhere.

The U.S. offense involved Marcel Gagnon's alleged participation in a conspiracy to possess, for purposes of distribution, 2.2 pounds of pure heroin in the State of New York. From past experience, State Department officials knew that, with extradition cases, Canadian defense counsel would usually argue the unfairness of the American penal and corrections systems. Sentences in the United States tended to be more severe and the conditions in the prisons there considerably worse than in Canada. To top things off, the U.S. Congress had recently enacted an anti-racketeering law that significantly broadened the range of offenses carrying stiff mandatory sentences.

Once the formal extradition request was complete in Washington, it was carried by diplomatic pouch to the American embassy in Ottawa where official copies were made. One was delivered to the court, another to local counsel retained by the United States justice department through the American consulate in Montreal. Yet another was sent to Gagnon's counsel, Guy Doucet. As a courtesy, additional copies were distributed to the federal ministers of justice and immigration and to the attorney general of Quebec.

The copy sent to the Canadian department of justice didn't reach the deputy minister, Miles Corbett, until late in the afternoon on Thursday, January 17. Appointed to his government post just before Christmas, Corbett was the former dean of law at Dalhousie University in Halifax. A rotund, paunchy little man with a ruddy complexion and a keen mind, already he had proven a valuable asset to his new minister, Joan Forrester, who was still making the transition from her downtown Toronto law office to Parliament Hill.

As a professor of criminal law, Corbett had enough sense to raise a red flag on the Gagnon file. He dashed off a detailed memorandum to Forrester indicating that she should be prepared to get into the nitty gritty and not let immigration take charge just because Gagnon may have been in Canada illegally. He warned that the RCMP would find it very convenient to cooperate with immigration and get him out quickly through deportation, if only to save costs and help out their friends in the DEA south of the border.

Forrester called him into her office within minutes of receiving Corbett's memorandum. "Miles, I'm just on my way to dinner with the minister of immigration, and I don't have time to read this tome of yours. Take me through it — I want to make sure I understand the issues before I see the minister. You can talk while I tidy up here," she said.

"Minister, I'll try to give you the highlights." This wasn't the first time Corbett had to discuss important issues while Forrester organized her desk. Once again he was impressed by her ability to concentrate on two things at the same time. "It's important to know that although the U.S. charges in the Gagnon extradition request closely parallel those in our criminal code, the American penalties tend to be much more severe. The minimum penalty for Gagnon would be ten years, with no eligibility for parole until after nine years. In Canada, the penalty would be in the range of ten to fifteen years, with leniency for a first offender, and parole might come after four years if he's well behaved. In fact, he could be out on day parole in a halfway house in two years."

"I see. What else?" Forrester put a fat folder into her already overstuffed briefcase.

"The U.S. system has another complication. Many judges and academics say the mandatory sentencing guidelines are an infringement on the traditional independence of the judiciary and might therefore be unconstitutional. The U.S. justice department has responded by invoking that anti-racketeering statute that was just enacted by Congress. This means that the penalty would be twenty years with no parole. I noticed a reference to this statute in the Gagnon extradition request."

"So the plot thickens, Miles. There really is a different standard that would apply." Forrester had finished tidying up her desk and crossed the room to the mirror. She began to fix her hair, pinning up a loose strand.

Miles, barely noticing, went on. "That's right, Minister. Seems particularly harsh, given that Gagnon appears to be a relatively minor player in the Bertolini scheme of things. I think he'll just be cannon fodder, in the hope that he might cooperate with the Americans in return for more lenient treatment."

"That's fair enough, isn't it?" Forrester said, touching up her eye shadow.

"Not really. Gagnon still could be jacked around, then blasted with those mandatory sentences," replied Corbett. He pursed his lips disapprovingly. "Not a nice business."

Forrester uncapped her lipstick. "I see. Now, Miles, what will our main difficulty be if the deportation order is stayed and we have extradition proceedings under our Act?"

"Defense counsel will probably argue that the anticipated U.S. presentation will be for an offense of a political character. They'll raise the 'cannon fodder' issue. Even if that fails in court, they can appeal to you on — let me read the words carefully — 'any ground that could be relevant to the minister in making a decision with respect to the possible surrender.'"

"What the hell does that mean?" Forrester turned, lipstick in hand, and looked at Corbett.

He shrugged. "Anything you want it to mean. You know how ingenious defense counsel can be. Don't forget, they can appeal if the court decision is negative. And if Gagnon is charged here in Canada for violating the Immigration Act because of the false passport, the extradition request can't be dealt with until the immigration infringement has been dealt with, by acquittal or expiration of sentence — unless you order otherwise."

Forrester reached for her overcoat. "It strikes me that we can apply justice Canadian-style better if we go through the extradition process, warts and all. If we allow deportation, we're just throwing Gagnon to the American wolves. That's not the Canadian way, is it, Miles?" She smiled.

"You're right, Minister. That's the conclusion I came to in my memorandum. You can look it over on your way to dinner." Corbett helped Forrester on with her coat.

"Many thanks, Miles. Good work. I'll deal with these immigration opportunists from the top. Baldwin can be turned around."

When the extradition request arrived on January 17, Guy Doucet was already well prepared. Madame Landry had surprised him and had done her research well. Guy figured that with any luck and a sympathetic minister of justice, his legal maneuvering could hold off Gagnon's extradition for at least three years. By then, both American and Canadian justice officials might tire of the fray.

In the meantime, he'd have to deal with the immigration adjudicator the following Monday by requesting an adjournment, usually a sure thing.

Miles Corbett had taken the precaution of sending a blind copy of his Forrester memorandum to his counterpart at immigration, Douglas Morrison. It had arrived on Morrison's desk on Friday afternoon, exactly two weeks after he had ordered an inquiry before an adjudicator, now scheduled for the following Monday. The inquiry was a week later than he'd wanted, but he could live with the delay. For one thing, it would appease Gagnon's counsel Guy Doucet, who had complained about undue haste.

Skimming the incredibly detailed memorandum from this Dalhousie academic, whom he despised as an outsider and intruder in his domain, Morrison simply smiled. If the immigration adjudicator did his job on Monday, Gagnon would be headed straight for the U.S. border in the company of the RCMP. He would have saved the Canadian taxpayers hundreds of thousands of dollars in legal costs and aggravation, not to mention the potential for political embarrassment to Forrester, Baldwin and the Savard government as a whole if extradition were allowed to proceed.

Miles Corbett didn't learn until the following Tuesday that an immigration adjudication had been held in Montreal the day before and that Gagnon had been ordered deported immediately. Gagnon's defense counsel, Guy Doucet, had argued before the adjudicator that it was an abuse of process to proceed with the hearing in view of the extradition request received through formal channels in

Washington and Ottawa. He had been unsuccessful.

"Surely," Doucet had argued, "my client is entitled to the procedural protection contained in the Extradition Act. The process contemplated by that act should not be usurped by an immigration inquiry ordered by the deputy minister and involving a summary procedure leading to a quick deportation."

The adjudicator, who was due for a promotion, had quietly received word that Morrison wanted this case to proceed expeditiously. Presumably the deputy knew what he was doing. So he denied Doucet's request for an adjournment and directed that the case begin immediately.

Doucet was also unsuccessful in attacking the grounds on which the deportation order was based. He had no evidence to rebut Marcel's admission to the Mounties in St-Jean-sur-Richelieu that he'd used someone else's passport when entering Canada the previous April. The deportation order was issued at the conclusion of the hearing, and Marcel was taken back into custody to await the next step.

Guy Doucet was left with two remedies, one legal and one political. He immediately applied for an injunction in the trial division of the federal court to prohibit the carrying out of the deportation order. Unfortunately, the earliest court date he could get for a hearing was Monday, January 28, almost a week away.

The other remedy involved calling his friend and former partner, Alan Chant, to ask the minister of immigration to rein in his zealous deputy and delay the implementation of the deportation order.

Early Tuesday morning, Guy tried desperately to reach

Alan in Ottawa. Unfortunately Alan was locked up with the minister and senior officials dealing with sensitive cases. Unknown to Guy, he would be in Montreal later that day to attend the sixtieth birthday party of his father Sam. Alan's mother Laura had organized a lavish party at the Queen Elizabeth Hotel. This party, in fact, was a convenient excuse for Alan. He wanted to spend some extra time with Susan, who seemed preoccupied. He suspected that she knew something about her sister's difficulties but wasn't quite sure what.

Alan was also secretly worried about both his safety and Susan's. He'd made the connection between Antoinette's problem and the money hidden in the closet at Peel Street. Now it seemed others might be on to him and were prepared to get to him through Susan. He was convinced that the attempt to run her down on Côte-des-Neiges was no accident.

Unable to crack the bureaucracy in Baldwin's office in Ottawa, Guy found himself finally being put through on the phone to Miles Corbett, Deputy Minister of Justice, late Tuesday afternoon. Guy's insistent reference to the formal U.S. request for extradition against his client Marcel Gagnon got him by Corbett's executive assistant and gatekeeper, an unusual occurrence.

Corbett wasted no time in getting straight to the point. "Mr. Doucet, I'm shocked to learn that an inquiry under the Immigration Act had been commenced and that the adjudication proceeded yesterday. Certainly no one in our office was aware of it. Nor would we have concurred in it. I'll brief Minister Forrester on this as soon as possible and get back to you."

"Thanks for your help, Mr. Corbett. I'm sorry I had to call you direct. I thought I could break through at immigration because Minister Baldwin's executive assistant is my former law partner. But I haven't been able to contact him. Obviously the immigration department has a head of steam up that's going to be difficult to dampen down. I would have thought that the procedures in the Extradition Act prevailed over those in the Immigration Act. That's the basis of my argument in the federal court on the injunction application I filed today. But I can't get a date for a hearing until next Monday."

Privately, Corbett was annoyed for not knowing that Gagnon's counsel was the former law partner of Baldwin's assistant. He should have included that in his briefing memorandum to Forrester. He wondered if Morrison and his gang knew. He kept his tone professional. "Well, Mr. Doucet, perhaps we can combine our efforts and our contacts to persuade ministers Forrester and Baldwin to have a chat and sort this one out. In my experience, there is little point in reasoning with the immigration bureaucracy — and that applies right up to the level of deputy minister."

Corbett's refreshing candor was not lost on Doucet. He decided that he should arrange for Alan Chant to speak to this guy as soon as possible.

"Goddamn it, Tom Baldwin, I want to see you immediately. Remember that potential problem I raised with you outside Henry Burger's last week — that your department, with the blessing of the RCMP, might use the summary procedures of the Immigration Act to usurp my powers under the Extradition Act?" The phone fairly crackled with Forrester's anger. "Well, they've gone and done it. And it's a goddamned travesty, a subversion of justice. I hope you're briefed on this one, Tom, because I'm going to raise royal hell. When can we meet?"

Across the river in Hull, Baldwin had already had a full day: more sensitive cases that morning, courtesy calls from three ambassadors prior to lunch, a difficult question period in the afternoon during which he'd been hammered by the opposition immigration critic on the Milanowski and Singh cases, followed by a cabinet committee meeting in which his proposal for a more open immigration policy had come under attack from his colleagues. He had a meeting with the deputy at seven following a brief supper of a couple of tired-looking sandwiches and an apple at his desk. He was looking forward to going back to the Park Lane, perhaps watching a movie and going to bed early. "Joan, I've not had a proper briefing on this yet. Alan Chant's away until tomorrow morning. Can it wait until then?"

"No fucking way. I'm coming over there to your office and I won't leave until we work this out. If that doesn't suit you, I'll go straight to Savard. You choose."

Baldwin sighed. "Listen, Joan, I'm meeting with the deputy at seven. Should be done with him by eight-thirty. Is that too late to meet at my office in Place du Portage?"

"I'll be there. No officials — and that goes for you, too. Understand? Your omnipotent Douglas Morrison, that asshole, seems to be the cause of the problem. You'd better get briefed between now and eight-thirty. And I wouldn't trust Morrison any farther than you can throw him. Bye." The phone clicked and went dead at the other end.

As it turned out, Morrison had a full agenda of other items and didn't even raise the Gagnon case at their seven o'clock meeting. Heeding Forrester's admonition, Baldwin didn't ask for Morrison's advice, and they finished at seven-twenty.

Forrester arrived late, closer to nine o'clock, long after Morrison and his driver had cleared the building. For the next hour, with just the two of them in Tom's grand office overlooking the Ottawa River, its mid-winter turbulence still visible under the lights from Parliament Hill, she lectured. Tom Baldwin got a seminal lesson on the meaning of the rule of law, procedural due process and the supremacy of the Extradition Act over the Immigration Act. And for good measure, she threw in some gratuitous advice concerning interdepartmental courtesies.

"The fundamental principle," she concluded, "is that any person present in Canada, whether a citizen, landed immigrant or just a visitor, is entitled to the protection of the Canadian Charter of Rights and Freedoms and Canadian criminal law and procedure. It's an extraordinary infringement on human liberty for an individual to be surrendered to a foreign state — particularly if that other state's sentencing laws are draconian. This should only happen when all the statutory requirements have been met — including the minister of justice independently determining that surrender is appropriate in the circumstances."

Tom stared out the window at the river. How could he argue with her? He was no lawyer. "Fine," he said at last. "I'll talk to Alan in the morning, and we'll get Morrison to stay the deportation order until the Extradition Act proceedings are completed or until any criminal charges against Gagnon up here are dealt with."

"Good." There was a hint of triumph in Forrester's smile. She picked up her coat.

Tom felt drained. "You know, Joan, I'm not sure I'm suited to this game, particularly this portfolio. Sometimes I wonder what the hell I'm doing here in Ottawa. There are a lot of strong, intelligent people here with a powerful message, particularly the professional women." He put his scarf on, then paused. "You're not the only one, you know. Francine Côté, the director of counter intelligence at CSIS, sold me a bill of goods on another drug dealer, this one from the Orient. He's running loose here and abroad because of the special services he provides to CSIS. The DEA want to jump all over me on that one."

"Well, Tom, that's the way it goes." Joan smiled as she buttoned her coat and adjusted the collar. "These are tough times requiring tough decisions. But was it any different back at the hospital in Regina when you'd pick up your scalpel and start a complicated operation?"

"Lots of difference. There, the choices were clear — at least for me. Here, they're murky. Also, I get the feeling that some decisions I make in Ottawa are two-edged — helpful to some parts of the community and harmful to others. To me, understanding and pursuing legal principles is a bit like trying to nail jelly to the wall. There are never any clear answers, no one course of action that's right and beyond dispute." He shrugged on his heavy overcoat and picked up his briefcase.

"It's not that complicated, Tom. You remember what I said when we found out we were both going into Savard's cabinet? Whatever the decision, whatever the field — try to be fair. Follow your gut instinct and you'll survive." She smoothed back a stray wisp of hair. "Now, let's go home." As she pulled on her gloves, she gave Tom a faint peck on the cheek. "You're lucky to have Carolyn. All I've got are four walls at the Chateau Laurier and those jelly-like legal principles."

"Yes, I suppose I am lucky." Tom smiled wryly, remembering the heated discussions he'd had with his wife over his new job.

Joan moved towards the door, then turned back to Tom as though she'd just remembered something. "Oh — I sent my driver home. Can I hitch a ride back across the river?"

For a moment, she seemed oddly vulnerable. Baldwin called down for Denis Forget to bring the ministerial car up from the basement to the front door. "No problem, we'll drop you off at the Chateau, Joan. Matter of fact, why don't we have a drink together in that little lounge across from the Adam Room while we're at it? I'll send Denis home and walk back to the Park Lane. Could use the exercise."

In the dimly lit lounge at the Chateau, the flickering candle wafted lazy shadows across Joan's face. She looked radiant and powerful. Tom sipped his scotch.

"Do you really enjoy this, Joan? All this controversy, the cut and thrust, the give and take that goes on around here — do you actually find it enjoyable? I've had a terrible day — my department, visiting diplomats, question period, cabinet colleagues — everyone wanting to give me hell!"

"It goes with the turf, Tom. You can't let it get to you. For me, it's not much different than a tough day in court. I actually find it quite stimulating." Joan leaned back and quaffed down the remaining heel of Cutty Sark and soda in her glass. "It's the power thing, probably. Almost like an aphrodisiac. But then, I've got a few years on you. You'll cotton on to it over time," she said, with a wink and knowing smile.

"Guess I have a lot to learn. Good thing I've got a capable teacher." Tom returned her smile. He felt totally comfortable and secure in the company of this attractive older woman. Before going to Ottawa, he'd heard from friends that the relationships and friendships spawned by politics were powerful and bonding. He hadn't for a moment thought that bond might be with an older person of the opposite sex.

"Well, come on," Joan admonished him playfully, "let's stop being wistful. It's late. Walk me up the stairs to my room on the second floor. It wouldn't look good to see two ministers of the Crown going up the elevator together this time of night."

When they reached her room, Joan slowly unlocked the door and turned to face Tom. "You know, we need each other, more than you think," she said in a low voice, gazing intently into his eyes. "You're welcome to stay and talk for a while, if you want." She put one long graceful arm about his shoulders and slowly moved towards him.

Tom couldn't move. Instinctively his arms went around her waist. Their kiss lasted a full twenty seconds before Tom realized that her tongue was moving too fast and her hips too actively to leave any doubt as to the meaning of her invitation. He quickly drew back.

"Joan, I can't. Please try and understand. I find you very attractive. But I owe too much to Carolyn. And this would be very complicated. It's not what I came to Ottawa for."

There was a long, pregnant pause. Forrester slowly exhaled. "As I said earlier, Tom, it's your choice. You'll have to live with it." Her voice hardened as she backed away, her warm smile becoming icy. Tom could feel a barrier rising between them. He was not sure their friendship would ever be the same again.

"Joan, please—I—"

"Good night, Tom. Thanks for the ride home and the drink. And stay on top of that extradition case. We'll be gunning for you if your department tries to deport that guy before he's had his day in court." Joan wheeled about, leaving Tom speechless. She walked quickly into her room and, without looking back, closed the door firmly behind her.

As he left the Chateau and headed past the National Arts Centre towards the Park Lane, Tom felt the damp January chill that only Ottawa, one of the most northerly national capitals in the world, could deliver. There were colder nights in Regina, to be sure — it was only −28° Celsius — but none quite as biting. He'd call Carolyn to see how she was doing as soon as he got to the Park Lane. It would be only ten o'clock in Regina.

There was no answer at the Baldwin house. He wondered what Carolyn was up to that evening. He felt a pang of guilt. Whatever she was doing, it surely didn't involve embracing some other man. Tom poured himself a beer, turned on the TV and slumped into the easy chair. It was four o'clock before he fell asleep.

Chapter Twenty-Five

S ince the election, weeknights together in Montreal had been a rarity for Alan and Susan. Except for the Christmas season, their life together had been mostly a weekend routine — usually a party at a friend's on Saturday night, maybe a movie, sometimes dinner for two at Susan's or a special bistro like L'Express. Inevitably, they would drift home hand in hand, glad to be close when one week ended and the other was about to begin.

Susan was happiest at night when he slept, after they had made love. She would nestle her head in the warm crevice of his shoulder, listening to his heart. All that energy, that passion, that striving to contain power, to be fair, to be in control. All that was at rest. And she was at peace with him.

On Sundays, they always tried to plan something special. After a full breakfast and *The New York Times*, they might go cross-country skiing on Mont-Royal or in the country up near St-Sauveur — Susan didn't enjoy downhill skiing, one of the few things Alan could fault her on. Sometimes they'd take in the art galleries on Sherbrooke Street or the Musée d'Art Contemporain on Ste-Catherine.

On one occasion, Susan had actually dragged Alan to a concert of chamber music, her true classical love, at Basilique Notre-Dame. He had gone along reluctantly and actually enjoyed it. Susan, meanwhile, mused that her father might have been pleased. This was only the second time she'd been in church since they had parted ways on the issue.

Sunday evenings they spent quietly at Susan's place — lasagna, maybe a pizza ordered in. She would work on her case files preparing for interviews or court appearances in the morning. He would become totally absorbed in reading confidential cabinet documents to prepare his minister for key meetings on the following days in Ottawa.

On the day of Sam's birthday in late January, Alan had arrived back in Montreal from Ottawa in the early afternoon. He'd gone straight to his parent's house to give Laura a hand with final arrangements for the surprise party at the Queen Elizabeth Hotel. Then he'd picked up Susan at her law office sharp at six and they'd driven down to the hotel. The party came off without a hitch. Sam was truly surprised and thoroughly enjoyed himself until three in the morning. Alan and Susan had begged off, citing work obligations early the next day.

Back in the living room of Susan's apartment, Alan was uptight and distracted. He tried to immerse himself in a background report prepared for the cabinet's economic development committee, which had met earlier that day. Meanwhile, in the dining nook, Susan had spread out some papers on the table.

She broke the silence first. "Alan, I might have to call you later this week for some advice."

He'd been half expecting that sort of request for some time. Until then, Susan had been remarkably circumspect in maintaining an arm's-length professional relationship and not putting him in a difficult position because of her personal access. In fact, the few times she had called him in Ottawa, it was usually to discuss immigration procedures in general terms. She never referred to the name of her client or the specific details of the case.

Alan would do his best to help her, also using general terms. They had both agreed, as a matter of professional ethics, that their relationship should be kept as quiet as possible. Her clients could draw the wrong impression if it became widely known that she was sleeping with the man running the immigration minister's office in Ottawa.

Even her dinner in Ottawa the previous week with Alan and the two cabinet ministers had remained a secret, and she resisted the temptation to "shop" this information with clients or friends.

"Alan," she said carefully, "this isn't a client. It's my crazy sister, Antoinette. She's got herself into a terrible jam. The RCMP have charged her for helping some big-time drug dealer get into the country using a phony passport. He's an older guy, Marcel Gagnon." She stood up and gripped the back of a chair tightly. "I negotiated a deal for her with the Mounties: her evidence — about the guy, his source of supply for the heroin, the financial details and their New York customer — in return for a guilty plea on a charge of aiding and abetting the use of a false passport. Plus an agreement to ask for a suspended sentence and two years' probation."

Alan tried to appear disinterested as he looked up from the couch. He could feel his stomach tighten. "How long have you known about this?" he asked.

"Since Christmas Eve. Antoinette came home after she'd just split with the guy. Seems that a few days earlier, he was picked up by the Mounties coming back into Quebec from upstate New York after making a drop in Plattsburgh. I've met with the Mounties three times, including this afternoon."

"Why didn't you tell me?"

"I don't know, it's been like a bad dream."

"Seems like you negotiated a pretty good deal. That's the sort of work I used to do on Rue St-Pierre." He tried to humor her.

"Alan, there are a few things you should know. First, the phony passport. It belonged to my father. Antoinette disappointed him for most of her life, and now this, even after the poor man's dead — all for a romp in the sack and a chance in the fast lane with this big shooter from the south of France. Would you believe it, she brought him into Canada posing as Roger Belair? Bitch!" In a sudden burst of anger, she pushed the chair into the table. Alan put his report down and came over to her.

"Second, you know what I think this ties into?" Susan was clearly agitated. "I've got this feeling it has something to do with the drug deal. Antoinette's been a little vague with me, but remember those two guys in the red Alfa Romeo who tried to run me down? The second time they shouted out at me: 'Next time, bitch, it'll be your fuckin' lawyer boyfriend!' I've just got this feeling in my bones that these guys know about Antoinette and her boyfriend and the drugs, and they're somehow involved."

"Susan, that's a bit of a stretch, don't you think?" He put his arms around her.

"Alan, I don't know. But I'm scared. And maybe you should be too." Her eyes were round with fear.

"You're right, my love." Alan kissed her and held her close.

Susan pulled away. "Let me tell you the third thing that really complicates matters. It's the reason why I met with the Mounties this afternoon. Since cutting the deal, Antoinette has had pangs of guilt at throwing her lover to the wolves to save her own skin. Against my advice, she's visited him several times in the holding cells downtown. This morning, she showed up at my office and broke down crying. Apparently Gagnon is about to be deported to the States after his immigration hearing yesterday. He's terrified he won't get a fair trial there and she's bought into that and desperately wants to help him."

"Will that affect the deal you negotiated for her?" Alan's inner turmoil was beginning to surface.

"It shouldn't. The changed circumstances aren't her doing. It's more of an emotional thing. I don't understand it, but I think she's still infatuated with the guy. Oh, and guess what else? Marcel told Antoinette to contact his legal aid lawyer, who turns out to be Guy Doucet."

"Did you speak to him?" Alan looked surprised.

"Yes, I called him this afternoon to find out what the hell's going on. Seems he'd been frantically trying to reach you in Ottawa for most of the morning."

"We were dealing with the sensitive cases. The rule is no interruptions unless it's an emergency."

"Well, he said he would ask you and Baldwin to stop the deportation so Gagnon's rights under the Extradition Act aren't compromised. Sounded pretty excited. You may want to think twice about talking to him. I didn't let on I knew where you were, or he would have been all over you then and there." Susan's voice suddenly took on a direct and deliberate tone. "But on behalf of my client, I'd like you to look into it first thing tomorrow when you get back to Ottawa."

Alan was not sure what terrified him the most — the prospect of Susan finding out about his one-night stand with Antoinette and the fact that he was holding Roger Belair's estate papers, which he now realized to his horror were the proceeds of an intended drug deal, or the realization that the mob was on to him and his life was in serious jeopardy. Sooner or later he was going to have to come clean with Susan. It was only a question of when.

"Antoinette's living with Maman on Carré St-Louis." Susan had calmed down. "She's under some kind of police protection, maybe for bigger trouble than I'd ever imagined possible. Maybe they're still collecting evidence. I hope to work things out for her in the next few weeks and I'll try not to lean on you any more than is necessary. Personally, I'd be just as glad if Gagnon was gone tomorrow. But hustling him out of Canada that way does seem a little extreme."

Alan and Susan clung to each other for an extra long time that night before falling asleep. But they didn't make love.

Chapter Twenty-Six

As Alan rushed into the minister's office following his arrival on the mid-morning train from Montreal, Baldwin was uncharacteristically blunt. "You picked a hell of a time to be away. There's less than two hours till question period so let's get into it." Alan looked puzzled.

"What's the problem, Minister? And how can I help?"

"Well, the opposition caucuses are probably all revved up today from their regular Wednesday morning meeting. I'm told by some of the guys in the press gallery that my number's up today — they want to hone in on some juicy immigration controversies. And there are a couple of things sticking in my craw."

"Like what, Minister?" Alan was beginning to think he should have taken the earlier train back that morning — or even the midnight plane the night before.

"Let's start with last night's crisis. Our omnipotent deputy is at it again. But this time he's got the justice department breathing down his neck. Forrester came over personally to see me last night and was here until nearly ten o'clock chewing my ass off. It seems our bright lights in immigration cooked up this scheme against a small-time foreign drug dealer who's been living in Montreal for the better part of the year."

Alan began to sweat. This sounded too close to home.

"They went to a quick and dirty inquiry and got a deportation order so they could toss him right into the hands of the DEA in the States — even though we, along with justice and the Quebec attorney general, had been served with a formal extradition request from the U.S. State Department. Our people ignored due process and the principles of fairness. In other words, Morrison ignored the Extradition Act. Forrester's mad as hell. We're afraid that the drug dealer's lawyer may go to the press." Tom tugged uneasily at his bow tie.

"Well, Minister, he's already been on the phone to me. We spoke briefly this morning when I was in Montreal. The lawyer's name is Guy Doucet. He's my former law partner. I think he's got a good point as a matter of legal principle. But I don't think the public will be too sympathetic to his client. The deputy may be doing you a favor." Alan had already chosen the easy way out even though it meant some compromising of his principles.

Tom still looked uncertain. "I told Forrester last night that I'd meet with you as soon as possible today and we'd try to get a handle on things. Told her you'd call her people once we decided what we're going to do."

"Have you got a briefing note from Morrison on this one?" Alan was curious to see how much they knew. Baldwin handed him the thin red file.

He skimmed Morrison's short briefing note. Sure enough, the name of Antoinette Belair, Marcel Gagnon's live-in girlfriend, appeared as the principal informant. So did the name of her lawyer, Susan Belair. There was no reference to anything from Forrester's deputy Miles Corbett, just Morrison's brief comment on Gagnon's overly generous rights under the Extradition Act.

Morrison had concluded that deportation was the quickest, cleanest and least expensive way of getting rid of this guy and that, if the matter became public, the Savard government and the minister of immigration would stand to benefit politically as a result of decisive action.

"I'm sorry I wasn't here the last twenty-four hours." Alan looked apologetic. "Last night was my father's sixtieth birthday party. You could have called me in Montreal — Martha can always reach me through my beeper. I'd have loved to have been there when Forrester came over. Did you two actually come to some agreement?"

"Well, I thought so. But now, I'm not sure. Did you say your former partner is representing this guy? Maybe we could enlist his cooperation."

Alan tried to hide his disbelief at Baldwin's naiveté. "I don't think that would be entirely ethical, or even smart, for that matter. If I were Guy Doucet, I'd simply demand that you, as minister, stay the execution of the deportation order so due process can run its course. This would buy Gagnon at least two, maybe three years in Canada and give Guy time to cut whatever deal he can with the Quebec prosecutors. That'd avoid the clutches of the DEA, the unfair procedures in the American courts and their mandatory sentencing guidelines. I'm sure that's what Forrester was suggesting, or at least her officials were."

Tom felt he was beginning to catch on. "Yes, exactly. So what's our counter-argument?"

"Well, you have to look at the politics of the situation. Here you've got a foreign drug dealer who comes into Canada with a false passport, intending to use Montreal as a base for supplying the Bertolini family in New York. He gets caught because of some fancy police work by the RCMP and the DEA, who've got enough evidence to throw the book at him in the state of New York." Alan paused. He realized that the line between his legal argument and his own self-interest was blurring. Gagnon had rights, but Alan had to admit that, for the sake of Susan and her sister, he'd like to see him deported.

Tom looked at Alan expectantly.

"Sorry." Alan smiled uncomfortably. "I got distracted. Anyhow, your deputy orders an inquiry, which he's entitled to by statute. The adjudicator rules that Gagnon came here with a false passport so he issues a deportation order. There's no claim to refugee status here. Immigration officials simply want to get him out to the first country willing to take him. France doesn't want him back but the Americans sure will take him. As a country, we owe Gagnon nothing. Let the American justice system do the dirty work."

"But that's what Forrester was complaining about. Alan, we can't be seen to be abandoning Canadians to the U.S. justice system, at least not without good reason."

"Minister, what do you think the voters of Regina East would say? If they knew all the facts, would they want you to support your deputy? Or would they want you to support Joan Forrester and her attempts to provide due process at taxpayer expense? Remember, he's not a Canadian. And he came here illegally."

"You're not making it very easy for me, Alan. If you'd been here last night and seen and heard the Forrester explosion, you might not be so glib about it today."

"Not a question of being glib, Minister. Forrester was just doing her job. She has the integrity of the Canadian justice system to uphold. But you have your job to do as well — to maintain the integrity of the Immigration Act."

"Are you saying I have no discretion in the matter, that

I must support Morrison and the adjudicator?"

"No, I'm not saying that. You have very broad discretion — on compassionate and humanitarian grounds. That's in the statute. And you have discretion based on higher legal principles of fairness that transcend the Immigration Act. Remember the Charter of Rights and Freedoms."

Tom remembered it very well. It had been less than three years since he'd watched the television ceremony during which the Queen and the prime minister had signed the Charter into law. "Wouldn't the Charter's provisions take precedence over other statutes?" he asked, brow furrowed.

"Not necessarily — it's complicated. At any rate, you also have an obligation to protect Canadians from foreigners who enter this country illegally to engage in criminal activity. You can go either way on this one, Minister."

Tom look dismayed. "Can I have a little more time?"

"Sure. Think about it overnight. It's a big decision. What's fair — to the Canadian people, to the legal system and to Gagnon? This is the kind of case where law, politics and morality intersect. The smart thing politically, Dr. Baldwin, would be to back your deputy, and take your lumps from Forrester."

"Alan, I thought we were going to use first names with each other."

"Sorry. Got carried away, Tom."

Tom leaned forward. "I have to ask, though — how can you be truly objective about this case? I couldn't help but notice in Morrison's briefing note that it's your friend Susan Belair who's counsel to the informant — her own sister — against Gagnon. How do you think the voters of Regina East would react if they knew this little tidbit?

Wouldn't they question my objectivity if they knew I was relying solely on you for advice in this matter?"

"Well, I suppose—"

"And while we're at it, Alan, let me tell you about a disturbing conversation I had with the PM this morning, who pulled me aside after caucus. He wondered why we're not running a tighter ship in the immigration minister's office and why there are so many leaks of information that seem to be damaging to our friends."

Alan began to feel sick.

'Surprisingly, he mentioned his good friend Senator Semeniuk, who continues to be attacked regarding the Winnipeg airport contract by Fred Milanowski. And he said he'd had an angry call from his Toronto fundraiser Henry Street. He didn't mind that we let Street's nanny stay but he didn't like the way the press made him look like the villain and me like the compassionate hero."

Alan's expression remained calm, but he nervously twisted his pen in his fingers. "It's unusual for the PM to get into this kind of detail regarding individual cases. He must have been really pissed off. Did he mention my name?"

"Matter of fact, he did. He wondered why I was having all this trouble keeping a lid on things when I had you to run the shop — someone he had trained personally and then handpicked for the job. Alan, I'll be straight with you. I told him you're in charge of case flow. He seemed comforted by that but asked me to speak to you anyway. I know you've been doing some quiet leaking. You told me as much regarding Firestone and that Cuban spy ring."

"I'll try to be more careful." Inwardly, Alan winced. He knew the rule around the Hill: leak to your heart's content, just don't get caught. "But these cases are never easy

— always at least two sides to them. Gagnon's a classic example. Let's come back at that one in a day or two. Tell Morrison you want to think about it over the weekend and to delay the deportation till Monday." Alan was undeterred by Baldwin's allegation of conflict.

"Forrester may not let me wait that long. I'm seeing her in cabinet tomorrow morning at ten."

Chapter Twenty-Seven

Alan and Susan decided to have a quiet dinner at her apartment the night he got back from Ottawa, the last Friday in January. For Alan, it had been a short but difficult week after the break to attend his father's birthday party. For Susan, Antoinette's situation continued to worry, particularly her sister's erratic behavior.

Alan was concerned. His boss was having an increasingly difficult time. While Alan could take care of scheduling briefings, dealing with visiting delegations and clearing time to consider sensitive cases, he had been unable to do anything about Tom's lackluster performance in the House during question period. The new minister's inexperience and insecurity showed — he read most of the answers from his cue cards. Moreover, he lacked spontaneity and humor and failed to counterattack.

That week, the opposition had brought up the Millicent Wright case. The critic for immigration, demanding to know why this illegal immigrant was allowed to stay when others were deported, made much of the Henry Street connection. Tom fumbled his response and blurted out some vague statement about humanitarian and compassionate grounds, which elicited groans from the House.

"You mean compassion for Henry Street?" the immigration critic shot back. His opposition colleagues clapped and hooted. Tom could only stammer out a lame denial.

He looked equally shaky on Thursday when the opposition raised the Chen case. The RCMP, who were still smarting over losing out to CSIS, obviously planted the question. All a surprised Tom could do was plead "national security" in so many words and sit down, an abrupt and peremptory approach that pleased no one.

Not that Tom was going to get the Savard government into real trouble. But he looked more and more like a fish out of water. For Alan, his boss's dithering over the Gagnon case was just going to make matters worse. Tom still hadn't made up his mind by the time he headed for his constituency in Regina on the Friday afternoon plane out of Ottawa.

For Susan, the week had also gone downhill after Alan's rare midweek visit and the fun of Sam Chant's birthday celebrations. Her office was inundated with Haitian refugees. All deserving cases, they had no money for legal fees and Legal Aid was becoming increasingly tough about granting certificates. Her income for this month would barely cover office rent, telephone and secretarial expense, with nothing left over for food and apartment rent.

Then there was the biggest non-billable file of all — her sister. Antoinette continued to call the office, worried about a possible visit from the Bertolinis after what Marcel might have told them, and uncertain that the deal struck with the RCMP would actually keep her out of jail. For some reason, Antoinette kept asking Susan about her relationship with Alan Chant. Perhaps she thought Alan's political connections might help her if the RCMP deal didn't work out.

"It's so good to be back," Alan said, bursting through the door at Côte-des-Neiges. "Wish the hell I'd never gone up to Ottawa this week. My weak-kneed minister is beginning to get to me. How about your week?"

"Not much better. The refugees just keep coming in waves and I can't afford them all. And my sister's beginning to drive me nuts."

Susan was in the kitchen already preparing dinner. She had stopped on her way home to pick up fresh salmon, some St. Antoine's paté and, for a salad, a Boston bib lettuce, sweet peppers and pine nuts. Before leaving Ottawa, Alan had grabbed a bottle of Pouilly-Fuissé from the liquor cabinet in the minister's inner office. It had been left there by Baldwin's predecessor and remained untouched since the government had changed.

"Thought I should clear out some of these old staples from Baldwin's office before they turned bad," Alan said with a wink. He placed the wine in its temporary resting spot in Susan's refrigerator, then grabbed a knife. "Here, let me help."

"Alan, remember our first lunch together at Les Filles du Roi last June? You had rabbit and I had fish. You tried so hard to impress me by ordering *'pour madame la brandade de morue aux raves, avec une salade verte.'* You were so refreshingly idealistic then. Now, after just seven months, it seems you've had half a lifetime of experiences. Still got those ideals that turned me on?" She headed for the dining nook, carrying the salad bowl.

Alan followed. "As I recall, you were looking for symbols — the tortoise and the hare, and so on. Best I could do was observe that you swim fast, I run fast, either way we get where we want in a hurry." Her question about his ideals had made him uneasy. He wanted to avoid a direct answer. "Also, I seem to remember something about us not being in competition with each other, maybe doing a lot of things together. That was my dream then. Now, I'm beginning to believe it."

For an extraordinarily long moment that cold January Friday night on Côte-des-Neiges in Montreal, they clung to each other. The frustrations of the week melted away.

Later, after they'd enjoyed the paté and salad, Alan proudly served the fresh poached salmon on a bed of saffron rice with his homemade hollandaise sauce. The conversation remained light. When they'd finished eating, Susan cleared the table leaving their wineglasses. She refilled Alan's glass.

"Alan, let me tell you more about the deal I've been able to negotiate for my crazy sister. Promise you'll keep this to yourself. It could jeopardize her deal and embarrass me if this one got out and around the community, let alone circulated in official circles in Ottawa." Susan saw Alan's quizzical look. "Don't worry," she added quickly, "it probably doesn't affect your department, at least directly, so I won't have to call on you." She took a sip of wine.

"You already know about Gagnon and the passport, and the attempted drop in Plattsburgh. Anyway, Antoinette told me for the first time this morning about the advance payment they received almost a year ago. Since there'd been a foul-up on the delivery, she's concerned that the Bertolinis'll try to recover it. I don't think Gagnon's a problem since he's still in jail downtown. As I told you the other night, she still goes to visit him — against my advice. By the way, is that deportation going ahead?"

"Talked briefly to Guy on Wednesday afternoon. Nothing's going to happen until Monday. After that, I can't predict. Forrester and Baldwin are in a real cockup over that one."

Susan looked thoughtful. "Well, that does affect Antoinette's case, at least indirectly. I'm trying to get the Crown to agree to a date when we can go before a judge. Then I'll enter a guilty plea and get that suspended sentence I negotiated with the RCMP. But they're both dragging their feet till they see where Gagnon will be brought to court first — here or the States."

"I can't help you on that one. It's in Baldwin's hands." Alan poured the last of the wine into their glasses.

"But Alan, I thought you were running the show there! The deportation order's been issued — what's the problem?"

"Well, Forrester's got a point too — about due process under the Extradition Act and all that."

"But he's a drug dealer!" Susan leapt up angrily from the table.

"Look, I know you're worried about Antoinette—" Alan's tone was sympathetic but Susan interrupted.

"Damn right!" She took a deep breath and sat down again. "Okay, I'll admit I'm biased here, but Marcel Gagnon's removal would be one less problem. I want to get her court deal done, get her out of Montreal, maybe send her to Whistler to work at one of the ski resorts or something. She's out of her mind with fear. Most of all, she's scared because of the money, the advance payment — she won't even tell me where it is or how much there is. Just tells me that Marcel and the Bertolinis know and will stop at nothing to get it back."

Sleep did not come easily to either Alan or Susan that evening. At four in the morning, Alan couldn't take it any longer.

"Susan, about the advance money . . ."

Susan rolled over sleepily. "What about it?"

"Haven't the Mounties been pushing Antoinette about where it's hidden?"

"No, not really. I think they're using it as bait — to keep Antoinette in line, and also just in case one of the Bertolinis shows up." She yawned. "I'm sure Maman's house is wired to the hilt. Antoinette can't take three steps outside without being followed."

"Do you still have any leverage left with the Mounties regarding your plea bargain deal for Antoinette?"

"Probably, yes. What do you have in mind?"

"I have this sneaking suspicion where that money might be, or at least where there are clues as to its location," he replied, sheepishly.

Susan propped herself up on her elbows and stared at him.

"How would you know? Is this something to do with your buddy Guy Doucet?"

"No, not at all. It's something Antoinette told me — long before you and I had lunch last June. Guess I'd better come clean with you, Susan. I was one of those guys at Tremblant that Antoinette was referring to. Only once, mind you. But I'm afraid that's on the record. I gave her a ride back to the city the next day."

Susan sat bolt upright. "What? You mean you slept with my sister?"

Alan sat up too. "I'm sorry you had to find out this way. We talked briefly about your father on the way down. She seemed pretty mixed up at the time. Even wanted me to do some legal work in connection with his estate. I told her I couldn't."

"You bastard! My own sister — and you didn't have the guts to tell me!"

"I'm sorry, Susan." He reached out to touch her but she

pulled away. "The problem is that Antoinette gave me important information on the ride down from the Laurentians that I can't even tell you about. She made me promise. And I agreed as a lawyer."

"I think you'd better leave, Alan. I'm not sure I want to see you again." Susan was close to tears, held back only by the anger welling up inside her.

"Susan, I know you're mad. But just listen for a moment. When I asked whether you have any leverage left with the RCMP on Antoinette's deal, I wasn't fooling around. Ask them to give you their surveillance records on all her movements during 1984 to see if you can help them figure out where the money might be."

"Why should I believe anything that you tell me now?" She blinked hard.

"I know they had her under surveillance as early as last February when she was going up weekends to Tremblant. They obviously kept records on her because her name came up in my security clearance interview with CSIS last November. I'm sure I only got the job because I didn't try to deny knowing her. I was surprised at the amount of detail they seemed to have." Alan rambled on desperately. Although part of him sensed it was futile, he hoped somehow to win Susan back. But she had stopped listening.

"Get out. Now." Her anger finally erupted.

Alan began to dress hastily. "Susan, listen—"

"I don't want to hear it!" She stormed out of the bedroom. Alan grabbed his overcoat and left. She slammed the door behind him.

It was still two hours to daybreak, and the temperature outside was so low the engine of the black BMW barely turned over. As Alan headed out of the parking lot onto Côte-des-Neiges, the red Alfa Romeo was not far behind.

Chapter Twenty-Eight

E arly that Saturday, there wasn't much doubt where Alan was headed. Normally he would have let his car engine run for a minute or two before taking off on such an icy morning. But with an angry Susan probably peering out the window and with a sick feeling in his stomach, he felt the need to get away quickly. He gunned the engine mercilessly before heading down Côte-des-Neiges and across Docteur-Penfield to Peel.

Damn Antoinette Belair, he thought, angry at himself for not having dealt with her sooner. If he had pushed her to make up her mind, he wouldn't be caught up in this web now.

It was bad enough trying to deal with the growing rift between the justice and immigration departments caused by the Marcel Gagnon case. But now he was personally implicated. The PMO would want an explanation. Baldwin would freak out. And Susan was probably beyond the pale.

He parked in a no-parking zone at the curb on Peel Street just north of his apartment. On this January weekend before sunrise, the university hadn't really begun to stir and there was little traffic.

Less than halfway down the block, Luigi Leonardo was sitting in his car. Ever since the Saturday before Christmas, he and Bruno had taken turns each weekend watching the comings and goings at the Peel Street pied-à-terre and Susan Belair's apartment. They'd watch from six o'clock on Friday night through till Monday morning when Alan would leave to catch the six-fifteen train to Ottawa. They knew sooner or later they were going to have to break in at Peel Street. In the meantime they wanted to make sure that Alan didn't trot out the door with all Bertolini's money.

Alan was too distracted to notice the red Alfa Romeo parked down the street. It may have been the darkness. It may also have been the fact that highly trained professionals like Alan often miss the signs and signals around them they'd be quick to recognize when watching out for others.

Within seconds of getting inside, Alan dug out Antoinette's attaché case and opened it. Even though he'd broken open the lock a few weeks earlier, the sight of one and a half million dollars in denominations of thousand-dollar bills took his breath away.

"How could I be so goddamned stupid to get sucked in by that little bitch?" he said aloud.

Alan looked for a letter of instruction, a handwritten note, anything that would provide more information about the money. But there was nothing except the small white envelope, grown slightly yellow, with the instructions "Deliver to Father Phillipe Péloquin one year following my death" and Roger Belair's signature in shaky handwriting.

What would he have done if he'd opened the attaché case the day he'd returned from Tremblant? Or in his office back at Rue St. Pierre? Or when he first moved these files to Peel Street? Should he have contacted police when he finally saw the contents?

These were all hypothetical questions now. He had chosen to fall into Antoinette's trap — he'd held onto the attaché case and done nothing. Why him? Had she targeted him because he was a young, single lawyer? Because she had been to bed with him? Because he was headed to Ottawa to work for Savard, the next prime minister? He didn't think Antoinette was that clever — unless she was directed by others.

What should he do now? What was his professional duty? Should he go to the police and turn over the money? Should he seek out Father Péloquin and give him the small white envelope? Maybe the simplest thing would be to go right over to Huguette Belair's on Carré St-Louis and hand the whole thing back to Antoinette. But that would immediately tip off the RCMP watchers who'd want an immediate explanation. It might jeopardize her deal.

Should he deliver the package to Susan? She was Antoinette's lawyer, even though it was apparent that her "client" had chosen not to tell her about it. Besides, he had a sinking feeling that Susan wouldn't want to talk to him.

Should he tell Guy, even though Antoinette said she'd broken off with Marcel, according to Susan? No, he concluded quickly, he had no professional duty to Gagnon and should really keep his distance from Guy, given his representations to the department on the deportation order.

Maybe he should consult a trusted third party who didn't know Susan or Antoinette. Should he get his own counsel? Perhaps it might be more prudent if he quietly sought advice from the *bâtonnier* of the Montreal bar or from the Barreau du Québec.

One thing was for sure. The PMO and Baldwin would

come down on him hard if this got out. If this wasn't handled correctly, he'd be blown out of Ottawa before he even had time to pack up his briefcase.

The events of the week flashed quickly across Alan's mind. Sam's smiling face as he cut the cake at his sixtieth birthday party. The warm and understanding face of his mother, Laura, who'd arranged it all. The troubled face of Baldwin, still smarting at the battering received from Joan Forrester the previous evening. Susan's determined face as she spoke confidently of defending her sister, and then later as she reacted angrily to the revelation of his prior involvement with Antoinette.

Strangely enough, the one face that provided the most guidance to Alan in this time of greatest need was his mother's. What would she advise if she were standing here trying to help him?

It had been a particularly tough day at Selwyn House. Alan was well into his final year of school and he'd had trouble juggling his heavy academic demands with his responsibilities as a prefect.

There'd been one particularly severe case of bullying that troubled him. One of the more aggressive younger students had injured a frail, bookish new boy, a recent immigrant from Europe. Alan knew that some form of punishment was required but agonized over what was appropriate.

He'd never forget his mother's advice at the end of that day: "Alan, sometimes the most difficult problems are easier to solve if you sleep on them overnight. Your mind clears up a little, your better instincts rise to the surface and the issues somehow come into perspective."

Alan remembered that lesson and began to master the art of the "delayed and measured response." Throughout school, his summer jobs at university and starting a law practice, this advice had served him well.

Alan carefully bundled the American bills and the envelope addressed to Father Péloquin back into the brown manila envelope marked "Belair Estate Papers" and stuffed it into the attaché case. He reckoned that nothing would occur in the next day and a half that would alter his ability to choose the right course. On Monday morning he would take decisive action.

Luigi Leonardo craned his neck in an effort to observe all movements in and out of the pied-à-terre while Alan was inside. Thirty minutes later, Luigi was surprised to see Alan emerge empty handed — no files, no boxes, no briefcases. And he was wearing the same leather jacket that he'd had on when he entered.

"Maybe he's just checkin' out some information or consultin' some file," Luigi whispered into his car phone to his brother, Bruno, who was back at the store at St-Denis and Rigaud.

"For chrissakes, you dummy, we can't put up wit' this anymore. He coulda taken all the dough. Did you follow him?"

"Nah, didn't wanna give up watching the front door. You never know who he might give the key to. You were the one who told me I woulda seen a big bulge in his jacket if he'd taken the money with him. Your words — 'it's a million and a half, asshole.'"

"Luigi, we're almost at the end of the line. Bertolini'll be pissed off. He needs an answer by Monday. Can't wait no longer. We're gonna have to go in soon or the lawyer or the girl'll grab the dough and run. Get back to the store soon as you can. We gotta talk."

Alan tried to call Susan that afternoon, to offer an olive branch in the form of a quiet dinner at the St. Amable. Really he just wanted a chance to talk. There was no answer all afternoon and evening, right through to midnight when Alan finally gave up.

Susan had kept her date for her usual squash game at the MAAA, then surprised herself by asking her partner, a young, eligible stockbroker, out for an early dinner that night. They enjoyed a fine meal in the Café de Paris at the Ritz Carleton and he picked up the tab over her protests. She excused herself at ten o'clock to catch a taxi to mother's where she'd arranged to stay overnight so she could finish some business with Antoinette. Also, she didn't want to be at her apartment when Alan called.

Chapter Twenty-Nine

"Maman, I think I'll go to evening mass tomorrow at Notre-Dame. It's been almost five weeks since I began hiding out here. I was just thinking it'll be a year to the day tomorrow that Papa passed away."

Huguette knew full well that the next day, Sunday, was the first anniversary of her husband's death, and she dreaded the prospect. She was surprised that Antoinette had remembered and that she'd again want to take refuge in the church during this painful time.

"Antoinette, your father would be so happy to know you're going to mass, but the police said you should stay inside. So did Suzanne."

"Maman, I'll be fine."

Huguette frowned anxiously. "You must be very careful, *ma petite.*"

Antoinette gave her mother a quick hug. "Stop worrying."

Huguette sighed. She knew she could not change her stubborn daughter's mind. "By the way," she said, "Suzanne called this afternoon when you were sleeping. I told her to call back later. She'll probably stay here tonight. Seems she and her boyfriend had a bit of a fight. She sounded a little concerned — said she had some important information for you about Marcel Gagnon." Huguette was secretly happy that both her daughters would be with her at home on the eve of this most difficult anniversary.

Antoinette's heart skipped a beat at the mention of Marcel's name. Despite her decision to trade her evidence against him for her own plea bargain, she still felt a lingering affection for him, remembering fondly their relatively tranquil eight months playing house on Terrace St-Denis. As well as being her lover, Marcel had become a father figure. He'd provided kindness and emotional security, and he understood her inner need to love and be loved.

Only after he became preoccupied with the drug deal with Gus Bertolini did their relationship begin to sour.

Still, she missed him — his warm smile, his sense of humor, the expressive right eyebrow that arched sharply whenever he was excited or amused. Poor Marcel. She had gone down to the holding cells on two occasions but their every word had been closely monitored. They did not discuss the money deposited with Alan Chant. Marcel didn't tell Antoinette that the Leonardo brothers had been regular visitors and, after agreeing to cut him in, knew virtually everything Marcel knew about the money. They had negotiated their deal on small scraps of paper, so as to avoid detection through monitoring.

The RCMP had indeed warned Antoinette not to go out. They feared that the Bertolinis or their men would abduct her and force her to retrieve the money or even kill her so she couldn't give evidence against Marcel Gagnon.

Susan arrived by taxi at ten-thirty that night. Huguette kissed her warmly. But she had the good sense, or perhaps motherly instinct, to retire early for the night and leave her two daughters alone at the kitchen table.

"So what was it that you gave to Alan Chant on the drive down from Tremblant last February after you screwed him? Come clean with me, Antoinette, or I'm going to bail out. You'll be on your own." Susan was unforgiving.

Momentarily stunned, Antoinette searched for an answer. Nothing came out. She closed her eyes, furrowed her brow, bit her lip — then suddenly collapsed into an incoherent heap. A torrent of tears began to stream down her face. She lay her head on the table, just as she used to as a small girl after her father would punish her. Convulsive sobs wrenched her entire body so intensely that Susan began to wonder whether she was seriously ill. Finally Antoinette began to talk, choking out words between sobs.

"You know what I gave Alan to look after? Guess it's time you knew . . . There was something . . . evil going on in this house all those years when you were the golden girl — CEGEP, Manoir Richelieu that summer, McGill Law School, your job in Toronto — and Marc, the charming, holy prince away at school. And I — I was the bad girl, the slow learner, left at home. For him, for Papa, *le salaud!*" She began to cry harder. Susan gasped, the horror of Antoinette's story beginning to dawn on her. Her eyes were frozen on her sister's face. Antoinette took a deep breath and found her voice again.

"You know how old I was when he first came into the bedroom and put his hand under my nightie, first my breasts, then between my legs? I was twelve! You'd just left for Toronto for the summer, Maman was at church and Marc was away at Brébeuf. That was the beginning of almost weekly visits. . . . He forced me to do things —

you can't imagine."

Susan took her hand across the table. "Antoinette, I'm so sorry . . ."

"I was trapped. I complained once or twice to Maman but she accused me of making it all up. She was afraid of Papa, Susan. He hit her several times. I remember one time — they had an argument about changing your name from Suzanne to Susan. He bruised her quite badly when she objected to his little campaign to turn you into an Anglo."

"Antoinette, this is horrible." Susan felt unsteady, as though the world had turned over.

"When Papa was dying a year ago, I came home — not to comfort him. I wanted to confront him. I wanted him to apologize — to actually hear him say he was sorry for what he did to me. Five days before he died, he scribbled out a total confession, let me read it, then put it in an envelope for Father Péloquin at Notre-Dame, to be delivered a year following his death."

Susan tried to focus. "Antoinette," she said gently, "I'm so glad you got your apology. But what's this got to do with what you gave Alan?"

"That was the envelope that I gave him at Tremblant for safekeeping. And the one year is up tomorrow."

There was a long pause as each sister contemplated the enormity of her father's transgressions. It put so many other things in perspective.

"Where's the envelope now, Antoinette?"

"It's at Alan's place on Peel Street. I'm going to get it tomorrow before I go to mass."

"So you've been there too. When was that?" Susan's anger was beginning to well up again.

"The Saturday before Christmas, in the afternoon, just

for a few minutes. I called him in Ottawa — I wanted to see him to make arrangements to get the envelope at the right time." Antoinette wiped her eyes. "Remember, Susan, I gave him the envelope long before you two got together and started seeing each other seriously. I had no idea that you'd become close. He seemed honest and trust-worthy — that's all."

"Wish I could believe there wasn't more to it than this, Antoinette. You should have told me earlier."

"Well, I didn't think this was going to be part of the deal — and frankly, I've been trying to block it out of my mind. I'll close the book on it after I see Father Péloquin tomorrow after mass." Calmer now, she reached for a cig-arette. "Now, come clean with me, Susan. What's happen-ing to Marcel? Does he stay or leave?"

"We won't know till Monday. Even then it might not be clear. But he shouldn't really matter to you anymore, should he?"

Antoinette began to cry again, another relentless tor-rent. "Of course he matters. After Papa and all the jerks who only wanted to get me into the sack, Marcel was won-derful. He's the only man who ever really cared for me."

"But you told me at the end he seemed to care more about the money than about you!" Susan exclaimed.

"I know, but — I can't help it, I miss him!" sobbed Antoinette.

Despite mixed feelings, Susan touched her sister's arm. "Come on, Antoinette. Let's go to bed. We'll both have to take it one day at a time from here on in."

Chapter Thirty

The RCMP were taking no chances in their surveillance of Antoinette and any visitors to the Belair household. They'd planted a high-tech bug in the light fixture in the kitchen as well as in the table lamps in the living room. Virtually every word spoken between Antoinette and her sister that night was picked up on the tape monitor in the unmarked RCMP van parked just around the corner.

By the time Antoinette emerged from the front door of the Belair residence on Carré Saint-Louis Sunday evening, the police had an unmarked car parked just up the street ready to follow her as inconspicuously as possible.

Susan had left at ten in the morning. She dropped by her office on Park Avenue where she worked for a couple of hours, then headed back to her apartment on Côte-des-Neiges. There had been little point in tailing her, although the RCMP did file a report confirming the connection between Alan Chant, executive assistant to the minister of immigration, and Susan Belair, lawyer and sister to Antoinette Belair, implicated in the Bertolini/Gagnon international drug ring.

Expecting Antoinette that evening to walk or take a taxi going south down St-Denis towards Basilique Notre-Dame in Old Montreal, they were surprised to see her swing right onto Sherbrooke. There she hailed a cab that continued westward, past the McGill University gates, and turned up Peel Street. To the RCMP surveillants in quiet pursuit, this could only mean one thing — a surprise visit to Alan Chant's apartment.

The Leonardo brothers also had plans that Sunday. Luigi was beginning to second-guess himself. He worried that Chant might have somehow taken the money when he visited the apartment early the previous morning. Bruno dismissed this possibility. He knew from experience that a million and a half's worth of thousand dollar bills was not so easy to stuff into a jacket.

"That's 1,500 pieces of paper, idiot. If he'd had it on him, you woulda seen it. Too bulky," Bruno admonished his younger brother, but not without a little doubt of his own.

At about five that Sunday evening, after darkness had fallen, they checked out the rear entrance to 3509 Peel Street. This was the best place to break in. It was not visible from the street, yet was still at ground level so they could easily use their acetylene torch and other tools of the trade.

The rear door targeted by Luigi and Bruno proved to be difficult to force open. Made of heavy metal, it wouldn't budge with the crowbar that had worked so well on other jobs. This door obviously hadn't been opened for many years. Something large and heavy seemed to be blocking it from the inside. This would create another barrier even if they did get the door open — unless they could somehow remove or cut through it.

"Luigi, we've had bigger challenges than this. Four big

cuts with the torch and then the crowbar to remove the piece of metal. I'll shove aside that big thing there, and we're in. It'll take fifteen minutes, tops."

Antoinette got out of her taxi at the corner of Sherbrooke and Peel and headed north on foot. The evening was biting cold. There were no stars and her heart was pounding. She hoped she'd find Alan by chance at his apartment, but that was unlikely.

If he wasn't there, maybe she could talk the building superintendent into letting her in on the pretense that she was picking up something for him. Or maybe she could break in, undetected. Somehow, she had to get the money. He'd never know. The Bertolinis and their henchmen could go screw themselves. She'd go out west, start fresh with an assumed name, maybe at a resort at Whistler Mountain where there were lots of jobs for skiers like Susan suggested. But first she would deliver her father's deathbed confession to Father Péloquin at the Basilique Notre-Dame.

She was nervous. This was more important than anything she'd ever done before. Maybe there wasn't any super — the building was pretty small. Maybe she could ring the bell of one of the other tenants and use her feminine charm to get them to let her in.

Susan had assured Antoinette that morning that the deal would be settled in another month, once Marcel's situation was clarified and they could get a court date for Antoinette. A month seemed like an eternity to be holed up like a prisoner in her mother's house. Maybe she could put up with it. But it'd be nice to have that money in her own closet so she could do what she wanted when her ordeal was over.

She wondered whether Susan had figured out where the money was hidden. Hopefully the revelation about her father's confession was enough to throw her off the scent. Susan was really steamed about Antoinette's one-nighter with Alan. She must have been serious about him.

Antoinette had taken some comfort after her brief meeting with Alan just before Christmas in knowing that he had no idea what he had been safeguarding for ten months. But yesterday, Susan was so persistent about Alan's involvement in Antoinette's life — something must have provoked her. God knows what he'd discovered or what conclusions he'd drawn.

Susan had been back in her apartment on Côte-des-Neiges for only five minutes when the phone rang. She agonized over whether to answer. The shattered images of the two most important men in her life were still flashing in front of her. The phone kept ringing. She decided to pick it up.

"Susan, I've got to see you. Truth is, I can't do without you. Can we talk?" Alan spoke breathlessly, before she could hang up.

"I'm not ready to forgive you so quickly, Alan. Not even sure I'm ready to talk. This weekend has been devastating in more ways than you can ever know. But I don't want to leave things the way they are." She hesitated. "Be here at five. If I can't stand talking to you, maybe we can manage a movie." She had not slept at all the night before.

Their first few minutes together were frosty. But she did allow her hand to touch his arm briefly as they turned the pages of the entertainment section of the newspaper. They had decided that a movie was a good, neutral first step towards trying to patch up their relationship.

The hot film at the Imperial was called *St. Elmo's Fire*, a story about seven friends, recent college graduates, searching for a place in the "real world" as they faced issues of career and commitment. Despite its lighthearted moments, the message that came through loud and clear was how the closest of friends could save, betray and love one another, all at the same time.

"I'm not sure that was the best movie for us right now," observed Susan, selecting her words carefully as they left the parking lot.

"Susan, listen," Alan pleaded. "There's so much happening, so much going on that we just can't allow our relationship to get derailed because of Antoinette and Marcel."

"Easy for you to say. Gagnon's just another third-rate dope dealer to you. But Antoinette's my sister — in case you didn't notice."

Turning on the car radio, Alan tried to change the subject. "Let's go get a pizza and some beer at Amelio's, just like we used to do in law school after studying late." Alan turned the dial till he found some classical music. She shot a faint smile across at him.

"You never took me to Amelio's when we were in law school, Alan. You were usually too busy studying or putting the hustle on some Anglo girl. But I'll give you a chance to make up for it now."

An unusual emergency meeting that Sunday at the

Langevin Block in Ottawa had been called by Michael Smith, the prime minister's quiet but efficient chief of staff. At three o'clock that afternoon, Smith had received a call from the commissioner of the RCMP about a possible security problem involving the executive assistant to the minister of immigration.

Rather than bother Savard, who had committed that Sunday afternoon to the Super Bowl, Smith decided to handle the matter himself. A mini cabinet shuffle was in the offing and Savard had told Smith that he didn't want any negative incidents to get in the way of the positive spin he hoped to give this major announcement.

Attending Smith's meeting were André Ouimet, chief of security in the PMO, Douglas Morrison, deputy minister of immigration, Frank Legault, director of control and intelligence from the immigration department and, on the protected line from Ottawa, Jean Thibault, Montreal regional director of the RCMP.

The meeting lasted only thirty minutes. The recommendation to the prime minister was clear. Alan Chant was to be immediately relieved of his duties as executive assistant to the minister of immigration and assigned to unspecified duties in the PMO pending clarification of his association with Antoinette Belair, Marcel Gagnon and an international drug ring that included the Bertolini family in New York and Victor Chen of Toronto and Hong Kong.

Once Smith had secured the prime minister's approval, Morrison would immediately call his minister in Regina. Ouimet would try to reach Chant in Montreal that evening to advise him to report to the PMO first thing Monday morning. Staff in the minister's office and at the department would be advised first thing Monday morning by Legault, but no details would be provided.

Chapter Thirty-One

After turning left off Ste-Catherine, Alan drove north on Université. It was eight-thirty Sunday evening, and he and Susan were headed for Amelio's. The classical music on the radio was interrupted by local news on the half hour. One item caught their attention: "Eyewitness News has just learned of a flash fire burning out of control close to the McGill campus at the corner of Peel and Docteur-Penfield. As we speak, flames are shooting out of the roof and the windows of a three-story rooming house believed to be home for several McGill professors and senior graduate students. More on this later as details are known."

"Christ, Susan, that's right near my place!" gasped Alan. "Let's see how close we can get."

As the black BMW edged northward on Peel, Alan and Susan could see the police barricade about two hundred yards south of Docteur-Penfield. Three fire engines with hoses spewing foamy water were lined up along the east side of the street. An ambulance stood by.

"Susan, that's my house! That's the one that's burning! Christ, all my clothes, my files, my personal papers. . . ." Alan was stricken. He barely heard the radio announcer.

". . . the fire department believes that the blaze was the result of an explosion of a fuel oil tank on the ground floor at the rear of the building, caused by two men apparently trying to enter with an acetylene torch. Ambulances are on the scene but police don't hold out much hope for the survival of the two men whose bodies were found at the rear of the building."

Susan grabbed Alan's arm and tried to suppress her panic. "You don't suppose . . . Those guys in the Alfa Romeo . . . I wonder . . ." Her voice trailed off as she tried to focus on the news report.

". . . have also recovered the body of a young woman in the first-floor hallway. The building appears to be totally gutted and will have to be demolished. Most of the seven residents appear to have been absent at the time of the fire. Police have not yet released the identities of the young woman and of the two men, pending notification of next of kin." Alan had a sickening feeling that the fire was connected to the hidden money. For a terrible moment, it crossed his mind that the woman who died could in fact be Antoinette. He tried to push the thought away.

Alan and Susan went straight to Susan's apartment. When they arrived at Côte-des-Neiges, Alan was first on the line to Sam and Laura. "Have you heard the news? There was a big fire near McGill!"

"No, Alan, we had some friends over for dinner," Laura said. "Your dad's still savoring the pleasant aftertaste of his sixtieth birthday party. What's this about a fire?"

"It was my building on Peel Street. Luckily I wasn't there when it happened. Didn't want you to turn on the news and think maybe I—" Alan stopped, cold sweat beading on his forehead. Was Susan right? Had someone been after him, or were they just trying to get the money?

"Alan — this is awful! Are you all right? What about Susan?"

"I'm fine, Mom, and Susan's right here with me. But apparently there were three people killed. The building's just a shell."

"Oh my God! Who were they, do you know?"

"No, I don't. They're not releasing the names until the relatives are notified."

"What can we do to help? A fire's a devastating thing." Her concern rippled over the phone. "Do you have to go to work tomorrow?

"I don't think I can get out of it. I'll get by, Mom. Don't worry."

"You could stay with us tonight," Sam said. He'd picked up the extension when he heard the anxiety in his wife's voice.

"That's okay. I'm hoping Susan will put me up until I get things straightened around." Out of the corner of his eye, Alan watched Susan. She didn't blink, and he thought she might have actually nodded her approval, although he wasn't sure.

Laura persisted. "Are you sure there's not something we can do, Alan?"

"Well, there are a couple of things I might ask Dad to do for me."

"How can I help, Son?" Sam's voice was gruff with concern.

"I may need the help of your accountant or secretary at the dealership to help me deal with some of the paperwork — you know, insurance policies, unpaid bills and so on."

"No problem, Son. That's what we're here for. Give me a call anytime. And by the way, once you get settled, maybe you can deliver an important message to the prime minister regarding a fund-raising problem here in Montreal. Call me at the office tomorrow when you're back in

Ottawa."

"Well, Dad, as soon as I sort myself out I'll do what I can."

It was a different story at the Belair residence. Huguette was watching television when there was a firm knock on the door. *"Qui est là?"*

"Inspector Jean Thibault, RCMP. Could we have a word with you, madame? It's important." RCMP surveillance had followed Antoinette to Peel Street and watched in horror when the building erupted in flames. They had quickly called Thibault to inform him.

Huguette opened the door quickly, knowing instinctively something was wrong.

"Bonsoir, Madame Belair, there's been a tragic fire over on Peel Street. We've just learned that your daughter was trapped inside. We're very sorry. God rest her soul."

"Mon Dieu! But how . . . why was . . . ? Huguette was stunned.

"It was the building where your daughter's friend Alan Chant lives. Seems there was an explosion."

"Ma petite fille. This is awful. Was Alan with her? Is he all right, or did . . . ?"

"He was not there, madame. You should know that it—"

Just then, the phone rang. It was Susan on the line.

"Maman, there's a terrible fire at Alan's apartment. Two men were killed. And someone in the hall on the first floor."

"Mon Dieu — I thought it was you. There's a man from the police here. He said that my daughter had been killed. What's—" The relief suddenly drained from Huguette's face. *"Ah, non* — could it be Antoinette?"

"Sorry if there was confusion, madame," Thibault broke

in. "It was your younger daughter. We don't quite know why she was there. But yes, our men have identified her. I'm very sorry."

"Did you hear that, Suzanne? Please come home right away."

"We'll be there, Maman, just as soon as we can."

"*Venez tout de suite!* I'm scared." Huguette was trembling.

Susan struggled to make sense of what had happened. "Maman, did you know Antoinette was going out?"

"She told me that she was going to mass at Notre-Dame, and to see Father Péloquin." Huguette began to weep.

Alan returned to Susan's apartment about eleven-thirty that evening. Susan had decided to stay with Huguette at Carré St. Louis for the night. He had spent a difficult and emotionally draining two hours comforting both Huguette and Susan as the police completed their interrogation. They also had to make arrangements with the coroner's office and the funeral home. There would be a small funeral for family and friends the following Wednesday.

As he turned the key to enter Susan's apartment, Alan felt numb. He could barely contemplate the horror of all that had happened. Visions of the radiant and seductive Antoinette standing on the threshold of his pied-à-terre kept reappearing. He flopped down onto the couch, mindlessly turned on the TV and began flipping channels, as if hoping the television images would blot out the others. Had he let her down? Those two men who tried to blast their way into his place were obviously after the money — did they have friends who would come after him? What was in the sealed envelope addressed to Father Péloquin? And how much did Susan really know from her last conversations with Antoinette?

Just as he began to drift off, with sleep slowly falling over him like a protective net, the telephone rang. He hesitated through three rings, then picked it up. "Hello?"

"Is this Alan Chant?" the female caller asked, in an official tone.

"Yes it is. Who is this?" Alan demanded, somewhat hesitantly.

"Just one moment, please. It's the prime minister's office. We've been trying to reach you for almost four hours. We finally got this number from your secretary, since there was no answer at your apartment and no response from your pager. Mr. André Ouimet, head of security in the PMO, would like to speak with you."

It seemed like an eternity before he heard Ouimet's voice. Alan had met him on several occasions in the PMO before being assigned to Baldwin in November.

"Mr. Chant, I'm sorry for calling so late on a Sunday night, but the prime minister has asked me to contact you on an urgent matter. Because of an alleged security problem, he's asked that you not go into work in the immigration department in the morning. You're to report directly to me in the Langevin Block, third floor. What time do you think you can make it in?"

"I can be there by nine-thirty. What's this about? Sorry if I sound tired but there's been a terrible fire at my apartment here in Montreal. Everything's gone."

"Sorry to hear of your loss. I can't provide too many details over the telephone except to say that it involves your girlfriend's sister Antoinette Belair and her companion Marcel Gagnon. I believe you know both of them. Please don't contact either of them before you see me in the morning, or it may adversely affect your situation. Do you understand?"

"Don't worry, sir. I won't be contacting Antoinette. She's dead. She was killed in the fire."

Chapter Thirty-Two

Alan parked his car at the side door of the Langevin Block in one of the spaces normally used by official government vehicles, the dark Chevrolets, Pontiacs or Oldsmobiles assigned to ministers or deputy ministers. The spaces were not authorized parking areas; rather, they represented an unofficial federal appropriation of part of the wide sidewalk at the busy corner of Wellington and Elgin. Ottawa police almost never tagged these cars. Still, to be safe, Alan left one of his business cards clearly visible on the dashboard to show that the vehicle belonged to the executive assistant to the minister of immigration.

The drive up from Montreal that cold January Monday morning had been hair-raising, with gray sheet ice on the Trans-Canada for most of the trip and the sun nowhere in sight. Three tractor-trailer transports had jackknifed along the way. One had slammed into an overpass support pillar, resulting in a spectacular fire that lit up the cold gray dawn and continued Alan's nightmare. A vision of Antoinette clutching the attaché case amidst the roaring flames flashed before him.

The steps leading to the side entrance of the Langevin Block, an unimpressive, turn-of-the-century, redstone building, were covered with that grimy mixture of sand

and salt that coats every ground-level exterior surface of Ottawa's government buildings in the winter. Alan took the steps slowly, rather than bounding up two at a time as he used to when working there briefly in the fall or, more recently, when he accompanied Baldwin to cabinet meetings. The commissionaire at the security desk was ready for him.

"Yes, Mr. Chant, Mr. Smith and Mr. Ouimet are expecting you. Please go to the third floor, at the far end."

The meeting lasted only forty minutes and was over well before ten. Although Ouimet had been fully briefed by the Mounties about the mysterious Peel Street fire and the death of Antoinette and the two men, this did not deter him from his mission.

He confronted Alan about his friendship with Antoinette and knowledge of Marcel Gagnon, and their connection with the Bertolini family in New York, known international drug dealers. He asked Alan if he remembered the case of Victor Chen and Chen's connection to the Bertolinis. Ouimet suggested that Alan's relationships may have been a factor in Baldwin's decision to allow Chen to stay in Canada despite his involvement in an international drug ring.

Alan shook his head emphatically. "That's just not true."

Ouimet paced a little, then turned to face Alan.

"Mr. Chant, is Susan Belair, sister and legal counsel to Antoinette Belair also your girlfriend?"

"We have been dating for a few months, but—"

"And is Guy Doucet, Marcel Gagnon's lawyer also your former law partner?"

"Yes, we were partners in the firm of Chant & Doucet for over two years, until I resigned to work for Mr. Savard."

Alan was not sure where this was leading.

"And are you aware that deportation and extradition proceedings have been started against Gagnon?"

"Yes, that's part of my job," Alan replied defensively.

"And you privately discussed Gagnon's situation with both counsel, Susan Belair and Guy Doucet, and offered to intercede with your minister." Ouimet concluded his indictment.

"Well, I'm not sure I'd put it quite that way, Mr. Ouimet," Alan said, looking away. Ouimet was close enough to the truth to make Alan uncomfortable.

"Mr. Chant, I trust you realize the seriousness of this situation," Michael Smith intoned judiciously. "The prime minister has asked me to temporarily relieve you of your duties with Minister Baldwin until matters are resolved, one way or another. Mr. Morrison has already been in touch with Minister Baldwin in Regina. Mr. Legault will advise senior officials in the immigration department later today that you've been temporarily assigned to unspecified duties in the PMO. Do you have anything to add?"

"Well, I regret that the prime minister has had to involve himself personally in these matters. There are heavy demands on him and I'm sorry that he's had to devote valuable time to my somewhat complicated situation," Alan said, looking directly at Smith, who looked down and began to nervously rearrange his notes. Alan had suspected that the PM had not been fully briefed and that Smith and Ouimet, prompted by information provided by the RCMP, were acting very much on their own. Smith's apparent discomfort at Alan's response confirmed this.

"You'll understand, Mr. Chant, that the government

must be beyond reproach in these matters. The prime minister has important high-profile announcements to make later this week and he does not want to be blind-sided by an unexpected public revelation of rather bizarre circumstances surrounding a senior ministerial staff member in a sensitive portfolio." Smith rose from his chair, suggesting the meeting was about to end.

"I'm not sure I understand, Mr. Smith, but you're the boss. What would you like me to do here for the next few days?"

"Well, Mr. Chant, we really don't have an office or any assigned duties for you here, at least not right now while the investigation is continuing. It would probably be appropriate for you simply to stay home for a while until we get in touch you. You may want to assist the Belair family with funeral arrangements. I'm sure the death of Antoinette has come as a terrible blow to Madame Belair and her daughter Susan. I'm very sorry."

Before getting into his car, Alan spied the final indignity. A twenty-dollar parking ticket, courtesy of the City of Ottawa, adorned his windshield. Some extraterrestrial force must have already advised local authorities that he'd been stripped of his responsibilities as EA to a minister and no longer entitled to the usual ministerial immunity.

His first thought was to head immediately for Montreal. Then he remembered his mother's favorite maxim: "slow, measured response." His small bachelor apartment on Slater Street really wasn't an option. The phone would most certainly be tapped. He stopped at the pay phone at the corner of Elgin and Laurier. Punching in his credit card number, he reached Baldwin at home in Regina.

"Alan, I got the word from Morrison last night. What's this all about?"

For fifteen full minutes, Alan spilled out the relevant details, leaving out what he knew of the contents of Antoinette's attaché case. He finished with the fire at his Montreal apartment the previous night and the tragic death of Susan's sister.

Baldwin gasped. Then, recovering, he offered some advice. "Go to my apartment — you've got a key — and feel free to use the phone. Surely to God they're not tapping *my* line. In addition to Susan and your family, I'd suggest you try to reach Forrester — she may have some advice. But give me a few minutes to contact her first. I'll call you at the Park Lane with her reaction and her private numbers in Toronto and Ottawa if I think she can help. I don't know how she'll react — she's not happy with me these days, primarily because of our good friend Marcel Gagnon."

"Thanks, Minister." Alan was touched by Tom's loyalty. "I appreciate this more than you can believe. Don't count me out yet. Quite frankly, I don't believe the PM knows anything about this. I think Smith and Ouimet got the 'heads-up' from the RCMP and now they're operating on their own. I'm going to sniff this one out."

Since returning to the Centre Block at three-thirty after question period, prime minister Jacques Savard had been on his personal telephone for the better part of an hour.

The first call to Savard had come in from Sam Chant in Montreal, who'd already faxed ahead short briefing notes from Susan Belair and Guy Doucet. The prime minister always gave priority to calls from his key fundraisers. Until this call, he had not been aware of the Alan Chant suspension, let alone any of the background.

The second call had come from Joan Forrester. She knew Alan Chant personally and had been fully briefed on the situation by Baldwin. She regarded the situation as a travesty, and demanded that Savard re-think his decision. She also suggested that he call Baldwin in Regina to get his views. Savard had taken her advice immediately.

The third call came from the director of CSIS, this one on the protected line. He reiterated the importance of Victor Chen as an informant and double agent who was vital to CSIS for preventing threats to the security of Canada. Linking Chant's suspension to his knowledge of Chen as an international drug dealer would be very damaging to CSIS interests. Besides, the director noted, it was Baldwin and not Chant who had made the final decision that Chen could stay.

Francine Côté had obviously been tipped off and had gone to the top to preserve her vital national security operation. The commissioner of the RCMP, previously unaware of the case's national security aspect, had been fully briefed by CSIS earlier that afternoon.

Finally, Savard was able to put in a call to his chief of staff. Smith picked up the phone after one ring. "Michael, you and I have worked well together on most matters," the prime minister said, "but we seem to have come apart on this one. I've just read Alan Chant's file. Why didn't you tell me you had suspended him using my name and authority?"

"Prime Minister, the evidence provided by the RCMP seemed pretty clear, and I wanted to get it out of the way quickly before your announcement on Wednesday. Chant's only suspended, not fired. He'll have his day to try to prove we were wrong."

"Well, he may have already done that, Michael. In the last hour alone, I've talked to two ministers, the director of CSIS, the commissioner of the RCMP and I've received written submissions from the lawyers representing Marcel Gagnon as well as Antoinette Belair. Unless you can persuade me with additional information that isn't in this file or is directly contrary to what these people have told me, I'm inclined to reinstate Chant immediately. What do you think?"

There was a brief, awkward silence at Smith's end.

"No real objection, Prime Minister. It's your call. I was simply trying to protect you politically. Sounds like you've already built in that protection."

"Thank you, Michael. I didn't get this far in politics by being oblivious to these things. Now, have the switchboard track down Alan Chant and give him the news. If he's in Ottawa, see if he can come in today before we all go home. He's owed an apology. I'll deal with it personally, if you don't mind."

Chapter Thirty-Three

"Alan, the last two days must have been terrible for you. I'm very sorry about this. Go back to the immigration minister's office and try to pretend your suspension never happened. Fortunately, we were able to intercept the intended memo to senior officials in your department before it was distributed." Savard spoke to Alan in a fatherly way.

They were comfortably ensconced in large leather chairs in the prime minister's office in the Centre Block. Alan gratefully sipped the steaming coffee the secretary had brought in and glanced around. They were directly below the opposition offices Savard occupied when Alan came to work for him. Alan remembered that Savard had barely unpacked in his office there, so confident had he been of a short stay. He had certainly moved into this space, however. Besides the photographs of former prime ministers, pictures of Savard now adorned the walls and desk: Savard with his family, Savard campaigning, Savard victorious on election night. Looking at the elegant, gray-haired prime minister, Alan saw a man who clearly relished power and who had settled in for the long haul.

"You know," Savard continued, "we've worked very effectively together ever since you first came up here last July. I'm sorry my staff members appear to have over-extended themselves. I'll try to make it up to you." Alan smiled for the first time in three days.

"Prime Minister, I really appreciate your intervention. It's been a very distressing time for me, what with the fire, my girlfriend's family problems and now this. I appreciate your support, particularly so quickly before any real damage was done to my reputation. I can't thank you enough. I hope I can repay you somehow."

Savard looked intently at Alan. "Well, the only payment I need, Alan, is for you to be the best executive assistant you can be over there in immigration. I know it's a tough spot but both Forrester and Baldwin tell me you're doing a great job."

"Thank you, Prime Minister. And if there's any special direction you'd like me to take or any particular immigration problem that's causing you or the government any aggravation, please feel free to contact me directly, at any time of day." Alan was beginning to feel useful again.

"Now that you mention it, Alan, there are a couple of matters I'd like you to keep an eye on. Be proactive if you have to. My staff have noted your adroitness in engineering selective leaks to the press — for example, the situation with the late Professor Firestone and the Cuban consulate," Savard said dryly. "There are a couple of other situations where friends of mine seem to have come out on the short end of the stick. That illegal Jamaican nanny in Toronto who used to work for my friend Henry Street, for example."

"I remember that one," Alan noted.

"Then there's that U.S. criminal the Mounties brought into Canada with a new cover. Lots of publicity there, too. In addition to being a crook, he's now trying to embarrass Senator Joe Semeniuk."

"Yes, I'm familiar with that case as well, Prime Minister."

"Alan, do what you can for me, please. I'd appreciate it."

"You bet, no problem. Message received, Prime Minister."

As he left the Centre Block, Alan wrestled with the task of reconciling his sense of justice with his immediate feeling of gratitude. It was not going to be easy.

Alan did not get back to his office until well after six. He had called in earlier to explain that personal problems would prevent him from getting in till late, but he certainly didn't want to give details. Martha Kulyk had already left for the day. Dominique Rodriguez was still working. She came right to the point.

"Alan, the minister wants to see you at ten tomorrow morning on the Marcel Gagnon file. He's obviously been agitated all weekend. I think Forrester must have called him in Regina and laid another trip on him. He called me at home yesterday afternoon when he couldn't reach you. He seems obsessed with this one — maybe he needs some other cases to distract him. You could do an update on some of the sensitive cases we handled recently. Ministers always like to see the results of their handiwork, particularly if the news is good. Got time for a short briefing?"

"Sure, Dominique, could use a little diversionary good news myself. Let's get right into it."

"First, the good news items. Millicent Wright, the Jamaican woman with children in Toronto. She's still on a minister's permit. She's gainfully employed as a hospital orderly, has her own small apartment on Vaughan Road, her kids are in local schools, there's no noticeable increase in abuse of the fiancé class provision since the changes were introduced. The Toronto Star gives our minister a 'laurel' in its 'darts and laurels' analysis on the editorial page last Saturday. No reference to Henry Street, the illegal employer. No call from the PMO."

"Well done, Dominique. Now what about the others?"

"Well, a couple of other good-news results. Remember the Polish ship jumper in St. John's, Stanislaw Zawacki? Well, after our people sent him back to the ship, we were concerned that his young bride, Bernadette Kelly, would be devastated and that the local media would be all over us."

"Who could forget that one, Dominique?" Alan smiled.

"Anyway, Bernadette, perhaps with a little encouragement from her parents and the local parish priest, has written the minister a letter of thanks. Seems the priest told her that there'd be no difficulty having the marriage annulled." Dominique's usually serious gray eyes twinkled. "Ah, the ways of love. Case closed."

"Guess it pays to be tough sometimes, Dominique. The minister will be pleased — I know he was worried about that decision."

"There's one more, Alan. The minister will be only too aware of the young Indian woman in Regina, Rauinda Singh. Her wealthy uncle back in New Delhi posted a bond of $250,000 that was sufficient to satisfy the Saskatchewan ministry of health about any possible dependency on the provincial health system. So the ministry sent a letter supporting Baldwin's decision to allow her to stay on a minister's permit with an expectation of landing after five years. Her family in Regina has gone on local television to thank the government and they named the minister in particular. Won't hurt him at all in Regina East, come election time, even though I know the minister had misgivings on this case because she lied on her application about her medical condition."

"Dominique, you're getting good at this. Perhaps you'll join the campaign team when the time comes." Alan couldn't resist this friendly jibe at a professional colleague who so steadfastly eschewed involvement in party politics.

Dominique laughed. "No way, Alan. You know I'm a lifer in the department here. Partisan politics is for the birds. If I'd accepted the same kind of invitation from Baldwin's predecessor last September, you wouldn't have kept me on. Right?"

"Right. And we can't do without you now — you know that. Now give me the bad news."

"The bad news is Fred Milanowski, the convicted commodities broker. Remember him?"

Alan nodded, though he wasn't about to admit to Dominique that Savard had reminded him of this case only an hour earlier.

"He's doing his interview tomorrow night with W5 about his involvement in the Winnipeg airport scandal. Unfortunately, Senator Semeniuk — the PM's friend — is certain to be front and center. Now, he's likely to fight back and point out the nefarious background of his accuser. The whole deal about Milanowski being in Canada will be laid at the minister's feet. I don't see any way out on this one except to go to ground with no comment."

"I'm not sure I agree with you, Dominique. We may have to be proactive on this one." Alan paused and looked away. "Maybe I'll have a word with the people who control CTV and try to get the story pulled. It's not in our interest to have the senator embarrassed."

Dominique looked at Alan in disbelief. He was clearly uncomfortable with the prospect of blowing away Milanowski in the interests of political expediency without permitting him to air his story publicly. "Isn't that risky?" she asked.

"Yes, but it's worth the risk. It's what Savard wants, anyway."

"If you say so."

He hurriedly changed the subject. "Are there any others?"

Dominique nodded. "The case we should really be worried about is Victor Chen. Somehow, *The Globe and Mail*'s onto the fact that we know Chen's a drug dealer in southeast Asia and yet the minister has allowed him to stay. Someone from the department or the RCMP must have leaked. The *Globe* reporter wants to interview the minister tomorrow. That'll be tricky to avoid, especially if you plead national security as your excuse for not talking. I don't know what to suggest on this one. Maybe you and the minister should ask CSIS for advice."

"Thanks, Dominique, but since when did CSIS get into the political advice business? We'll take a fresh look at this one tomorrow. See if you can delay the *Globe* reporter for another day. In the meantime, you might try to set up a direct, face-to-face meeting between Baldwin and Francine Côté of CSIS. She's the one who talked Baldwin into softening his decision in the first place."

It was now close to seven o'clock. Alan had had enough ups and downs for a week — perhaps for a lifetime. He was exhausted. He closed his briefcase. Before calling Susan in Montreal, he went for a long quiet walk in the snowy park next to the Ottawa River. The magnificent parliament buildings, in all their symbolic splendor, looked down impassively from the hill above. Tomorrow would come soon enough.

Chapter Thirty-Four

It was nearly ten o'clock Tuesday morning. Alan could see from his office that the minister had not yet arrived. He wondered what was keeping him. He knew that the minister was in town because Alan had called him at the Park Lane late the night before to confirm that he'd arrived from Regina.

Martha came in to say that Denis Forget had phoned from the minister's limo. Apparently Baldwin had been unexpectedly called to a meeting at the PMO just before nine but should be finished in less than half an hour.

At a quarter past ten, Baldwin rushed into his office, calling for Alan to join him in the inner office immediately.

"What is it, Minister? You look upset. It's not the Marcel Gagnon case, is it?"

"Well, yes and no." Baldwin gripped the back of his chair as he spoke. "I don't know what Forrester's been telling the folks in the PMO this last week. But whatever it was, I'm toast in this portfolio. There'll be a mini cabinet shuffle announced by the PM at eleven tomorrow morning. I'm being appointed minister of state for health. The PM says it's so the government can take better advantage of my professional credentials in the medical field." Baldwin looked glum.

"Did he really say that?" Alan asked, incredulously.

"Fact is, Alan, it's a demotion. Must have thought I'm not up to the job here. He mentioned my weak performance in the House and the difficulties we've had in keeping the lid on controversial immigration cases. Just think — less than three months since the swearing-in and I'm being shuffled sideways. Carolyn will be even more cynical now."

Alan was still in a state of disbelief, shocked that the minister who had gone to the wall for him less than twenty-four hours earlier was now himself a victim.

"Tom, I'm extremely sorry to hear this. You had all the right instincts on the difficult cases and were a quick study. It's not fair to move you at this early stage." Alan realized after he said it that this was one of the few times he'd addressed Baldwin by his first name. "Did the PM tell you who else is being shuffled?"

"Apparently this is just a mini shuffle. Only three of us involved. My position as minister of state for health is new. It's ironic that I'm being replaced by Joan Forrester. The PM says she's seen as a tough, high-profile lawyer from Toronto and better able to deal with the growing immigration mess — much of which is centered in her city. Fact is, I think the PM still feels threatened by Forrester and this is a good way to marginalize her. Bit of a demotion for her, too."

Alan tried to sort through the implications of what he was hearing. "Who's taking over at justice?" he asked, frown lines creasing his forehead.

"She's being replaced by Terrence O'Donnell, the veteran law-and-order MP from Calgary. He used to be a trial lawyer in his early days but he hasn't seen the inside of a court room in ten years. The PM says he wants to give a stronger regional balance to the cabinet — says we need more voter support in the big population centers in western Canada. To me, this is his code for a real shift to the right in the justice portfolio." Baldwin sighed.

"I agree. Forrester will be unhappy. Guess the leadership convention is still going on. But the real tragedy is losing you at immigration. It's just not fair."

Tom managed a grim smile. "I'm beginning to see that 'fair' isn't central to this business after all."

"Well, one blessing in disguise is that you don't have to spend a lot of time on the sensitive casework I'd planned for you this morning." Alan tried to sound upbeat. "But there are still one or two matters we should go over. When do you want to tell the staff?"

"Don't breathe a word to anyone on the outside until just before eleven o'clock tomorrow when they actually make the announcement at Rideau Hall. We'll get the staff together in the boardroom at five today, but swear them to secrecy. Savard would go bananas if anything leaked out officially before tomorrow morning, although no doubt the PMO will be leaking its own unofficial version of the shuffle at midday today."

"No doubt," said Alan, wryly. "But that's the way it is at the top."

Baldwin looked philosophical. "I guess I can accept that, Alan. There can only be one boss. How can I help clean things up around here in the next few hours we have left?"

"Well, while we have a few minutes this morning, perhaps we should try to resolve the Marcel Gagnon situation, particularly with Forrester becoming the new minister tomorrow. I've thought about this case a lot over the last few days. And it's not based on anything said to me by Guy — you know, his lawyer, my former law partner. Frankly, I think you can save Forrester a big headache if you take action today."

"Like what?"

"Well, you can stay the deportation order issued by the adjudicator. That would allow the proceedings under the Extradition Act to follow their normal course over the next year or so. Morrison and the enforcement people in the department won't be happy. But now you can tell them that's what Forrester would do anyway, starting tomorrow."

"But Alan, you're the one who wanted to deport this guy. You said that, politically, this was the best way to do things." Tom began to pace uneasily.

"Well, I've been re-thinking. Why not let Forrester come into this portfolio with a clean slate, with you taking the heat for overruling your deputy? Besides, I now believe it's the right decision on a matter of legal principle. I was wrong first time around. He may be a criminal, but Marcel Gagnon's still entitled to the full protection of Canadian law and justice."

Tom stopped pacing and stared out the window across the river. Alan continued. "If our guys really want to help the DEA deal with the mafia and its drug trade, the Canadian system gives Gagnon just as good an opportunity to sing as part of a plea bargain. His information can be presented on a silver platter as commission evidence, if that's what the Americans need. More likely, all they'll really want are names, dates, telephone numbers and methods of distribution — the details."

"Agreed, Alan. I don't mind overruling Morrison on the way out. In fact, I might even enjoy it." Tom turned from the window to face Alan. "And I appreciate your honesty in admitting you've changed your mind. It's a bloody shame this portfolio's going to lose you, too. I'm assuming that you'll come over to health with me, even though it's just a minister of state's office and not a full-blown department."

"Well, I'll have to think about it overnight, Minister. I appreciate the offer. I'm still a bit disoriented myself."

Alan stayed late at the department that night, preparing to clear out his files, not knowing quite where his future lay. The meeting with staff at five had been difficult enough. Baldwin had spoken bravely and well, but the general atmosphere was one of incredulity. Alan, responding on behalf of all the staff, had choked up. And Dominique Rodriguez, a veteran of ministerial changes, had left the meeting in tears.

Alan received three significant calls. The first was from Guy Doucet.

"I want to thank you and your minister, old boy. I just got word this afternoon. You did the right thing — saved me the time and expense of having to go to court to get an injunction. Call me when you're next in the city and we can get caught up."

"Don't thank me, Guy. It was Tom Baldwin who made the decision in the end. Had to overrule his own deputy. Hope you guys at the bar remember that."

"Don't worry. Duly noted. And Alan, sorry to hear about Susan's sister and the fire at your place on Peel Street. I'll bet there's more to it than appeared in the papers. "

"Thanks, Guy." He didn't want to think about that

now. "Good luck with Gagnon. You'll need it. And keep a small corner for me on Rue St-Pierre. I may have to rejoin you sooner than you think." Alan didn't have the heart to tell Guy how the Gagnon decision had come about. Nor did he want to tell him outright that he might not have a job in Ottawa next time he saw him.

The second call came from Susan. "I met with the Montreal coroner this afternoon. He said Antoinette died from smoke inhalation . . . God, I hope she didn't suffer too much. There'll be an autopsy and a coroner's inquest. Apparently the two guys killed were brothers. They were trying to break in at the back with an acetylene torch. You know that deli at the corner of St-Denis and Rigaud? It's run by their mother. Inspector Thibault of the RCMP tells me that these guys were bad actors tied in with the Bertolini family. Antoinette must have wanted that envelope for the priest pretty badly. Don't know why, for the life of me, she didn't ask me to get it from you. I guess I'll never know."

"I guess not, Susan. Please — you of all people must understand that my lawyer's duty to her doesn't end with her death."

There was a long, heavy silence. Alan could almost hear Susan's mind working as she struggled to accept his decision. Finally he heard a reluctant sigh.

"Of course I understand *intellectually*. Emotionally, it's harder . . . but that's something we'll just have to live with." Her tone changed. "But you should know, Alan, that I took up your suggestion about asking the RCMP for their surveillance records on Antoinette."

"You did? What'd they tell you?"

"I saw your name associated with the trip coming down from Tremblant last February. I think I know where the money went. And you'll be interested to know that I'll be visiting Father Péloquin tomorrow morning to make the confession for my father that Antoinette was never able to deliver."

There was a long pause as she waited for a response that never came. Susan had guessed that the money had been at Peel Street and had burned in the fire but was content not to force his admission. The fewer people who knew the better.

"Maman's still in pretty bad shape. I've moved in with her until at least the weekend. The funeral's at three on Wednesday afternoon in the small side chapel at Notre Dame. Father Péloquin has agreed to preside. Can you come?"

"Susan, I'll be there for sure. I have to stay in Ottawa until at least noon but I can make it if I get away by one and the roads are okay. Don't tell a soul, but there's a mini shuffle in the works tomorrow. I'll hightail it down right after. I may never come back. Lots of strange things happening here."

"And, Alan, there's one last matter."

"Yes, Susan?"

She hesitated. "I love you. And — you're going to need a place to stay in Montreal. If you want to move in with me for a while —"

"Susan, I love you too, more than you know! Starting tomorrow night, you've got a new room-mate."

The third call came just before ten. Alan had just begun to clean up his desk in preparation to leave his office, perhaps for the last time. Joan Forrester was on the line.

"Alan, have you heard what's happening tomorrow?"

"Yes, Minister. Congratulations!"

"Alan, I'll come right to the point. I'd like you to be my executive assistant. I've already checked it out with the PMO and they've okayed it. I haven't spoken to Baldwin about this, although I did call this afternoon to congratulate him on finally taking the right decision on Gagnon. Bet you had a hand in that." Alan avoided responding to her speculation.

"Minister, Baldwin has asked me to go over with him to health. I haven't given him an answer yet."

"Don't be stupid, Alan. The minister of state for health isn't entitled to a full-fledged EA. He's a junior minister at the beck and call of the minister of national health and welfare. You'd be a mere special assistant at reduced pay and you'd have no programs to run. And a lot of good your legal training would be on esoteric issues of national health policy."

"True, but Tom stuck by me through this mess—"

"Oh, Alan, don't be a wimp. Baldwin's going nowhere. He'll be back at the hospital in Regina full time before the end of this Parliament — trust me. Stick with immigration. You're good at it."

"You don't have to do this, Minister. You're very kind, but it's not necessary." Alan felt a pang of guilt. Tom *had* been loyal to him, and now he was being tempted to jump ship.

"Alan, it's not a question of being kind. I need you. The system needs you. Canada needs you." There was a very long pause as Forrester waited for his answer.

Once again, his mother's advice rang in his ears. But she had also said, "Only when the way is clear should you act quickly." The way was clear — the lure of power was too strong. "Agreed," Alan said quietly. He knew this decision would not change overnight.

"Fine! Take tomorrow off and we'll meet first thing Wednesday." Forrester sounded relieved.

"It's not that easy, Minister. Can we meet at the department for half an hour at noon tomorrow, just after the swearing-in? Before I leave for Montreal, I have to brief you on some sensitive matters that just won't wait."

Alan knew that if he were going to continue running the department and dispensing justice in a way that was also compatible with the political interests of the Savard government, he would have to stay ahead of his new minister. She would be a challenge indeed.

"Agreed, Alan. Tomorrow at noon," she said with no hesitation.

As he left that night and drove back across the Ottawa River, the lights illuminating the majestic parliament buildings seemed particularly bright.

Acknowledgement

Like so many first-time novelists, I have come to depend on the kindness and generosity of friends. The first to be acknowledged is my best friend, my wife Marie Rounding who dared me to take on this project some time ago and provided encouragement and support, reviewed the manuscript several times and took on a disproportionate burden of managing our household and children Matthew and Jennifer to allow me time to write.

It has been my good fortune over the years to have been given the privilege of access to Canada's political and legal system from a variety of perspectives. Many friends and colleagues have been helpful, some unwittingly, in allowing me to observe and occasionally participate in the fascinating process of politics and government. This in turn has fueled my imagination leading to the creation of the fictitious characters and situations in this book. I shall always be in their debt.

My first allegiance professionally is of course to my colleagues at Osler, Hoskin & Harcourt, the best law firm in Canada, where I happily earn my daily living. Recently the firm had the good sense to establish a sabbatical policy for partners to avoid burn-out and sustain personal motivation and energy. I was an early beneficiary and the freed-up time available to me at Craigleith enabled this project to proceed when it might otherwise have floundered.

In August 1993, the Creative Writing Program under Greg

Gatenby and Joe Kertes at Humber College provided insight and inspiration that was invaluable. Direct daily exposure for a week to Margaret Atwood and Graeme Gibson, two icons of Canadian literature, was an unforgettable and somewhat humbling experience, not to mention the constructive criticism of fellow classmates Alessandro Carrera, Anne D'Andrea, Shaena Lambert, Brenda McCrank, Irene Parikhal, Marilyn Sciuk and Eva Stachniak, which continued in a helpful and enjoyable way long after the formal program was finished. These individuals are all wonderful writers and will continue to be heard from I'm sure.

At risk of embarassment to them, I should acknowledge those friends who, when asked, dutifully read earlier versions of the manuscript and offered helpful comments and suggestions which contributed to authenticity: Cathy Beehan, Jan Dymond, Simon Potter, Clay Ruby, Effie Triantafolopoulos, Michael Levine, Sally Brown and John Tory. There were also special and unique contributions from Erin Atkey, Martha Sharpe, Cally Jordan and Jonathan Atkey. Of course, I bear total responsibility for any remaining errors or oversimplifications, and these friends are hereby exonerated from any criticism that may be directed at me or liability for this work.

One of my great pleasures was working with Alison Braden and Carole Hamilton who typed most of the manuscript on their own time and, as insightful readers, courageously told me what seemed right or wrong while maintaining confidentiality.

A first-time novelist in Canada could not ask for a better publisher than Little, Brown and Company (Canada) Limited. Together, Kim McArthur, Sarah MacLachlan and Ann Ledden and their staff comprise a formidable team who provide creative ideas, support and confidence, which can only buoy an author in approaching the unknown. They have been totally professional in settling contractual arrangements, organizing the substantial editorial work involved and communicating their enthusiasm for the project to booksellers and to the public. I am fortunate they decided to take a chance on me.

I am also grateful to them for introducing me to Greg Ioannou, Marie-Lynn Hammond and Madeline Koch who provided sound structural advice, meticulous copyediting and a sense of humour as the project neared completion. Their considerable and relentless efforts led to significant improvements for which I am deeply grateful.

Finally, a word of thanks to readers who have made it through to the end of this book, and who have enjoyed the experience enough or been curious enough to read this Acknowledgement.